THE

DEFINITION

OF WIND

Also by Ellen Block

The Language of Sand

Praise for
The Language of Sand

"*The Language of Sand* has something for everyone: myths, mystery, community, humor, grief, and, ultimately, healing. I found myself rooting not only for Abigail but for the whole community of Chapel Isle. In the wake of unspeakable tragedy, Ellen Block manages to hold sass and heartfelt emotion in perfect equilibrium."
—BRUNONIA BARRY,
New York Times bestselling author of *The Lace Reader*

"Abigail Harker's life is filled with darkness, yet on a remote island of North Carolina's Outer Banks, amid a cast of vividly drawn characters, brightness eases its way into her lighthouse home and into her heavy heart. In subtle, graceful prose, Ellen Block gives us a tale that is both filled with longing and hopeful."
—CATHY BUCHANAN, author of *The Day the Falls Stood Still*

"[A] book-club-friendly read that will have readers itching for a sequel." —*Booklist*

"Block explores . . . the notion of how losing oneself in a new adventure can help heal wounds. . . . Block writes gracefully about heartache and the mending of an injured soul, and the smalltown backdrop is pleasant without being kitschy." —*Publishers Weekly*

"A delightful, highly recommended read." —BookLoons

"This is a wonderfully intelligent, sad, sweet novel, a sort of emotional detective story. A woman who lives in her intellect, suddenly alone and bereft, allows her professional skills as a lexicographer to lead her into a new life—as a lighthouse keeper. Terrific secondary characters, possibly including a ghost." —*Sullivan County Democrat*

"A phenomenal novel! . . . The dialogue is emotionally charged and the plot intense with drama and mystery. . . . The story leaves some threads open as we wait for a second novel about Chapel Isle, which follows in 2011. So much is going on here that delights the reader with each turn of the page. A brilliant character-driven novel, *The Language of Sand* is a Perfect 10." —Romance Reviews Today

"There's more to *The Language of Sand* than just a dip in the waves. . . . Block has melded her storytelling skill with a passion for language. . . . Readers of *The Language of Sand* will look forward to seeing how words will continue to serve Abigail in her life ahead."
—*Fredericksburg Free Lance-Star*

THE

DEFINITION

OF WIND

A Novel

Ellen Block

Bantam Books Trade Paperbacks New York

The Definition of Wind is a work of fiction. Names, characters, places, and incidents either are the product of the author's imagination or are used fictitiously. Any resemblance to actual persons, living or dead, events, or locales is entirely coincidental.

A Bantam Books Trade Paperback Original

Published in the United States by Bantam Books,
an imprint of The Random House Publishing Group,
a division of Random House, Inc., New York.

BANTAM BOOKS and the rooster colophon are
registered trademarks of Random House, Inc.

RANDOM HOUSE READER's CIRCLE and colophon is a
registered trademark of Random House, Inc.

Chapter-opener definitions are from
The Random House Webster's Unabridged Dictionary, 2nd edition
by Random House, Inc., copyright © 2001, 1998, 1997,
1996, 1993, 1987 by Random House, Inc. Used by
permission of Random House, Inc.

Library of Congress Cataloging-in-Publication Data

Block, Brett Ellen.
The definition of wind: a novel/Ellen Block.
p. cm.
ISBN 978-0-440-24576-6
eBook ISBN 978-0-440-42338-6
1. Self-realization in women—Fiction. 2. Lighthouse keepers—
Fiction. 3. Lexicographers—Fiction. 4. Widows—Fiction.
5. North Carolina—Fiction. I. Title.
PS3602.L64D44 2011
813'.6—dc22   2010053290

Printed in the United States of America

www.randomhousereaderscircle.com

9 8 7 6 5 4 3 2

Title-page art from an original photograph by Jolka Igolka

For my parents.
With love.

THE
DEFINITION
OF *WIND*

Anneal (ə nēl´), *v.t.* 1. to heat (glass, earthenware, metals, etc.) to remove or prevent internal stress. 2. to free from internal stress by heating and gradually cooling. 3. to toughen or temper. 4. Biochemistry: to recombine (nucleic acid strands) at low temperature after separating by heat. 5. to fuse colors onto (a vitreous or metallic surface) by heating.—*n:* 6. an act, instance, or product of annealing. [bef. 1000; ME *anelen*, OE *anælan*, to kindle, equiv. to *an*+ *ælan* to burn, akin to *āl fire*]

◆　◆　◆

There was a word for what Abigail Harker had.

Trouble.

She'd been looking forward to the summer on Chapel Isle since moving there nine months earlier. Quiet strolls on the beach, spectacular sunsets, balmy evenings—those were some of the principal reasons she'd settled on the remote island in North Carolina's Outer Banks. To her dismay, by the last day of June the pleasant weather had been replaced with a heat wave so intense that the thermometer was inching toward eighty degrees by daybreak. Abigail's fantasy of a season full of fun in the sun had turned into a total scorcher.

She awoke to a humid breeze drifting through her open bedroom windows. Yawning and already sticky with sweat, she padded into the bathroom to discover that there was barely any water in her toilet and it wouldn't flush.

"You have got to be kidding me."

Abigail jiggled the handle, then removed the tank's lid and tinkered with the inner workings, clueless about what was awry. Despite her best efforts and a few mumbled pleas, the toilet refused to work.

From the very moment she'd taken up residence at the caretaker's cottage attached to the island's lighthouse, the property had had its issues. There were the outdated appliances, the squeaky floorboards, the faulty wiring, and, most notably, a supposed resident ghost. But in the time she'd been renting the place, Abigail had acclimated to the home's eccentricities. At least, most of them.

She'd weathered the fall and winter well, not an odd noise or bump in the night to be heard. Though the power went out occasionally when a bad storm would barrel in off the Atlantic and the brick front stoop was crumbling after its tenure exposed to the elements, life on the isle's southern bluff had been relatively uneventful. That was until the toilet went on strike.

Downstairs, Abigail rummaged around for her landlord Lottie Gilquist's phone number. She thought she'd put it in a drawer in the cherrywood end table in the living room. The end table, along with the rest of the home's handsome antiques, had belonged to Wesley Jasper, the former caretaker rumored to haunt the property. After Abigail had renovated the house with paint and elbow grease, she carted his possessions up from the basement, where they'd been languishing for decades, covered in sheets like fun-house ghosts. The tufted settee, the mahogany dining set, the comfortably worn-in wingback chairs—she enjoyed having them around. They spoke to the true character of the house, to its history. She thought Mr. Jasper must have appreciated them too. Why else had he left her alone all these months if not as a thank-you? That was what she told herself on the days she believed the gossip. More often than not, she didn't give it much thought. Her mind was occupied with other matters.

Lottie's number wasn't in the end table, so Abigail tried the console by the door. The drawers were wedged shut, the wood having expanded with the climbing temperature, which was confirmed by a haze of condensation glazing the windowpanes. Outside, the over-

grown grass was a dewy emerald, the ocean in the distance an electric azure, as if the water molecules in the air refracted the colors.
The brochure Lottie had sent before Abigail came to Chapel Isle
didn't mention how steamy it got in the summertime. Abigail
would have come anyway, but a little forewarning would have been
nice.

Advance notice wasn't Lottie's forte. Petite, plump, and preter-
naturally cheery, she appeared to be the essence of sweetness and
innocence. Her pastel tracksuits and white-blond hair, always
combed into a tall bouffant to give her a couple of extra centime-
ters in height, were the perfect disguise. Under her floating heart
pendant and bedazzled bosom lay the soul of a pint-size master ma-
nipulator.

Lottie made a habit of dropping by unannounced on the pretense that she had an urgent issue to discuss. In reality, she was con-
ducting spot inspections of the caretaker's cottage, ironic given that
the house had been practically uninhabitable at first. Abigail had
refurbished most of the place with no assistance or gratitude
from Lottie, so when she'd questioned the motivation behind these
surprise visits, Lottie simply laughed her signature high-decibel
chuckle, then waved away any insinuation like a pesky gnat.

"A single lady out in the middle of nowhere all by her lonesome?
Heck, it's my civic duty to check on you, Abby. Make certain you're
A-OK."

Like many of the locals, Lottie had checked Abigail's left
hand for a wedding band as soon as she arrived. The absence of a
ring told people she was unmarried. It didn't tell them the whole
story.

A house fire had claimed the lives of her husband, Paul, and their
four-year-old son, Justin, a year earlier. After recuperating from injuries sustained during the blaze, Abigail had retreated to Chapel
Isle and told no one of her past. Better to be considered single than
to divulge the painful truth. While apt, the noun *widow* didn't feel
befitting of her. As a former lexicographer and lover of words, Abigail understood the effect language could have on a person, how it

could define someone. Even she didn't call herself a widow. Then again, she didn't refer to herself as a brunette, label herself a lefty, or consider herself a Capricorn, yet she was all those things. Certain traits in her life were a given. Widowhood now figured prominently among them.

Lottie's phone number was buried under a stack of papers in the console drawer, which had taken five minutes to coax open. Anxious to get her toilet problem resolved, Abigail dialed the antiquated rotary-model telephone, numbers spinning backward slow as syrup. By the seventh digit, she was growing impatient. The outdated aspects of the caretaker's cottage exasperated her only at moments such as this, when the speed and ease of the modern world felt a million miles away.

"I'm sorry," a computerized voice droned. "Your call cannot be completed as dialed. Please hang up and try again."

"Not you too," Abigail said, reprimanding the phone. "Maybe the heat toasted the wires."

The third time she hung up and redialed, she finally got a connection. Static flared as Lottie answered, drowning out Abigail's voice.

"Lottie, it's Abigail. Can you hear me?"

"Barely. Sounds like you're fryin' bacon."

"I'm not cooking, Lottie. It's the phone. Something's wrong with the line."

"You're doing fine? Is that what you said?"

"No, never mind about the phone. My toilet is clogged. Can you send a plumber?"

"A plumber ain't gonna fix your phone. Do you have a cell?"

"Yes, I have a cell phone, Lottie. That's not the point. My toilet won't flush. That's why I need a plumber."

"Mercy me, Abby. I got six summer renters with pipe, drain, and crapper woes, and this here island's got only two plumbers to its name. I'm afraid you're at the bottom of the pecking order. Summer folks come first."

"I'm a renter too," Abigail protested. "Those people are here for only a week. I'm here all the time."

"Precisely, darlin'."

Abigail had become a fixture on Chapel Isle, a known quantity, notwithstanding the fact that she'd been holed up at the cottage for months. All the progress she'd made since the fire had slowly ebbed away before she even realized what was happening. Staying inside one afternoon and reading turned into hunkering down for *days* and reading, her coping mechanism of choice. Abigail hadn't merely lost track of time. She'd lost track of months.

Turning over a new leaf, making a fresh start, beginning a new chapter—the idioms allowed her to categorize what she was trying to do, yet they didn't help her do it. Her husband's life insurance and a pending payment from the lawsuit against the company that installed the defective oven responsible for the fire meant she didn't have to get a job, so actively ignoring reality had become Abigail's preoccupation as much as her occupation. Flexible as this "career" was, she was consumed by it. There were no weekends off, no vacations, no sick days. She ventured into town only to get groceries or to stop by to see her friend Ruth Kepshaw, the waitress at the Kozy Kettle café. Otherwise, she stayed at the caretaker's cottage, alone, plying her new trade.

"You certain the toilet's broke and not being finicky?"

"Everything in this house is finicky. I wouldn't know the difference. That's why I need a plumber, Lottie."

"Okay, okay. Try Duncan Thadlow," she suggested over the fizzing static. "He might be able to lend a hand."

Abigail hadn't heard that name in ages. She'd helped paint his house with Nat Rhone last year, a trade for Nat moving Mr. Jasper's antique furniture up from the basement with her. She and Nat had argued bitterly throughout the painting process, racing to see who could finish slapping coats onto the home's exterior first. Days later,

Nat was arrested for the murder of his best friend, Hank Scokes, but Abigail had gotten the bogus charges dropped after learning Hank's death was actually a suicide. She and Nat had barely spoken since then. The heady memory of those events drained Abigail's focus for a second.

"Doesn't Duncan repair boats for a living?"

Lottie clucked her tongue admonishingly. "A boat and a toilet are more similar than you'd imagine."

It seemed Abigail's imagination was as useless as her logical nature on Chapel Isle, a place where common sense wasn't exactly common, especially for Lottie.

"Of course. How narrow-minded of me."

"Bring him a brownie or a muffin and the man'll bend over backward for you. On second thought, Duncan wears his pants kinda low on account of how much he fancies his desserts. You may want to skip the bending-over part."

"That's an image I'll cherish," Abigail grumbled.

"And if the phone's giving you a pain in your posterior, least you have your cell."

"It doesn't work either. I'm too far away to get reception at the lighthouse."

Because the majority of Chapel Isle's stores were dedicated to fishing or souvenirs, Abigail had been forced to order a new cell phone from a catalog. Along with the phone, she'd ordered a slew of other items for the house, including drapes, a microwave, new towels, bedding, and a steady stream of books. Of her many catalog purchases, the striped cotton-duck window dressings looked great and the extra housewares were a boon, but the phone was a waste.

"Try standing outdoors, dear. The cell 'waves' travel through the air. I know technology can be confusing. You have to try to stay abreast of these innovations, dear."

With that, the line went dead. Either Lottie had hung up or the phone had disconnected, as if even an inanimate object couldn't take that much of Lottie's talking.

"I feel your pain," she told the receiver before setting it in the cradle. "So now I'm the one who's behind the times? Typical Lottie."

Hoping to fix the telephone herself, Abigail unplugged the cord from the handset and attempted to reinsert it for a tighter fit—except one of the tines on the connector snapped off and she couldn't get the cord back in. She felt as if she broke everything she touched.

Worse off than before she'd called Lottie and needing to go to the bathroom, Abigail dressed to go into town. Her khaki shorts and cream tank top were her most recent mail-order acquisitions. She'd had no warm-weather clothes when she moved to the island, only a selection of bland basics her mother had bought her after the fire, while Abigail recovered in the hospital. Getting new summer clothes should have been an enjoyable experience. It turned out to be a downer. The shorts were too loose. The cotton Ts and tanks hung tentlike off her shoulders. Everything was the wrong size. Abigail had lost a lot of weight. She hadn't noticed.

As she fussed with the baggy tank top in the bathroom mirror, she said, "First the toilet. Now the phone is on the fritz. What next?"

Abigail half wished she hadn't asked that aloud. Not because she didn't want to invite more difficulties but because she hadn't thought about her "housemate" in quite a while. Could the ghost of Wesley Jasper be tampering with the home's archaic plumbing and wiring? She hated that the question sprang to mind.

"The average person doesn't automatically think a ghost is responsible when things go wrong around the house," she chided herself. "It's significantly more plausible that the telephone needs to be repaired, as do a multitude of things in this house."

After living in the rustic cottage as long as she had, Abigail understood that plausibility didn't carry as much weight as she wished it did.

Breakfast could wait. Abigail's bladder couldn't. She grabbed her keys and headed for the door. The instant she stepped outside, the sweltering sun was a slap on the skin. With no wind blowing in from the water, the humidity gave the air a solid dimension. The tall grass and unwavering trees seemed to tether the heat to the ground.

As she opened the door to her Volvo station wagon, already imagining the chilling blast of the car's air-conditioning, Abigail felt a sting on her wrist. She batted away a large black fly, revealing a growing red welt. Soon more flies were buzzing around, diving at her like kamikazes. She jumped in the car and locked the door. It was hardly necessary—they were only flies—yet it made her feel safe. And so would a big can of insect repellent and some treats to butter up Duncan Thadlow. Although she may not have wanted him to bend over backward, Abigail was prepared to do that and more to get her toilet running properly again.

By mainland standards, the ride into town was a brief fifteen-minute jaunt. On Chapel Isle, that was an eternity. But the drive was pleasant in a scenic sense—a decent consolation. Summer had turned the marshes and patches of scrub brush into lush green spans where herons waded through the shallow water and wildflowers bloomed in riotously colorful bunches. Abigail had come to appreciate living in a place where nature outnumbered people. Except these black flies were liable to change her mind.

The bug bite was itching ferociously by the time she neared the center of town. She was distracted, scratching, when she jerked her head up and saw something she hadn't encountered in months. Traffic.

Cars, minivans, and trucks filled the streets, along with throngs of tourists, making the normally quiet town square seem more like Times Square. People in Chapel Isle T-shirts were milling about and perusing shop windows. Beyond, in the bay, flashy yachts had replaced the weather-beaten fishing trawlers at the docks. Music blared from passing vehicles, and litter filled the mortar between the cobblestones. At last, Abigail was getting a taste of what the islanders dealt with year in and year out.

Between the itching, the urge to pee, and the annoyance that there wasn't a single parking spot to be had in the entire square, she decided to throw caution to the wind and double-park in front of the Kozy Kettle to go to the restroom and buy the sweets for Duncan. She abandoned her station wagon, blocking in a convertible, then dashed into the café.

The Kettle was packed. Heat seemed to glisten off the red-and-white-checked vinyl tablecloths, making the faux-wood paneling glow. Electric fans propped on chairs were churning the stagnant air, while behind the counter Ruth Kepshaw was taking to-go orders from pushy, sunscreen-slicked visitors, each in a bigger rush than the person beside them. They elbowed one another, vying for position by the register.

Are these people on vacation or on their lunch break? Abigail thought after someone stepped on her foot.

Chapel Isle billed itself as a peaceful retreat, off the beaten path compared to other renowned vacation destinations on the Eastern Seaboard. Its slow-paced appeal was a main selling point. However, this didn't appear to be a relaxing getaway for any of the tourists competing to get to the head of the line, and it definitely wasn't relaxing for Ruth. Past middle age yet able to pass for it, she had a pretty smile that shone brighter than the garland of rhinestone brooches pinned to her apron, and the warmth of her quick wit could soften even the surliest customer. Usually.

Abigail was about to wave to Ruth when one tourist loudly complained, "This isn't what I ordered. I wanted the sausage on the side."

"I bet you say that to all the girls," Ruth teased, whisking the bag away from the man. A lady in line snickered. "I'll get that changed for you in a jiffy, sir."

"Isn't there anybody else working here?" another guy asked. "This is taking forever."

"Son, you don't know what 'forever' means until you've listened to a country-music radio station play a commercial-free hour of Kenny Rogers. You hold your horses and I'll be right with ya," Ruth assured him as she made a break for the kitchen.

To the out-of-towners, her tone sounded like down-home Southern sass. Abigail knew otherwise. Thinking Ruth might return wielding a meat cleaver, she waded through the crowd toward the bathroom, where a woman in a bikini top and cutoffs beat her to the single-stall facilities by a split second.

Abigail cursed under her breath, then conjugated Latin as a diversion while not-so-patiently waiting her turn.

Maneo, manere, mansi, mansus.

Sto, stare, steti, status.

Irrito, irritare, irritavi, irritatus.

The two teenage girls who came and stood next to her in line quickly derailed Abigail's concentration.

"This place sucks," one said, a beach bag slung over her shoulder. "There's no movies, no shopping, no water parks, no nothing. I wish my parents would stop coming here. It's *bor-*ing."

"And, like, none of my text messages are going through," the other girl added glumly, as she typed on the keypad to no avail. "The reception here blows."

Tell me about it.

Abigail's connection to the world outside the island was as reliable as the cell service. Sometimes it was clear, easy to comprehend. Mostly it wasn't. This sudden swell of tourists reminded her of what life had been like prior to the move, when lengthy lines, noisy cell chatter, and jockeying for parking spots was part of her normal, everyday routine. *Normal* may as well have been an eternity ago. The frenetic existence she'd fled had descended upon her doorstep, and she wasn't sure she could stand the heat, literally or figuratively.

"There's no more toilet paper," the woman who emerged from the ladies' room reported. "Guess you'll have to go au naturel."

"Gross," the teen beside Abigail said.

"We're in Hicksville. What did you expect?" the other girl groaned, slinging her useless phone into her backpack.

Infuriated, Abigail realized that it was the collision of her *before* and her *after* that was bothering her so much. This wasn't the Chapel

Isle she'd signed up for. The mob scene was making her claustropho-
bic. Sadly, her only escape was the bathroom.

Post pit stop, she pushed her way to the counter and flagged
Ruth.

"My stars, Abby. What are you doing here? You're risking your
bodily safety coming during mealtime," she whispered. "These folks
will knock you down and walk over you for a cracker. It's like ice
hockey without the ice."

"I need a slice of cake or a crumb bun ASAP. Whatever you have
that could induce a diabetic coma, I'll take it."

Ruth raised a brow. "You got your—how should I put it—Aunt
Flo in town?"

"No, I do not. The food is for Duncan Thadlow. Lottie told me if
I bribed him with sweets, he'd fix my broken toilet."

"Hon, that doesn't make a lick of sense."

"Did you not hear me say *Lottie* told me to do it?"

"Gotcha. Well, we've got a cruller left," Ruth began. But as they
swiveled toward the dessert tray at the end of the counter, a tourist
lifted the lid and helped himself to the last remaining doughnut.
Score another point for the visiting team.

"Ma'am, my order?" a customer carped.

"How long does it take to make an omelet?" another demanded.

"This is the South, folks. We don't do nothin' in a hurry," Ruth
declared. On the sly she told Abigail, "Give me a minute. I'll find
you something tasty in the back."

Squeezed in with the angry customers, electric fans barely
drowning out their gripes about the service, Abigail began to dread
sharing the island, *her* island, with hordes of loud-mouthed, litter-
ing, toilet-paper-swiping tourists.

Ruth returned with a paper bag, ignoring the gauntlet of shouts
and requests as she delivered it to Abigail.

"Ever consider hiring another waitress? At least you wouldn't be
the only one under fire. You're running around behind that counter
like the carnival game where people try to shoot the ducks."

"What, and share my tips? Perish the thought."

"You may want to underline the 'perish' part."

Ruth noticed Abigail scratching her wrist and asked, "You get a black-fly bite?"

"Good grief, it's awful. The fly was the size of a silver dollar and I feel like it gave me rabies. Will the itching ever stop?"

"Eventually. Buy some calamine lotion and bug spray or else you're in for a world o' hurt. Black-fly season is usually done by the end of June. We must have offended the gods, 'cause it's late this year. Take this." Ruth passed Abigail an aerosol can of repellent. "Should hold ya until you can get an industrial-size jug for yourself. You're gonna need it."

"You keep insecticide next to the cream and sugar?"

"I spray a little in the customers' coffee if they're crabby."

"It's poisonous, Ruth! You could hurt somebody."

"Now you're the health inspector? Better than me spitting in their fruit compote."

"Should I be afraid to eat here?"

"If you weren't already, why start?" Ruth nodded toward the paper bag. "I scrounged this day-old apple turnover from the fridge. Duncan won't know the difference. Oh, and let him prattle on about whatever his latest passion is—fishing, sports, his cocka-mamie conspiracy theories. That should seal the deal if the turnover doesn't."

"Conspiracy theories? I'm not going to get stuck talking about the grassy knoll for three hours, am I?"

Before Ruth could reply, an elderly customer in a plastic sun visor hollered, "Yoo-hoo. I'm ready to place my order."

"I have a place for your order," Ruth said under her breath, retrieving her pad from her apron. "Listen, Abby, Duncan Thadlow could talk to a wall and believe it's a two-way conversation. You don't have to listen. You just have to *pretend* to listen."

As tourists continued to bark for her attention, Ruth could hold them off no longer and went to take more orders, disappearing behind a wall of hungry out-of-towners.

Abigail had never been an expert at pretending. Not when it came to pleasantries, chitchat, or how she felt. She couldn't pretend the "summer people," as Lottie called them, weren't bugging her more than her insect bite, the heat, or her broken toilet.

For Abigail, that was saying something.

B

Battology (bə tol´e jē), *n.* wearisome repetition of words in speaking or writing. [1595–1605; < Gk *battología* (bátt(os) stammerer + -o- + -logia -LOGY]

◆ ◆ ◆

Advice in mind, apple turnover in hand, and bug spray in the crook of her elbow, Abigail exited the Kozy Kettle to find Sheriff Caleb Larner leaning against the hood of her double-parked station wagon, arms crossed. Sweat glistened along the receding hairline of his buzz cut, and dark sunglasses hid his eyes. Abigail didn't need to see them to know what he was thinking.

"Massachusetts plates, illegally parked—I figured it was summer folks searching for a latte fix. Was about to start writing the ticket 'til I realized it was your car."

"I plead insanity induced by heat exhaustion and black flies," Abigail stated, stuffing the bag with the turnover under her arm so she could spritz herself with repellent. The spray quickly surrounded her in a chemical cloud that sent both Abigail and Larner into choking fits.

"What is that? Napalm?" he asked between coughs.

"I don't know. Ruth gave it to me," she hacked.

"Then it's probably pepper spray instead o' bug spray. She puts it in the—"

"Tourists' coffee. I heard."

"I'll let you off with a warning about the car, but no more double-parking. Can't have you encouraging any of the visiting yahoos."

"Hey," a male voice called. "Aren't you going to give her a ticket? She's been blocking my car for the last ten minutes."

Eyes burning from the noxious repellent, Abigail had to squint to make out the guy storming toward her as well as the cherished automobile he was so concerned about. The car was a sleek black Mercedes convertible coupe. Its driver: a ruggedly handsome man with a warm tan to match the leather interior of his two-door.

"My apologies, sir," Abigail told him, clearing her throat. Her oversize clothes and stubbornly itchy bite made her feel like a gawky adolescent under the gaze of the attractive guy. Plus, she felt a sneeze coming on from the bug spray.

He was about to lay into Abigail, then stopped once he'd taken his shades off and gotten a look at her. "Um, actually, it's not that big a deal, Officer."

"That's 'Sheriff,'" Larner corrected him. "Changing your tune now that you see it's a pretty lady, eh?"

"Is that a crime?" He shrugged, coy.

Larner put up his hands. "Only if she wants to press charges."

"Sir, huh?" the man said, focusing on Abigail with a flirty grin. "Is that Southern hospitality, or do I look *that* old?"

"Old? You? Absolutely not," she stammered, holding in the sneeze. "That wouldn't be the adjective I'd select. Far, uh, from it."

What is the matter with you? Abigail's brain was yelling. *A good-looking guy smiles at you and you turn to mush?*

Larner interrupted her conversational free fall. "Allow me to explain. I'm showing this woman some leeway seeing as she tends the island's lighthouse. It's a historic property. Got a lot of, whadaya call it, history behind it. Abigail Harker, this is . . . ?"

Smooth, she thought, trying not to grimace at Larner's ham-handed introduction. He'd mistaken the strain in her expression from trying not to sneeze for interest in the man with the Mercedes.

"Tim Ulman." He shook her hand, then Larner's. "A lighthouse? I wasn't aware Chapel Isle had one. All I heard was how terrific the beaches are. That's according to the friend who rented me his house, so I hope I wasn't being misled," he joked.

"Misinforming a tenant about a rental home on the island—who would do such a thing?" Abigail deadpanned.

Larner changed the subject. "Whereabouts you staying, Mr. Ulman?"

"Highbrook Road."

"Nice neck o' the woods." Larner puckered his lips, impressed, and threw Abigail an obvious glance, making her want to sneeze on him in retaliation. "Yessiree, we got the finest beaches in the state," he went on. "You can take that to the bank."

"Please, don't say 'bank,'" Tim said with a wince. "After my divorce and the beating the market's been taking, I don't want to think about anything except sand, sun, and some fishing."

"The market?" Larner volleyed the question, acting innocent, though he clearly understood what it meant. Tim may have wanted to go fishing, but Larner already was.

"The stock market. I'm a bond trader in New York. It's been such a roller-coaster ride that I'm thinking of hanging up my hat. Do some day-trading instead. I could work from home. Or from anywhere, for that matter. Even here."

"So you're single?" Larner confirmed.

Abigail wanted to melt into the ground. If it were a few degrees hotter, she could have.

"You say that like it's a bad thing." Tim glanced at Abigail. "I'll have to put the lighthouse on my to-do list. Maybe you could give me a tour sometime."

"It's not exactly open to the pub—"

"She'd be happy to," Larner answered for her. "Feel free to stop by. It's a big white building on the southeast side of the island. Can't miss it."

"A pleasure meeting you, Abigail. You too, Sheriff. Now, if you don't mind . . . ?" He gestured toward Abigail's Volvo.

"Oops. Right."

She started her car and coasted forward to allow the gleaming coupe to pull out into traffic.

Larner walked around to her driver's-side window and tipped

his sunglasses to prove Tim had passed muster. "He's divorced, looks like a movie star, and is renting one of them giant houses on Highbrook Road, which tells me he's loaded. Best part, he's got goo-goo eyes for you. I can tell."

"That's some crack police work, Caleb. But could you not invite strangers to my house? I didn't like having you there uninvited, and I *know* you."

"I'm only saying it might not be such a terrible idea for you to go on a date. Could do far worse than a man with a flashy convertible and cash to burn."

Neither flash nor cash had ever been Abigail's style, and it felt too soon to reenter the real world—let alone the dating world. She'd been avoiding all except the most basic responsibilities, anesthetizing herself by reading books, taking long baths, or staring at the ocean from her favorite wingback chair, a perch from which she could lose track of hours, days, even weeks.

Paul used to call her "Little Bear." Whether it was a bad cold or bad news, Abigail would withdraw to their bedroom and lock herself in to hibernate until she was well again. She needed to be by herself to heal.

"You don't have to be alone to get better," Paul would often remind her.

"But I don't have to get you sick in the process."

"I'd chance it if you wanted the company."

That was how seriously Paul took loving her. When Justin was born, Paul had slept on the floor because the hospital was short on extra cots and chairs. Afterward, his back was out for a week, but he never complained, not once. When friends and relatives who'd come to see the baby noticed him limping, Paul told them it was sympathy soreness from Abigail's labor.

Having someone to share her pain had made it bearable. Now Paul was gone, and his absence was like a missing limb. It hurt more because he wasn't there.

"Dating hasn't exactly been a priority," Abigail said.

"Seen Nat Rhone lately?"

"That's subtle, Caleb."

It wasn't hard to read between the lines with Larner. When Abigail had come forward to clear Nat's name, Larner suspected Abigail was in love with him, asked her point-blank. The answer was no. Though Larner had let Nat go, he continued to harbor feelings that Nat had had something to do with Hank's death. This ongoing bone of contention had prevented Abigail from ever fully trusting Larner, especially after she'd learned he was stealing from rental properties to pay for his daughter's cancer treatment. Their uneasy armistice had remained exactly that—uneasy.

"It was a simple question, Abby."

"Was it?"

He disregarded the comment with a sniff.

"I have to go," she said, patting the paper bag with the turnover in it. "I have a delivery to make."

"Drive safe. And no more double-parking."

"Yes, *sir*," she chirped, letting the jab about his age register.

Larner raised his sunglasses and ambled onward into the crowd of tourists.

As she nosed the Volvo through the bustling town square, she wondered why Larner's remarks perturbed her. Sure, Nat was notorious for being Chapel Isle's preeminent troublemaker, but Abigail had seen a side of him few witnessed. He had a good heart, even if he did hide it behind a belligerent, come-out-swinging façade.

"Who cares if I've been talking to Nat Rhone?" she announced aloud while idling at a crosswalk. A passing vacationer overheard her through her open car window and shot her a curious glance.

"Or talking to myself," she mumbled, embarrassed.

In the weeks after Abigail had helped free Nat from jail, she'd run into him at the Kettle and seen him driving Hank's truck, yet they never spoke more than to say hello or how are you. As a toddler, Nat had lost his parents to a car accident, then his best friend had committed suicide, so Abigail felt bonded to him in grief. Nevertheless, she didn't feel comfortable reaching out to him. She doubted he'd approach her either.

Nobody had been aware that she was a widow when she moved to the island, but somehow the natives had gotten wind and the news circulated—Abigail wasn't sure how widely. She'd found out only because she'd heard a few local women whispering about her at the market. She'd had trouble accepting that the two people privy to the truth would have exposed her secret. Somebody had, though.

Abigail didn't want to dwell on it, so she switched on the car radio and caught the tail end of her favorite call-in show broadcast from the mainland, hosted by the brazenly tell-it-like-it-is Dr. Walter. The program was a slim tether to the real world beyond Chapel Isle, one she could connect with when she chose. Abigail liked how its host could confront any subject head-on, no holds barred, a skill she had yet to perfect.

That day's topic was chronic pain. Callers were phoning in to grouse about everything from arthritis to sciatica to carpal tunnel syndrome.

"The surgeons told me that when they replaced my hip I was gonna set off the gosh darn airport metal detectors," a man railed, a twang in his accent. "What they didn't tell me was that my robo-hip was going to hurt like a—"

A protracted *bleep* masked the man's cursing until Dr. Walter could put him on mute.

"Ouch indeed," Dr. Walter intoned. "And our next caller is . . . ?"

"In agony," the woman pronounced. "I've given birth to three kids, so I'm on a first-name basis with pain. But this fibromyalgia is medieval torture. And the doctors can't make it stop. Some have said it's all in my head, that I'm making it up to get more pills. I wish I was. It's unfair that we get labeled as nutcases or prescription junkies because you can't 'see' what's wrong with us. Doesn't mean there isn't something wrong."

As the woman's aggravation seeped through the airwaves, Abigail had to ask herself if she also had chronic pain in the form of a sore spot for Nat Rhone.

◆　◆　◆

A single-lane road flanked by tall marsh grass led to Duncan Thad-low's clapboard cottage. His home backed up to the bay, creating an inlet that allowed boats to dock for repairs. Out front was a clear-ing where Duncan kept old parts scattered in the sand like lawn or-naments. A giant rust-caked ship's propeller greeted guests in lieu of a front gate.

Abigail and Nat's paint job had fared well over the winter. It was as crisp as the day they'd finished. She had to manhandle the mem-ory of that encounter out of her mind as she knocked on Duncan's door, apple turnover at the ready.

"To what do I owe this delight?" he asked, finding Abigail on his stoop. With a belly as round as the underside of a rowboat, there was no denying that Duncan enjoyed eating. His long brown beard skimmed his chest, a permanent bib.

"I have a favor to ask." She dangled the paper bag before him.

"Twist my arm, why don'tcha?" He joined her on the front steps and opened the bag to get a whiff of his gift. "Don't have to kill any-body, do I?"

"I may be from Boston, but this isn't that kind of favor."

Duncan took a bite of the turnover. "I'm all ears."

"It'll sound strange. Okay, maybe not that strange. Then again, it's been such a strange day. I mean, with my toilet not working and my phone breaking and the black flies and the tourists. What's with them, anyway? Are there always so many? Tourists, not black flies. There's no parking, and there are people everywhere. It's like a tsunami of sunburned out-of-towners in gaudy T-shirts. And they get the plumbers first, which strikes me as unreasonable. Unwar-ranted. Unjust. Frankly, I couldn't conceive of so many tourists being jammed onto this tiny island. It's all so strange. And, yes, I'm saying the word *strange* a lot. And rambling. A lot."

Remembering that Ruth had told her to let Duncan take the lead, Abigail reined herself in and put the brakes on her harangue. One time at a bank back in Boston, she'd been talking to a teller—and going on as she was with Duncan—when she looked back at the woman behind her in line and saw her roll her eyes dramatically. As an embarrassed Abigail had hurried to finish her transaction, the woman cracked, "You sure know a lot of ten-dollar words."

"It's what I do for a living," Abigail had explained with a repentant shrug.

"Whatever," the woman had scoffed, as if Abigail was lying outright, then took her turn with the teller.

Being a lexicographer didn't strike most people as a real profession, so Abigail was continually clarifying it for everybody, from the mailman to babysitters to total strangers. Her shorthand for the many facets of spelling, pronunciation, history, and connotations she dealt with was: "My job is to make words make sense."

For some, that sentiment didn't make much sense in itself. Saying she'd worked on legal dictionaries or as a consultant for media firms to fine-tune advertising copy was concrete yet vague. Like the woman in line at the bank, many simply couldn't grasp the concept or didn't want to. Without words, life would grind to a halt. Abigail's contribution to keeping the wheels of the world running was—albeit small—something she had been proud of, regardless of whether anyone fully comprehended it or not.

"'Bout that favor?" Duncan said, happily devouring the turnover.

"The toilet. Lottie told me you'd help me. It's broken."

"You tried a plunger? Might be cheaper than paying me to fix it."

Pay? Abigail had assumed any work would be covered by Lottie. That or the baked goods would suffice.

Duncan grinned knowingly. "Lottie's been your landlord how long? And you still can't tell when she's giving you the runaround?"

"You're saying this was a wild-goose chase? That Lottie set me up?"

"Can't complain. I got a turnover out of it."

Typical Lottie. Abigail should have seen it coming. She'd been duped by her before.

"Merle Braithwaite sells plungers at his hardware store, doesn't he?" Abigail asked, defeated.

"Indeedy he does. Assuming the summer people haven't picked the place clean. Piranha don't have nothin' on them. With the big

Fourth of July celebration hard on our heels, it's only going to get worse. Batten down the hatches. Chaos here we come!"

"Fourth of July. Right." Abigail had completely forgotten that the holiday was mere days away. The massive influx of tourists suddenly made sense.

"Most locals count the minutes until Labor Day. Not me," Duncan declared. "All the boats the tourists bring in means more business. Engines conk out, fuel stabilizers get shot, water pumps rupture, rotors bust, loads of problems."

He continued nattering on tediously, as Ruth had warned he would. Abigail was trapped and Duncan was oblivious to her utter lack of interest. She was partly able to tune him out, until he mentioned encountering fewer wreck divers this season than in years past.

"Wreck divers?"

"Yup, they come for the Graveyard."

The Ship's Graveyard was an unsettling nickname for the dangerous shoals off the eastern shore of Chapel Isle. Abigail had heard stories about the boats that crashed there and the many sailors who'd lost their lives. She couldn't fathom people intentionally setting course for a legendary death trap.

"They go there on purpose?"

"Bunch o' wackos with their scuba gear and their pricey gizmos and charter boats to search for sunken treasure. Can't recall any who've found more than seashells or starfish. Waste of time. Then again, if I'm the person they're paying to take 'em there, they can take all the time they want." Duncan polished off the last of the turnover and wiped powdered sugar from his lips. "They're all looking for the *Bishop's Mistress*. I'd wager they'll never find her."

"Did you say the *Bishop's Mistress*?"

"You heard of it?"

"In passing," Abigail answered noncommittally.

That was the ship that had sunk during Wesley Jasper's watch, more than one hundred years ago. Abigail had found his journals in the basement of the caretaker's cottage. They meticulously detailed every morning and night for months, all except for the evening when the *Bishop's Mistress* crashed on the rocks.

Mr. Jasper had fallen down the winding spiral staircase in the lighthouse tower earlier that day, an accident that almost ended his life, rendering him unable to light the beacon and sealing the *Bishop's Mistress*'s fate. Talk of his ghost standing guard at the lighthouse in perpetuity, even menacing Lottie after she'd let the place fall into disrepair, had spooked Abigail when she first moved in. Having the *Bishop's Mistress* crop up randomly in conversation struck Abigail as an inauspicious sign.

"I'd better be going," she said. "I've got a toilet to fix."

"Happy plunging," Duncan chimed.

His remarks about the *Bishop's Mistress* echoed in her ears on the ride back across the island. Kids were riding bicycles along the shoulder of the road. Passing cars had fishing poles lashed to their roofs, windows rolled down to snare the breeze. The summer people were blithely going about their vacations, unaware of the natives' mixed feelings toward them. Abigail envied the tourists that. For as much as she'd become a fixture on Chapel Isle, she was still an outsider, and earning the natives' trust seemed to cost her at every turn. Sometimes it was as little as an apple turnover. Other times much more.

Contumely (kon´tŏo-mə lē), *n., pl.*—lies. 1. insulting display of contempt in words or actions; contemptuous or humiliating treatment. 2. a humiliating insult. [1350–1400; ME *contumelie* (< AF) < L *contumēlia,* perh. akin to *contumāx* (see CONTUMACY) though formation and sense development are unclear]

❖   ❖   ❖

Duncan was right. Merle Braithwaite's normally quiet hardware store was full of summer people asking for every conceivable item, most of which he didn't carry.

"Do you have adapter cords for the PlayStation? We left my son's at home," a woman in a sarong confessed, zinc slathered on her nose.

Merle, a giant of a man whom Abigail gratefully counted among her friends on the island, blinked at the woman. "What kinda cords?"

Abigail tried not to laugh as Merle politely informed the woman that he was out of that particular "doohickey."

Situated in an old beach bungalow that had been gutted and remodeled, Island Hardware retained its homey feel, despite the power-tool displays, racks of wrench sets, and aisles full of supplies. Though Merle towered over everything and everyone in his shop, he wasn't brusque or scary. Unless he wanted to be.

"I have to hand it to you," Abigail told him, marveling at his ability to put on a sociable face for visitors when she figured he would have preferred to throttle them. "You're pretty convincing as a 'nice guy.'"

"Hey there, Abby," he said, thrilled to see her. "Thanks, but don't blow my cover."

She hadn't been in to see Merle in weeks, if not longer. Her excuse—that she genuinely didn't know where the time had gone—was weak albeit true. Abigail hoped he would understand.

"I'm sure they have jump ropes here, darling. Don't cry," a mother said to a teary-eyed little girl in a purple swimsuit as they scoured the shelves. "We'll get you a jump rope."

"You have those?" Abigail asked once the customers were out of earshot.

"Jumper cables. No jump ropes."

"Seriously, Merle, how do you handle this?"

"As you may have noticed, being gracious does not come naturally to me. It's a skill I've had to hone. Taken years of practice. Which has been worth it, because summer is a three-month-long typhoon that we islanders have to learn to weather if we want to eat when the storm is over. Grin and bear it, Abby. Grin and bear it."

"Safe to say, I'm not here for adapter cords or toys. I need a plunger. Lottie has me chasing my tail all over the island because I'm an ordinary 'yearly' tenant, not some fancy seasonal renter."

"Something wrong with the toilet?"

"Was that not implicit in my requesting a plunger?"

"You can use them on sinks too."

"This is precisely why I shouldn't be acting as my own plumber."

"John's stopped up?"

"Yes and when you've got only one, you'll move heaven and earth to have it fixed. That or I'll be forced to take a more 'naturist' approach, which doesn't bode well," Abigail stated, leaning into the counter. "For me or for nature."

"You, the great outdoors—not the best combo." She glared, and Merle put up his arms in defense. "I'm guessing," he added.

"Okay, I'm . . . indoors-y. Not outside-y. I can admit that. But this is too much. I've got a terrible black-fly bite, these tourists are making me berserk, and now my bladder is in danger of bursting because my landlord is a nutcase. Some sympathy would be appreciated. Try honing that skill."

"Hold that thought and cross your legs if you have to, missy," boomed a voice from behind Abigail.

Turning, she was met with the sunburned face of a man in a wheelchair. White hair poked out from under a green baseball cap with the Gilquist Realty logo on it, a stark contrast to the bright pink of his cheeks. This had to be Franklin Gilquist, Lottie's better half. Abigail had heard that he was injured in a car accident with a drunk tourist years earlier. Though Franklin was wheelchair bound, he had the confidence of a man who stood taller than Merle.

"Mr. Gilquist, I didn't mean—"

"For me to hear that? No worries. I'm married to Lottie, hence I'm hard to offend. Nice to finally put a face with the name, Ms. Harker."

She shook his hand. "Likewise."

"Trust me, I'm thoroughly acquainted with my dear wife's smooth talkin'. You can't believe what she's capable of, tiny as she is. She and my buddy Bert Van Dorst went to grade school together here on Chapel Isle, and he told me that when their teacher gave them an IQ test, Lottie beat him. Frightening, ain't it?"

Scary indeed, especially since Abigail knew that Bertram Van Dorst had been a professor of astrophysics at MIT.

"I feel bad about the toilet inconvenience," Franklin told her. " 'Cept every unit me and Lottie own is booked to capacity. We got our plates full with maintenance troubles or else I'd have a plumber at your place on the double. Hand to God, Abby."

"I think I hear a customer calling," Merle cut in, slowly backing away.

Abigail frowned. "I didn't hear anything. Oh, no, hold on a second." She felt an oncoming ambush. "You want something from me. I can tell. It's the Chapel Isle version of *Let's Make a Deal.*"

"True enough," Franklin said. "I have a proposal. It's a real win-win. If you're willing to act as a 'case manager' of sorts and visit the properties to troubleshoot, then I'll take care of whatever issues are bubbling up at the caretaker's cottage. You name it. I'll even have the house repainted. Heard through the grapevine you've been talking about that for a while."

The grapevine was less a vine than a single leaf—Ruth Kepshaw. Abigail had to wonder if Ruth also blabbed about her being a widow. It was hard to accept that one of the few people who'd gone out of their way to be kind to her could also be airing her secrets.

"Is nothing sacred on this island? Can a woman not make a confidential comment or two? Or five?"

"Not here," Franklin replied. "At least, not yet."

Yet was the crux of the matter for Abigail. As far as the natives were concerned, she was a temp, a trainee, someone not worth their full confidence or respect. Last fall she'd wound up as a de facto security guard after Merle had been hurt defending her in a brawl at the Kozy Kettle. Abigail had taken up his rounds, checking on Lottie and Franklin's vacant rental properties to make sure they hadn't been broken into. Now she was being offered a position as a junior maintenance man. It was hardly a lateral move. Favors were Chapel Isle's form of currency, and keeping to herself over the last months hadn't earned Abigail any credit or goodwill. If she wanted things fixed, she didn't have any choice.

"But I'm only a 'case manager,' right? No heavy lifting. I don't do heavy and I don't do lifting."

"I promise, Abby. And, hey, you never know. Could be fun. Get you outta that lonely caretaker's cottage more often. Might do you good."

"Then why do I feel as if I just signed a deal with the devil for a couple gallons of paint?"

"I may have a sunburn, but I'm hardly evil incarnate. That's Lottie," Franklin joked as he guided his electric wheelchair toward the door. "Give her a jingle and she'll make the arrangements. See you, Merle. Abby."

She waved goodbye, feeling like she was bidding adieu to her freedom for the rest of the summer.

"He's got a point about you being out and about," Merle said once Franklin was gone. "I haven't seen you since Moses threw the tablets off the mountain."

"Come on. It hasn't been *that* long."

"I get it, though, Abby. Hiding from the world, shutting down, living in your head. If there's anybody who can relate, it's me."

Merle had endured a painful divorce that cost him his son. While he might not have been willing to sympathize with her toilet woes, he could sympathize with loss.

"You have to get out of your comfort zone," he asserted. "What better way than getting hands-on with these wonderful summer renters? Here. I'll give you some incentive."

He lumbered down an aisle between the shopping tourists and returned to the register bearing a plunger.

"Hear ye, hear ye," Merle pronounced. "I induct you, Abigail Harker, into Chapel Isle's trade union." He pantomimed knighting her with the plunger, tapping her on each shoulder with the wooden handle. "Unofficially, that is."

"More like jack-of-all-trades union."

"Your staff, my liege." Merle ceremoniously proffered the plunger.

"Do you have any telephones to go with it? Mine's acting twitchy."

"Stopped carrying them 'cause everybody's got their cells and dingleberries."

"*Black*Berries."

"Same difference."

"Then how about an electric fan? This liege is sweltering."

"Sure do. 'Bout to run out. The last one's . . ."

A couple approached the register, prepared to pay for the sole electric fan Merle had left in stock.

"Can I use my debit card, bro?" asked a guy in swim trunks, a damp T-shirt, and flip-flops. As Abigail gnashed her teeth, the girl with him was perusing the color-coded display of paint samples.

"Ooh, honey. This color, Limitless Sky, it looks exactly like the sky here."

"Nope," Merle replied. "Only cash or credit."

"That's sort of old school. You'd do more business if you got up to date with technology. Take it from me, I'm in I.T."

"You're in *it*?"

"No, 'I.T.,' as in information technology."

"Well, I'm in D.C."

"What's D.C.?"

"Don't care."

"Whatever, dude."

The guy tossed some cash on the counter, then left with the ditzy girl and Abigail's fan.

"Shame on you, Merle. What happened to your years of practice?"

"It's too hot to be friendly to *every*body."

"Well, I'm glad you're friendly to me."

Even as she said it, she wondered if Merle was responsible for spreading the word that she was a widow. Her gut told her he wasn't, yet he *had* been the one who told her about how Nat Rhone lost his parents, a secret imparted to Merle by Hank Scokes. So perhaps Merle wasn't the most dependable confidant. Abigail just wasn't certain. She hated that.

Certain was a noun she cleaved to, a favorite among favorites. If a situation was certain, it was indubitable, irrefutable, satisfyingly incontrovertible. Even the synonyms smacked of reliability. The antonyms, however—words such as *cryptic, indeterminate, unclassifiable, anomalous*—just sounded ominous, like a science experiment gone awry. Abigail far preferred to be *certain* rather than the alternatives.

Once she'd loaded up on cans of bug repellent, electronic insect zappers, fly swatters, and citronella candles, she spotted the paint swatch the ditzy girl had been studying—Limitless Sky. The girl had put it back in the incorrect spot on the color chart. Abigail replaced it and took out a sample of warm white called Morning Mist. Even though Franklin's offer to have the caretaker's cottage's brick façade repainted was difficult to resist, the paint wasn't as important as changing her image in the community. Being the creepy woman who never left the island's secluded lighthouse was not an image she cared to cultivate.

Abigail tucked the white paint sample into her pocket and headed for the door, saying, "Stay cool, Merle."

"I was born cool."

"Then stay out of trouble."

"Excuse me," a tan woman in a sun hat chirped. "Do you sell batteries?"

What the woman failed to observe was the rack of batteries right beside the register, practically under her nose. Merle took a deep breath.

"Not my strong suit, Abby, but I'll try."

With the plunger propped on her shoulder and her insect munitions overflowing from two large bags, Abigail used her hip to open the door to the hardware store. Outside, she ran smack into Bertram Van Dorst.

Having not seen him for months, Abigail gave Bert a huge hug, nearly dropping her bags in the process. A brilliant man with a peculiar penchant for laundry, he'd become her friend after he helped protect the caretaker's cottage from a hurricane that blasted the island shortly after she'd arrived. Bert may have come off as Chapel Isle's resident eccentric; however, he was quite the contrary.

"Uh, hi, Abby."

The hug had startled Bert, and he let go quickly.

"Bert, you're boiling."

He was wearing heavy trousers and a short-sleeved buttondown, his sizable stomach pressing outward, straining his shirt. Despite the permanent expression of disapproval caused by his under-bite, Bert was usually upbeat. That day, his consternation was genuine.

"I am a touch hot." He daubed his forehead with a handkerchief from his pocket. "It's the humidity. The ratio of the partial pressure of water vapor compared to the saturated pressure of water vapor is decidedly off kilter today. Because, as I'm sure you're aware, when the absolute humidity changes, the air pressure changes, which is, of course, very inconvenient for chemical-engineering calculations—for example, in commercial dryers, where temperature can vary considerably—and that's a real bee in my bonnet. Heat and mass balance equations aside, it's just plain miserable."

"You lost me at ratio. But I'm on board for miserable. Say, I hear Lottie has a higher IQ than you."

"Will wonders ever cease?"

"Not on Chapel Isle," she said, balancing the plunger against her neck so she could adjust her grip on the bags of bug repellent.

"I haven't seen you in town, Abby. You been holding up okay at the lighthouse?"

"I've been getting by."

There was little more she could say on the topic. She wasn't intentionally being evasive. Except nothing in her life had changed. That seemed slightly reprehensible to her somehow.

"How's life at the laundromat treating you?"

Abigail had first met Bert there; she later learned he worked for free for Franklin and Lottie, who owned the place. It was a testament to his friendship with the Gilquists. If a soul as sensitive as Bert could befriend them, they couldn't be that dreadful. Could they?

"While I'm not the type to speak ill of strangers, these summer people have no respect for the delicate mechanisms involved in industrial-grade machinery."

"Let me decode. Are you saying they're breaking your washers?"

"Yeah. Really gets my goat."

"T minus two months until September. Then they'll be gone." Abigail patted his shoulder reassuringly and he perked up.

"So who's the guy?"

"What guy?"

"The one driving the convertible with the shaky exhaust. I heard it a half mile away."

Peeved that she was making local headlines again over a guy she had no interest in, Abigail promptly excused herself, saying, "I barely met him. His name is Tim something. Anyhow, Bert, I have to get going."

"But—"

"My toilet's clogged. Tons to do." She waved the plunger for emphasis.

"But—"

"Great to see you."

She rushed away before Bert could get in the question he appeared to be dying to ask. As she hiked to the side street where she'd parked, the noon sun beat down on her ruthlessly, as if accusing her of not trying hard enough to fit in. Though she'd been living like a hermit for months, she was becoming the talk of the town all over again. It seemed Abigail couldn't win.

The lighthouse stood impassively against the cloudless skyline, framed in the windshield of Abigail's car as she pulled into the long, gravel driveway leading to the caretaker's cottage. With the air-conditioning blowing and the blue ocean in the distance separated from the short spit of grass and trees by a breakwater of dark-gray boulders, Abigail almost forgot how hot it was. While every living thing seemed to wilt in the heat, the lighthouse, the boulders, and the sea remained impervious. Abigail wished she could be too.

With her brand-new plunger at the ready, she went upstairs to the bathroom and faced off with the toilet. The porcelain tank was sweating as much as Abigail. Having never done this before, she was unsure how to proceed. She positioned the plunger, then pumped the handle, sloshing what little water was left in the basin.

"Am I even doing this correctly? I feel like I'm churning butter."

Soon the water level began to rise and the toilet flushed, completely back to normal.

"Nicely executed! For a newbie."

While washing her hands at the sink, Abigail caught a glimpse of her reflection in the medicine cabinet she'd had Merle order to replace the old, warped mirror that hung there before. Eye to eye with herself, she had to wonder if she should be proud of unblocking a toilet. Given how little she accomplished on an average day, Abigail thought she ought to be.

When Justin was three, he'd had trouble learning to cut with safety scissors. With his small hands and slowly developing motor skills, he couldn't manage to get the angle of the scissors right, so the paper would just crunch between the blades. Frustration quickly set it and so did the tears.

Paul came to Justin's defense. "I have a PhD in applied mathematics and I can't even cut paper with those darn things."

"But he needs to learn," Abigail had insisted. "He wouldn't cry about it if he didn't want to do it himself."

For a week, Abigail practiced with Justin. First on construction paper, which turned out to be too thick. Then copy paper from their home-office printer, which was slick, causing the dull blades to crush rather than cut. Last she'd resorted to newsprint. Abigail sat her son down on the floor with the weekend edition of the *Boston Herald,* put her arms around him, and cut an article out of every single page until he could do it himself.

While her despair over her husband's and son's deaths wasn't as palpable anymore and her days at the cottage had been filled with small chores, such as fiddling with the faucets so they wouldn't drip, jerry-rigging the refrigerator so it wouldn't rattle, and a panoply of random tasks she'd never envisioned filling her time, Abigail's world hadn't bloomed into anything magnificent. Or anything at all for that matter. She might be able to unclog a toilet, but it was her life that was in need of unclogging.

Abigail splashed water on her face to cool off. Tendrils of wet hair clung to her forehead, and she could taste the sweat on her chapped lips. Being hot only intensified the simmering resentment she felt toward the summer people and the way they treated the

island. The reaction surprised her, mainly because she couldn't ignore the fact that the natives used to think—and might *continue* to
think—of her in much the same terms.

"When do I get to be like everybody else here?"

The real question was: Did she want to be?

Abigail had yet to make a conscious decision. She herself was
unclear whether she remained because of her husband's childhood
love for the place or because it was easier than starting life over
somewhere else. Paul had visited Chapel Isle during the summers in
his youth and had spun his vacation stories into a world that came
alive in Abigail's mind. He'd waxed about the endless beaches, the
stores that sold delicious homemade ice cream, and the incompara-
ble lighthouse that was like something out of a book.

"An author couldn't make up one that was more fantastic," Paul
had told her. "Words can't describe it."

"Really?" Abigail had said, dubious. "Consider who you're talking to."

"Okay, maybe I can't convince you with that argument. But one
day you'll see it and you'll know I was right."

There Abigail was in the lighthouse her husband had adored,
alone. It wasn't as if she was bound to the location or being there
was propelling her toward some goal. Was living there merely an
excuse not to move on in every sense of the phrase?

Staying there out of convenience was, indeed, convenient. So
was not deciding at all.

D Desuetude (des′wi tood′, -tyo͞od′), *n.* the state of being no longer used or practiced. [1425–75; late ME < L *dēsuētūdo,* equiv. to *dēsuē-,* base of *dēsuēscere* to become accustomed to, unlearn (dē- <u>DE</u>- + *suēscere* to become accustomed to) + -*tūdō* -<u>TUDE</u>]

◆　◆　◆

The cottage held the afternoon heat like an obligation. Even with the windows open, the sturdy brick walls wouldn't let the air go. The place had stood empty, unoccupied for years, prior to Abigail's arrival, and this was the first summer that somebody had been there to open the windows, which took a Herculean effort. Swollen in their casings, the frames wouldn't budge. When the heat wave first hit, Abigail had spent hours wriggling the windowpanes until they raised. Since then she'd been reticent to close them, for fear they would be permanently stuck. The humidity made everything stick—the windows, the cupboards, the doors. Getting a spoon out of a kitchen drawer could easily turn into a wrestling match. The one upside was that the floors ceased to creak, because the boards were pressed too tightly together to move.

Abigail hadn't eaten a thing all day but she wasn't hungry. The weather sapped her appetite. She poured a glass of iced tea, doused herself in more bug spray, then went and sat on her front steps.

Waves were languidly lapping against the seawall, wafting a weak breeze in from the water. The muggy wind wouldn't let Abigail linger on the stoop for long, as though urging her on to the business she dreaded. Calling Lottie.

There was no reception on Abigail's cell phone. The landline wasn't a significant improvement. Over the crackle of static, Abigail got Lottie's voice mail and left a garbled message about the deal she'd struck with Franklin.

"Now what?" she asked herself.

While she would have relished sitting in a shady spot and reading a book, she felt pressure to circulate in town. Merle, Franklin, *and* Bert had each commented on her perceptible absence. Their remarks weren't meant to be disapproving, yet Abigail took them as discreet criticism, a judgment call on how she'd been living.

"Don't I have a right to do what I want? I'm a grown woman."

She was entitled to grieve, entitled to be sad, entitled to feel sorry for herself. But not forever.

Hoping to dodge a return call from Lottie, Abigail drove back into town and was forced to park on a residential side street she'd never been on. That was as close to the town square as she could get. And it wasn't that close.

A string of fishing cabins lined the road, which abutted the bay. They were the sorts of houses that had paper-thin walls, no insulation, and saggy roofs that were fortunate to have survived the winter. Each shouted: *summer rental*. Seeing them for the first time reminded Abigail that there were still uncharted parts of the island, places she hadn't seen. Chapel Isle had more to show her if she was willing to look.

Reaching the town square, Abigail experienced another first. Trash cans. She'd never noticed them before, but since the crowds of tourists had subsided slightly, what stood out compared to the familiar sights were the overflowing garbage bins and the debris collecting in the gutters. More and more, Abigail appreciated the locals' love-hate relationship with the summer people. Lines at the ice cream shop circled the block. Bike-rental shanties had materialized overnight. Every candy wrapper and soda can was a sign of cash that was going into native pockets. But earning that money came at quite an expense.

Abigail headed to the Kozy Kettle, hoping the lunch rush had dissipated and she could give Ruth an earful for spilling the beans about her desire to have the cottage repainted. However, from the moment Abigail entered the café, she couldn't get a syllable in edgewise.

"Abby, Abby," Ruth called, motioning her to sit down at the counter. "Wait 'til you get a load of this!"

The place had cleared save a handful of islanders that Abigail recognized, each stationed by the fans, soaking in the tepid air. Among them was George Meloch, the island's ferry captain and father to Denny, who'd had a crush on Abigail since she'd come to Chapel Isle. George was perched at the end of the counter next to the two elderly men that Abigail had dubbed the "John Deere twins" because they each invariably wore John Deere caps and stared at her sullenly. The men's garb was barely affected by the change in season——work boots, canvas pants, and T-shirts with oil stains that would never come clean. That was their uniform, heat wave or no heat wave.

Ruth poured Abigail a glass of ice water in a jelly jar, saying, "I just found out that some famous treasure hunter from up north is on the island, and he's itching to get to the Ship's Graveyard."

"Please refrain from using the term *itching*," Abigail said, scratching her fly bite. "See. It's Pavlovian."

"Didn't get that calamine, did ya?"

"I forgot. That said, I do have enough bug-blasting ammo to cause a black-fly genocide."

"Let the annihilation begin, baby. Everybody 'round here'll thank you."

"You were saying?"

"The buzz is——"

"*Buzz* is verboten too," Abigail objected, and scratched some more.

"Fine, fine. The skinny is that this guy is searching for the *Bishop's Mistress*."

That was twice in one day that the ship had been mentioned.

Abigail didn't put much stock in omens or signs; otherwise she wouldn't have been able to reside in a house many claimed was haunted. Still, this did strike her as a noteworthy coincidence. The word *coincidence* simply referred to when two things *coincided*. Etymologically, it had nothing to do with providence or luck, although the meaning had evolved to denote exactly that.

"Problem is, nobody will take him," Ruth added.

"Is it really that risky? Don't the fisherman have to navigate around those shoals every time they go out to sea?"

"Go around the Graveyard, yes. Go into it, no. Too many a boat has met its fate in those waters, so any sailor worth his salt avoids it like a curse."

"I'll be damned if he gets any captain to take him," George Meloch croaked from the end of the counter. He and the twins had been eavesdropping on Ruth's update. In Abigail's scant dealings with the stern man, George had proven he was as tough and crusty as he seemed.

"He's paying a lot, but nobody wants in. It's a fool's errand," George snarled, leaving in a huff. The bell over the café door clanged, punctuating his exit. The twins chewed their lips and kept silent.

"Why does George have such a grudge against the wreck divers?" Abigail asked in a hushed tone. "And why is everybody so interested in the *Bishop's Mistress*?"

"Can't talk about it with those two in listening distance." Ruth nodded at the twins. "They probably couldn't hear a fog horn from this far away, since neither of 'em turns on his hearing aid, but I'm not taking the chance."

The bell over the door rang again, announcing the arrival of a family of seven, who rolled into the café like the circus coming to town. As the harried parents tried shepherding their rambunctious kids toward a table, each shot off in a different direction. That was the John Deere twins' cue to go. They were ambling toward the exit when one of the three girls started skipping circles around them, hampering their passage.

"Sweetie, let those men get by," the mother insisted, as the father attempted to keep one of the boys from yanking napkins out of the dispensers on the counter.

"We'd like to order some food to take for a picnic lunch on the beach. You're still serving, aren't you?" the father asked plaintively. He had a diaper bag hanging from his shoulder, a cooler under his arm, and was using his free hand to try to grab the other kids as they began a game of tag.

"You're it," they each shouted, running from table to table.

"That is not what we do in a public place." The mother's scolding didn't put a damper on the game.

Ruth took pity on the parents, saying, "Absolutely. We'll pack everything up for your picnic. What can I get you?"

A little girl ran past Abigail and said, "Tag. You're it."

"She's not playing," her sister said, then they went on with their game as their little brother entertained himself rolling a toy race car across the floor and up the legs of the bar stools fixed under the counter. He was about Justin's age. Seeing the boy contentedly making engine noises caused a bulge of sadness in Abigail's chest, like a balloon expanding under her ribs. This was why she'd stayed at the cottage. Contending with her memories was complicated enough. Reminders of her past were everywhere in the real world. Alone at the lighthouse, there were none.

Unable to resist the impulse to flee, Abigail hurried for the door and accidentally kicked the boy's race car in her haste. The toy went skittering across the floor and he burst into tears. His mother rushed to him.

"I'm sorry," Abigail repeated again and again. That only made the boy sob harder. Neither of the parents was mad. They were too busy to be. She felt terrible nonetheless.

Ruth now had to take pity on Abigail. She stepped in to redirect the attention, announcing, "How about cupcakes for everybody? Would you kids like that? On the house," she assured the father.

The door to the Kozy Kettle closed behind Abigail as she heard the kids cheering, "We want cupcakes, Daddy. Cupcakes!"

◆ ◆ ◆

Rattled, Abigail began to walk to her car, thinking her red face could pass for heat stroke instead of sheer mortification. Had those months alone totally eroded her social graces or, worse yet, her ability to be social?

"Is that you, Abby?" a voice hollered. Denny Meloch was jogging up behind her. "Hey, it is!"

Since introducing himself on the ferry ride over to Chapel Isle, Denny had been dogged about pursuing a friendship with Abigail. His sweetly innocent nature made it hard for her not to like him, yet she got the sense he wished she more-than-liked him. Abigail wasn't interested in reciprocating Denny's affections, but he was still a welcome sight. Tall, lanky, and ten years her junior, he had a baseball cap on backward, and tan lines from wearing sunglasses day in and day out had left bright circles around his large blue eyes.

"I just bumped into your father at the Kettle."

"We're on break before the next ferry run. This is our busiest season. I could drive that stretch of water between here and the mainland with my eyes closed. Morning, noon, and night, same thing back and forth. Between you and me, it gets kinda boring after a while."

The yearning for something different—Abigail saw it on Denny's face and recognized it because she'd seen it in her own.

"So how you been, Abby?"

"Good. Getting by."

Denny pulled off his cap and said solemnly, "I been meaning to pay my respects."

In an instant, he'd unwittingly closed the gap in time between that very second and the fire, ushering Abigail back to the funeral and the mourners offering their condolences.

Anger crept into her voice. "How . . . how did you hear about that?"

"Dunno. Around, I guess. People were, um, talking. . . ." Denny stuttered into a bashful silence.

"It's okay," Abigail said, hitching down the emotions that threatened to rear up. He didn't deserve her wrath or resentment. "I told only one person, and I thought that person would keep it to herself."

In reality, Abigail hadn't *told* anybody. Ruth had pegged her as a widow because she was also one herself and had revealed as much to Merle only so he'd look after Abigail. Although Abigail couldn't conceive of either divulging such a private matter to anyone else, one of them had.

Anxious, Denny was kneading his cap in his hands. "It was a secret?"

"Evidently it's not anymore."

"Didn't mean to piss you off."

"I'm not."

"I'd be! If you can't trust a person with something private, you can't trust 'em with——" He was about to curse. "Squat. Dad says I swear too much in front o' the visitors. Supposed to watch my mouth."

"I'm not a tourist, Denny."

"I know, but you're . . ."

There it was again. She wasn't a summer person, wasn't a native.

"A what?" she asked.

"A lady," Denny said, then checked his watch in a panic. "Listen, I gotta go. Don't want Dad to tear me a new one for being late. But I'm sorry about . . . well, the first thing. And I'm sorry about the second thing too."

"Thanks, Denny."

The second thing, Abigail thought as he trotted away.

She wasn't sure if she should blame herself for not being honest with people or if she shouldn't care what the islanders thought of her. Maybe the problem wasn't trusting other people. It was trusting herself to be able to handle whatever came her way.

Suddenly she felt a sharp pinch on her lower leg. Another black fly had bitten her. It was right by her shoe, where she'd forgotten to spray repellent.

"Very tricky. This is officially war."

Abigail was manically scratching the welt when she felt a tap on her shoulder and nearly jumped out of her skin.

It was Tim Ulman.

"Hate to interrupt your battle plans, but I thought I recognized you. Abigail, right? Lighthouse Abigail?" He was eating an ice cream cone, shades propped on the top of his head, pinning back his wavy chestnut hair.

"Sorry if I scared you. It's these loafers," Tim explained, modeling the soft leather driving moccasins. "If I'd worn my usual wingtips, I might not have been so stealthy on the cobblestones."

"And I apologize if I scared *you* by threatening armed conflict. I might have reconsidered settling on this island had I known these flying terrors were a factor."

"Come for the black flies, stay for the horrible parking. That should be Chapel Isle's new motto," he joked. "It can't be that hellish or you wouldn't have stayed, would you?"

Excellent question.

"This island definitely has its quirks. But it'll grow on you," Abigail replied, then tried to make her exit. "I'm sure you want to get back to your relaxing vacation, and I've got to—"

"Relaxing, you said it," Tim agreed, trying to keep the conversation rolling.

She caught a flicker of nervousness in his delivery. *Maybe he's lonely,* Abigail thought. She could certainly identify with that feeling.

"I only got here this morning, but hearing the ocean and smelling the fresh air, I already feel better. I can't tell you how badly I needed this trip. I don't know if you've ever gone through a divorce. It's the inverse of relaxing."

"Can't say that I have," she stated, looking to extricate herself from the conversation before some local spotted her with Tim and the rumors went hurtling across town. Abigail did, however, note his use of *inverse,* which was grammatically correct yet rarely used in modern English. The term stemmed from the Latin *invertere,* to turn upside down or inside out, which gave it a lively, visual feel in the noun form. She considered it a more succinct word than *opposite,* and for no other reason than that, Abigail suddenly saw Tim in a faintly different light.

"So you're single?" he inquired. A seriousness in his tone peeked through from behind the breezy banter. "I'm quoting the sheriff, I realize. Just wanted to make sure before I invited you to dinner."

Uh-oh.

While empirically attractive, Tim was almost *too* good-looking. Abigail had never gone for jocks or pretty boys. The geeks in the science lab were more her speed. Paul had majored in math. For her, a studious nature was sexy. When they were dating, Paul would self-effacingly say, "My brain is my handsomest feature."

To which Abigail would always reply, "I can't see your brain and I still think you're handsome."

Her husband had been the whole package—looks, smarts, and heart, a hard combination to find. And even harder to part with.

She could have used being a widow as a pretext, claimed she was in mourning, which she was, but what Merle said about getting out of her own head had struck a chord. Abigail didn't particularly want to have dinner with Tim. But going on a date would be categorically outside her comfort zone, so on that merit she thought she should agree. Even if it would set tongues wagging.

"Uh, um, yes," she answered haltingly. "I'm single. Ish."

"Single-ish? Are you separated? Have a boyfriend? Trying to nicely blow me off?" he asked cautiously, clearly hoping that wasn't the case.

Abigail didn't consider herself single, but she didn't consider herself married either. She didn't consider herself much at all, which was why she rarely looked in a mirror or cut her fingernails or brushed her hair. It was also why she was always forgetting to eat. Tim's ice cream cone reminded her that she was famished.

"No, it's that I haven't been asked on a date in a while," she said, evading a straight answer.

"I broke your streak. How do you feel about that?"

"I feel . . ."

Abigail searched her brain for some sort of emotion to describe. Verbs, nouns, and adjectives percolated through her thoughts. What surfaced was unexpected.

"Hungry."

Amused, Tim raised a brow. "Does that mean we're on for dinner?"

"I guess it does," she said, praying she wouldn't regret this.

For such a cute guy, he seemed relieved that Abigail had consented to go out with him. The cocky edge in his voice was gone. That made him decidedly less Grecian god and more approachably human. Abigail could handle *human*.

"I'll defer to you for the best restaurant in town," he said. "Any suggestions where we could go for a nice, quiet meal?"

"The mainland."

"You can't be serious, Abigail." Tim genuinely chuckled. "This island is renowned for its seafood. There has to be someplace."

"Honestly, I don't eat out that often. The only recommendation I can make is my kitchen."

"Terrific. What time should I come by?"

Well worded, Abigail silently reproached herself. Her language selection had painted her into a corner.

"Seven. Ish?"

"You're a woman who hedges her bets, I take it. Since I used to work at a hedge fund, I can handle that. Nothing wrong with being cautious. Seven-*ish* it is."

As they were agreeing on the details, a red SUV full of teenagers came swerving around a corner of the town square, the loud bass of a song radiating from the vehicle in syncopated sonic booms. The car jetted by and the side mirror nearly clipped Abigail's shoulder. Tim grabbed her elbow, pulling her to safety on the sidewalk. It was a close call that left her breathless.

"Are you all right?" he asked. "Are you hurt?"

She was about to make a harsh retort about *these awful summer people* but stopped herself because the *summer person* standing next to her had just saved her from being hit by a car.

"If I wasn't sweating already, *that* got my heart pumping." Abigail dusted herself off and straightened her tank top.

"I didn't pull your arm out of its socket, did I? Wouldn't want to make it harder for you to cook," he teased, trying to lighten the mood.

"I'll survive. The issue is: Will you? You haven't tasted my food."

"I'm up for a challenge." Tim toasted her with his ice cream cone, grinning as he walked away.

Am I? Abigail had to ask.

She watched him stride off, broad-shouldered, confident. Then, without warning, her mind slid back to a memory of Paul at their wedding. He was leading her to the dance floor for their first song as a couple. Abigail could practically feel the hard parquet floor underfoot and the gentle tug of Paul's hand. They'd selected a traditional waltz, taken dance lessons, memorized the steps. She could hear the music as clearly as she'd heard the radio blasting from the SUV.

Abigail had to physically shake aside the thought. Was this always going to happen? Would every new person and every new day be linked like a chain to her past? If so, was there an anchor somewhere at the bottom that Abigail would be able to untie herself from?

If she couldn't, she was destined to sink.

Esurient (i soŏr´ē ant), *adj.* hungry; greedy. [1665–75; < L *ēsurient–* (s. of *ēsuriēns,* prp. of *ēsurīre*) hungering, equiv. to *ēsur–* hunger + *–ent– –*ENT]

❖   ❖   ❖

With her first *first date in almost a decade looming, Abigail went* directly to Weller's Market.

The island's lone grocery store, Weller's occupied a large, barn-type building and was stocked floor-to-ceiling like a frontier trading post, complete with decorative wagon wheels mounted to the walls. Cracked linoleum floors and old-timey décor notwith-standing, the produce was shipped in fresh from the mainland and the shelves were always full. That afternoon, a few women trolled the aisles, locals and out-of-towners alike. For Abigail, telling them apart was a cinch. The natives wore regular clothes; the tourists, bathing suits and cover-ups, their hair wet from a swim. While the islanders were selecting vegetables and scrutinizing the packaged cuts of pork, the summer people tossed ground beef, hot dog buns, and jumbo bags of chips into their carts. Everyday food, vaca-tion food—there was a decided difference. Abigail just needed food, period. The fact that she was starving made everything look delicious, especially the candy, which she rarely ate. Ravenous, she ripped open a chocolate bar and gobbled bite after bite as she cruised the store in search of some low-stress entrée to whip up for Tim.

Having subsisted on sandwiches and cereal for months, the concept of cooking an entire meal made her stomach hurt. It was that or the candy bar. In the freezer section, frozen dinners sat behind glass, presenting themselves as an easy out. Could she pawn off beef teriyaki or parmesan-crusted chicken as her own cuisine? Maybe. Except the cardboard containers were so small that she would have had to buy a half dozen to make it appear as if she'd prepared the recipe from scratch.

In the past, Abigail's track record with frozen dinners had not been stellar. She'd massacred more than her share of turkey Tetrazzinis when she moved into the cottage. Because of her fear of the oven and its fateful connection to the fire that took her family, Abigail had eventually broken down and ordered a microwave, which she mainly used to zap water for tea rather than wait for the kettle to boil.

"You got yourself into this," she sighed, putting back a tempting box of beef stroganoff and letting the frosty air blast her skin. Abigail wanted to climb in next to the fish sticks and prepared piecrusts, not only to cool down but to hide from what she had to face.

Before the fire, she'd been a confident cook. When she and Paul bought their house, they'd had the kitchen stylishly renovated. Marble countertops, tiled backsplash, stainless-steel appliances, custom cabinets—a chef's dream. Or, in Abigail's case, incentive to become a chef. Friends gave her cookbooks as housewarming gifts, the perfect combination of the hobby she loved—books— and the craft she was trying to master. Paul had gotten in on the act too.

"Cooking is basically math," he'd told her one evening after a trip to the grocery store. "Multiply the number of cups of x by a certain amount of tablespoons of y, then presto. Dinner!"

Paul had been undaunted by anything involving numbers. Abigail, however, was more circumspect with numbers as well as food. Too much of an ingredient, a sprinkle of the incorrect spice, and a meal could go horribly amiss in a heartbeat. The last time she'd cooked for anybody besides herself was the dinner she made the night of the fire. It was penne pasta and prosciutto topped with creamy vodka sauce from a jar. She'd been running late from work and knew she could save a side of penne for Justin to eat with butter, then add the sauce to the rest for Paul and her. Abigail remembered thinking that evening, as she'd put the dishes in the dishwasher, the sauce wasn't that great, too much oil and not enough vodka. She'd reminded herself not to get that brand again and to try a recipe from one of the housewarming cookbooks next time. Abigail never got the chance.

"Simple," she told herself, forgoing the market's pasta aisle on principle. "Think simple."

She opted for a chicken, new potatoes, salad greens, vanilla bean ice cream, and a package of brownies from the bakery section. Into the cart also went her regular staples: bread, jam, peanut butter, and apples.

"No, I didn't bake the brownies myself," she said to herself. "That isn't technically cheating."

An older woman wearing plastic rollers in her hair shot Abigail a distrustful look while sorting through the cantaloupes and sniffing them to find the ripest melon. Her floral housecoat and orthopedic shoes gave her away as an islander.

"Ms. Harker," the woman said with a nod.

Although Abigail hadn't the foggiest who the woman was, she nodded back, then briskly pushed her cart away.

"She's wearing rollers in public and looking at me as if *I'm* the weirdo?"

What stung more was that she was known not for the attributes she prided herself on—her intellect, her kindness, her skills—but for being the widow who lived at the haunted lighthouse.

"Whose fault is that?" she asked introspectively.

"Whose fault is what?" the teenage girl at the checkout stand wanted to know.

Abigail hadn't realized she was next in line.

"Nothing. I forgot the salad dressing."

"'Kay. This be all?" The girl had her hair slicked into a ponytail, the loose pieces pinned down with tiny colored barrettes.

"Oh, calamine lotion. Do you have that?"

"Aisle three. You can go get it. I'll wait," she said listlessly.

"Thanks." Abigail went and grabbed a giant bottle of calamine lotion, then swung by the condiments aisle for some balsamic vinaigrette. When she returned to the register, the girl was picking at her sparkle nail polish, killing time.

"I'm supposed to give you this. It's free." She handed Abigail a map. "City makes us hand 'em out to tourists. The map tells you where the 'hot spots' are. There's, like, tons of beaches. Cute stores with stuff made outta seashells. We even have a lighthouse. It's kinda lame, 'cept some people like to go see it."

Abigail stared at her. The woman in the rollers could have picked her out of a police lineup, yet this local girl didn't recognize her at all.

"Ms. Harker don't need a map," a female voice stated.

It was Janine Wertz. She'd appeared at the register with a stack of coupon circulars to put by the front door. Her dishwater blond hair was pushed behind her ears to show off a set of dangly freshwater pearl earrings. The fancy earrings were too formal for her rumpled T-shirt and jean shorts, almost deliberately so, to draw attention to them. Abigail assumed they were a gift from Janine's husband, Clint, whom Abigail had caught cheating on Janine last fall. She hadn't told a soul.

"Pretty earrings," Abigail said.

Janine tried not to smile, though she was clearly glad someone had noticed. "Thanks. They're a birthday present."

Abigail was happy she'd guessed right and even happier to rouse a fleeting smile from the hard-as-nails Janine. During the winter, Abigail had occasionally run into her at the market or around town, but their acquaintanceship didn't develop beyond being civil to each other. The woman Abigail saw kissing Janine's husband, however, had ceased to work at Weller's. Something Abigail definitely took note of.

"Nice to see you eatin' something besides sandwiches," Janine observed as the girl bagged Abigail's purchases. Then the jar of peanut butter rolled down the conveyer belt.

Janine corrected herself. "Well, in *addition* to peanut butter and jelly."

Obviously, people in town had been keeping tabs on Abigail. Were the natives finally warming to her, or were they monitoring her every move for a sign that she couldn't hack it here?

"You haven't been at bingo," Janine commented, careful not to be overly friendly.

That's when Abigail figured it out. Janine must have heard she was a widow. Pity or indifference—Abigail couldn't decide which was worse.

She forced a grin as short-lived as Janine's had been, saying, "I'll try to make it to the next game."

Juggling the heavy grocery bags, Abigail started the trek back to where she'd parked. Couples with strollers and kids scampering about turned the sidewalk into an obstacle course. She was so focused on not knocking into any more small children that she collided with a man in a straw hat who was standing on a corner, scouring a bulky folding map. He stumbled, and Abigail lurched as the groceries threatened to slip from her grasp.

"Pardon me," the man said politely, as if the accident was his fault instead of hers. He tucked the map into the pocket of his fishing vest and graciously assisted Abigail in repositioning the bags in her arms. The brim of his straw hat cast most of his weathered face in shadow.

"No, no, I should be more alert," she maintained. "Please don't think mowing down tourists is a regular occurrence here."

"Oh, you're an islander?" he asked, hopeful.

Abigail couldn't settle on how to respond. She went with, "I've been here awhile."

"Then perhaps you could tell me where Pamlico Shores Beach is? This map I brought with me isn't as specific as I'd expected. It covers from here to Delaware. If I was flying a plane rather than walking, it might be more effective."

"Not a problem. Pamlico Shores Beach is on the northeast end of the island." She gave him directions, complete with the names of the streets and the approximate distances between the turnoffs, then sent him on his way. It was a gratifying moment.

"Maybe you are getting the hang of this place," she told herself, pleased.

Any satisfaction garnered from putting the man in the straw hat on the right path sloughed away as Abigail overshot the street where she'd parked and had to double back, using the bay as a guidepost. Twenty minutes later, arms aching from carrying the groceries, she got to her car, opened the door, and spotted her own island map tucked above the visor.

Humbling, she thought.

As Abigail packed the grocery bags into her station wagon, a truck pulled up alongside her. At the wheel was Nat Rhone. He rolled down the window.

"That's a lotta chow. You having a party? Because I didn't get my invitation."

Days spent in the sun out on the Atlantic had lightened Nat's hair to a sandy brown and darkened his freckles. Abigail might not have known it was him except for his hard-set jaw and the fact that he was still driving Hank Scokes's F-150. She'd heard through Ruth that Nat was drinking more and having trouble keeping Hank's fishing business afloat. She considered asking Nat how he'd been faring, financially and emotionally, but thought it imprudent. Though he may have looked different, she doubted his temper had mellowed.

"Just trying to eat better. For a change."

Abigail didn't know why she was lying.

"'Bout time. Your fridge was pretty empty last I saw it. Don't want you wasting away."

Nat had peeked into her refrigerator the day he'd helped her move the antiques upstairs from the basement. The memory of being humiliated by how poorly she'd been eating still made her cheeks burn. That day Nat had told her how he'd once been a short-order cook, one of many jobs he'd held as he traveled from place to place, seemingly unable to settle down in any particular spot for too long. He shared that tiny scrap from his past, then shut down. Nat had been wary about opening up to her. Little had he known she had as much to hide as he did.

Has he heard the rumors? He did say he didn't want you "wasting away." That's something you'd say to a widow. But he hasn't mentioned it. Knowing Nat, he wouldn't. Except you don't *know him. Not that well.*

Feeling as if Nat could see right through her and hear the questions jumbled in her mind, Abigail switched the topic.

"How's business treating you?" she asked, cringing on the inside. This was the very thing she'd instructed herself not to do.

"I've had more day trips and fishing tours, what with the season. Sad fact is, money's tight." He spoke with a measured calm, as if his voice knew better than to betray his feelings. "Fishing industry isn't what it used to be. I may have to pick up stakes and move."

"Move? As in away from Chapel Isle?"

"That is the general concept behind moving."

The news hit Abigail hard. Harder than she imagined it should. She struggled not to show it.

"I got this new gig, though. Some guy offering to pay big bucks to go to the Graveyard for a week of deep-sea diving. Way he spins it, we could each be in for a windfall if things run smooth." He gripped the steering wheel as if he could rein the possibility into reality.

Alarm bells went off for Abigail as she recalled what George Meloch had said at the café.

"Nat, don't! It's not called the Ship's Paradise or the Boating Oasis or the Yacht Spa. It's the *Graveyard*. It earned that name for a reason."

"The Yacht Spa?" he said sardonically. The deep green color of his eyes seemed perfectly suited to his mocking tone.

"Everyone claims it's too dangerous, that nobody should go there."

"Why?" he asked, smug. "You afraid I might get hurt?"

Abigail recoiled, realizing she'd displayed too much concern. "No. But if you're not going to survive to spend all the money you say you'll earn, why bother?"

Nat took the snub in stride, settling back into the driver's seat as though it was a trifling blow. "I can handle the Graveyard. Don't worry about me."

"I'm not."

"Good."

Their childish parrying ended in a draw. Almost every time they were together, they fought. She'd incited him to a fistfight at the Kozy Kettle, a battle of wills at Duncan Thadlow's house, and a duel of determination while they'd rearranged furniture at the caretaker's cottage. They didn't have conversations. They quarreled. Abigail didn't argue with anybody except Nat. She couldn't help herself. He made her want to have the last word, to be the one in the right. Abigail had felt wrong, victimized, and aggrieved for so long that being right was a reprieve. Even if it was only in a petty squabble.

"This 'guy' who's chartering your boat, is he searching for the *Bishop's Mistress*?"

Nat narrowed his eyes. "Didn't take you for such a sailing buff. You familiar with it?"

"A bit." Abigail shifted the last grocery bag in her arms, as if to distract Nat from the fib. "What's so special about that ship?"

"Beats me," he replied, cagey. "Whatever was aboard must be worth something, or else why would this guy pay to find it?"

There was more to the story that Nat wasn't telling her. They both knew it.

Abigail's cell phone rang, breaking the tension and making her flinch, which caused the contents of the final grocery bag to spill everywhere. The head of lettuce and the pint of ice cream bobbled across the sandy lane as the paper bag ripped down the center. She could either pick up the phone or clean up the mess. Abigail didn't want to do either. She was too embarrassed.

"Oughta answer that," Nat urged. "Oh, and don't forget your apples. They rolled under your car. Have fun getting 'em."

He rode away as her phone rang.

"God, I—"

Abigail was going to say *hate him*. Except she didn't. What she hated was the effect Nat had on her. He transformed her into somebody who was clumsy, inept, mouthy—characteristics she wouldn't remotely attribute to herself. If Abigail didn't know better, she would think she had a crush on the man.

"Coming, coming," she told the bleating phone. Lottie was on the other end.

"Abby, dear. Where are you? I need you to come quick."

Static sizzled the line, muddling everything Lottie said after that.

"Lottie, I can barely hear you. Did you say 'come quick'?"

What am I? Lassie? Abigail thought.

"Lottie, speak up. Where? Now? *Right* now? Okay, okay, I'm coming. Yes, quickly. Bye."

She hung up and started to collect her food from the street. Sand clung to the lettuce leaves and adhered to moisture on the rapidly defrosting container of ice cream. When she peered under the station wagon, Abigail saw that the apples had amassed in a furrow well beyond the range of her outstretched arm.

"Forget it. Why do I need fruit when I have brownies?"

She started the engine, cranked the air-conditioning, and retrieved the calamine lotion for her bug bites, which were itching nonstop. As she slathered the pale pink cream on her arm and leg, she wondered when her life would become normal again. Or did being a widow mean that a normal life would always be like the apples—just out of reach?

F

Farraginous (fə-raj´ə-nəs), *adj.* heterogeneous; mixed: *a farraginous collection of random ideas.* [1605–15; < L *farrāgin-* (s. of *farrāgō*) mixed grains (see FARRAGO) + -OUS]

◆　◆　◆

Thankful for the map she'd been ashamed of minutes ago, Abigail used it to find the address Lottie had rattled off over the phone. The tenant's name was Marion McNair.

"She's a real proper lady, like you," Lottie had said. "I'm sure y'all will get along."

Is that how I'm perceived? As a "real proper lady"? Abigail mused as she turned off a main road onto a sandy side street.

Lottie didn't do sarcasm, yet Abigail could discern the inherent slander, making her curious to meet this woman with whom she purportedly had so much in common.

The map led her to a hulking, modern house in the southwestern section of the island. A cookie-cutter copy of its neighbors, the place featured floor-to-ceiling windows facing a view of the marsh, glass-block insets, a sprawling wraparound porch, and steeply pitched rooflines. Built on tall pilings because the area was a flood plain, the home presided over the street imperiously.

As she parked, then climbed the front steps, Abigail realized this was the vicinity she'd toured while doing Merle's security detail in the fall. Even though she hadn't been back since, she could recollect testing doorknobs and inspecting windows as if it was yesterday. She should have been at the caretaker's cottage preparing for her date with Tim—a date she was beginning to dread more by the minute—but instead she was about to knock on a door she had been checking the lock to months earlier.

An attractive woman wearing a white linen sundress and coral necklace greeted Abigail with expectant enthusiasm. "Please tell me you're with the rental agency?"

"I am," Abigail replied.

Ish, she thought.

Polite and polished, this Marion McNair was a kindly comparison. In fact, it was very flattering to be likened to her. Except Lottie was as proficient at praise as she was at sarcasm. That put Abigail on guard.

Marion ushered her into the home's cavernous foyer. Travertine floor tiles stretched as far as Abigail could see. The décor was seaside chic, right down to the fluffy white slip-covered couches and the coffee table fashioned from driftwood. Wafts of cool air instantly enveloped Abigail, a respite from the heat.

"You have air-conditioning?" Her jealousy was difficult to conceal.

"Had. It broke down. And the toaster won't turn on. And the toilet in the master suite is blocked."

The toilet. Of course.

"It's so hot that I don't want to leave the house for fear of letting the cool air out. It's the same feeling as when you lose power and won't open the refrigerator in order to keep the food chilled."

Abigail appreciated her analogy. "I totally understand."

She felt at ease with Marion, as if she was the sort of person Abigail would have met in Justin's play group or at a book club or a wine tasting. Marion's elegantly beachy attire and her cultured comportment gave Abigail a taste of her former lifestyle, which she was luxuriating in until Marion said, "You're going to fix everything, right?"

"Fix? Me? No, no, I'm the 'middleman,' so to speak. The agency sent me to make a list of the issues for somebody else to address. I'm not a professional."

"Two seconds. Just two seconds and I'm sure you could have this taken care of."

Refusing to take no for an answer, Marion guided Abigail to the kitchen, where a black plastic toaster sat on the granite countertop, looking lowbrow against the backdrop of pricey contemporary finishes.

"The light won't go on when you press the lever." Marion pushed it down. "See? No light, no toast."

She was speaking to Abigail as though the basic mechanics of a toaster were outside her ken. Abigail had to defy the urge to defend herself, to extol the virtues of her advanced degree, her thorough proficiency in Latin, her encyclopedic understanding of language. She almost blurted out that her paper on theoretical lexicography's effect on American-Asian diplomatic relations was used as teaching material in undergraduate linguistics classes.

You think Marion here in her fancy rental house gives a hoot about your academic paper?

Abigail's indignation deflated into apathy. Lexicography had ceased to be her profession as well as her passion. She didn't really have a passion anymore. That weighed on her almost as heavily as the grief. Then it dawned on her that Marion viewed her as the "help," an insight that was followed by an appalling realization: What if this was the way Abigail had treated everybody when she first arrived on Chapel Isle?

Oh, no—am I as stuck up as she is? Is that what Lottie meant?

A guilty conscience spurred Abigail to utter a phrase she hoped she wouldn't regret.

"Okay, let me see what I can do."

An inspection of the toaster led her to discover that the plug wasn't fitted securely to the rear of the appliance. Abigail pushed it in and the light lit up. She wished things had gone as smoothly with the telephone at the caretaker's cottage as they had with this toaster. The thermostat wasn't quite as easy to conquer, but after resetting the timing mechanism, the air kicked on with a triumphant *whoosh*.

Marion clapped. "I knew you could do it."

That makes one of us.

"Now if you can get the toilet to work, you'll be my hero."

"Too bad I left my cape in the car," Abigail grumbled as she tailed Marion up the carpeted stairs to the master suite.

Vaulted ceilings and a color palette of cream and taupe gave the room a soothing ambience. A selection of swimsuits and summer outfits was draped on the king-sized bed, a tennis racket was leaning against the bureau, and Marion's jewelry was lying on top. A diamond bracelet and gold watch were placed apart from the rest, presumably because they weren't "vacation appropriate."

"Excuse the mess. We've barely unpacked," Marion explained. "The bathroom's in here."

A jet tub, glass-enclosed shower, and double sinks got Abigail thinking.

I didn't get a jet tub. Then again, I didn't even get a toaster.

The list went on and on in Abigail's brain as Marion lifted the toilet lid. The waterline hovered near the bottom of the basin. Since her skill level with toilets was limited at best, she was frank with the woman.

"If you don't have a plunger, you're out of luck."

"But I don't. I don't have a plunger. That's not something you pack when you go on vacation." Marion was growing testy. "I'm not paying four thousand dollars a week to plunge my own toilet."

That settled it. Abigail wanted the caretaker's cottage repainted the very next day. If Lottie and Franklin were raking in that kind of profit, there was no excuse for the dilapidated state of the home she rented.

Eager to stick it to Lottie, Abigail counseled Marion, saying, "You'll get no argument from me. Maybe you should ask for a deduction. You'd be well within your rights as a renter."

"I don't want a deduction. I want my toilet to flush." Marion's composed expression began to crack. She was on the verge of tears. "I want to put on a pretty dress and do my makeup and go out to dinner with my husband. Is that too much to ask? He's never around. Always at work. I had to fight tooth and nail just to get him to come here for a few days. I can't remember the last time we had dinner together. One stinking dinner."

Abigail felt for the woman. Although she wasn't looking forward to the meal she had planned with Tim that night, dinner was all Marion had to look forward to. So Abigail said it again.

"Okay, let me see what I can do."

No time to be squeamish, she told herself, then she removed the toilet tank's lid, dunked her hand in the water, and repositioned the parts inside, feigning that she'd done this before. A silent prayer on her lips, Abigail gave the handle a push. The toilet flushed resoundingly.

"Ooh!" Marion squeezed her arm. "You're the best!"

Delighted with everything that had been accomplished, Marion escorted Abigail to the front door, singing her praises.

"You're a miracle worker. This is such a relief, I can't tell you. Now if you'll excuse me, my husband will be home from golfing soon and I have to get ready."

At that, she sent Abigail packing. The door closed on her back. The heat was there to greet her on the porch.

"You're welcome," Abigail carped.

Wishing she'd had the chance to wash her hands, she returned to her car to discover that the top had come off the pint of ice cream. The contents were melting through the paper grocery bag, oozing onto her seats. With the rest of the food in danger of spoiling and nothing to clean up the spill, Abigail pumped the air-conditioning and raced home.

A pickup was parked in her driveway. Duncan Thadlow was planted on her front stoop. Beside him sat a cardboard box, a telltale delivery from Lottie.

The box undoubtedly held a sampling of Lottie's favorite romance novels, each reread so often that the covers had lost their color at the edges. Though Abigail wouldn't admit it, she had gone through every bodice ripper in the last batch from Lottie, more out of desperation than a genuine interest in the subject matter. They were the literary equivalent of potato chips—not terribly filling but available. She'd even circled back to them when she was tired of the books she'd brought, a meager set that had been stored at her parents' house at the time of the fire. Abigail's once-great collection had been burned along with her home, reducing years of careful cultivation in fiction, nonfiction, vintage encyclopedias, and memoir to ash.

One of the reasons she'd loved her house so much was the built-in bookshelves in the study. The home was modeled after Edith Wharton's estate, The Mount, with grand, spacious rooms and soaring ceilings topped with finely milled moldings. The library shelves were as tall as the room—nine feet. Abigail had filled every inch, with hundreds of volumes. Now she had less than thirty original books to her name. If she added in Lottie's contributions, the count nearly doubled, though that didn't improve Abigail's outlook on her greatly abridged collection.

Trashy romances as an olive branch, Abigail thought. *How high was Lottie's IQ again?*

Duncan waved and stood as Abigail pulled into the gravel drive.

"What on earth is he doing here?" she asked herself, glancing at the dashboard clock. She had only an hour before Tim would arrive.

"Wasn't sure if you got your john sorted, so I figured I'd be neighborly and stop by," Duncan intoned as she unpacked the car.

"That most definitely is . . . neighborly."

If you could only hear the other adjectives I was considering.

"Is that ice cream leaking through your bag or are you just glad to see me?"

Abigail let him give her a hand with the groceries, as well as with Lottie's delivery, while mentally willing Duncan to hit the bricks. She needed to get ready for her date. But he wasn't picking up on her vibe. Not by a long shot.

"You've done a lot with this old place," he remarked as he toured the downstairs living space, scrutinizing the antiques, commenting on anything and everything that caught his eye. "This ain't veneer on the table or them chairs. Nope, this is solid teak. The real McCoy. Is that bird's-eye maple on the sideboard?"

Pretend to listen, Abigail reminded herself. That was what Ruth had told her.

As Duncan blathered, drily itemizing the variety of woods, their global origins, and the tools traditionally employed for marquetry inlays, Abigail unpacked her groceries, throwing in an *uh-huh* at appropriate intervals. Then he segued into how wood not indigenous to the South was shipped to the Carolinas, a topic that circuitously brought him to a dissertation on the local waters.

"I know this stretch of the Atlantic better than the back of my hand. Have my dad to thank for that. He was raised here too. Matter of fact, his great-grandpappy helped build this lighthouse. The last caretaker wanted to interview my dad on account of it. Said he was writing a thesis or something. Long-haired hippie dude."

"Right, right," Abigail said, half listening as she unsuccessfully attempted to wash the sand off the heads of lettuce. Merle had mentioned the last caretaker too. His stint was short-lived, only two days, and he'd reputedly been run off the property by the ghost of Wesley Jasper.

"'Tween you and me, I doubt that hippie really cared much for the lighthouse or his thesis." Duncan was leaning in the doorway to the kitchen, unfazed that Abigail had her back to him and was basically ignoring him. "I think he was here looking for clues."

That got Abigail listening. She shut off the faucet.

"Clues to what?"

"Rumors been swirling for decades that Mr. Jasper kept notes about where the *Bishop's Mistress* sank. Anybody searching for the wreckage would want to get their hands on 'em in order to look for the cups."

The lighthouse, Mr. Jasper, the ship—this was all, quite literally, hitting too close to home for Abigail.

"Cups?" she asked, now fully paying attention.

"It's folklore, legend, the sorta stuff my dad told me to put me to sleep when I was young. Story goes that the great patriot and silversmith, Paul Revere, had been commissioned to make a decanter and set of goblets out of gold, rare in itself because he usually only worked in silver. Hence the title—"

"Silversmith," Abigail said impatiently. "Yes, and?"

"Supposedly, the set was never claimed. Revere's son held onto it until a North Carolina businessman bought the decanter and goblets, then shipped them down on the ill-fated *Bishop's Mistress*."

A Boston native, Abigail was familiar enough with Paul Revere to realize the significance of such a find. The decanter and "cups" would be worth a hefty sum. This had to be the reason why the much-talked-about treasure hunter wanted to go to the Ship's Graveyard and also why he was paying Nat so handsomely to take him.

Abigail had a sinking feeling about this sunken ship. She hustled Duncan out of the kitchen into the living room, saying, "Boy, am I beat. Tired. Bushed. Whipped. I think I need to hit the hay, so . . ."

"Bed?" Duncan inquired. "Aren't you fixing supper? By the looks of it, I thought you had a beau comin' over for a five-course meal."

Something in his tone changed, reminding Abigail that she didn't know Duncan well, nor was she certain of his motives. As the clock crept toward seven, desperate times called for desperate measures. She remembered Ruth asking what the sweets were for, and a foolproof idea emerged.

"Duncan, I have to be honest. I have my period. You know, a ladies' cycle? Monthly bill? I'd kind of like to be alone."

"Oh . . . absolutely." He scuttled toward the front door. "Have a good . . . um, take it easy . . . uh, feel better," he stammered, hotfooting it for his truck.

With Duncan gone and less than an hour until Tim was slated to show, Abigail ricocheted around the house, setting out plates and silverware and tidying up. Then it was time to turn on the oven—something she should have done the second she'd arrived home. Abigail had mentally glossed over the action, as if she could handle it without a problem. But when it came down to actually cooking, she was having second thoughts.

"Why did you pick a raw chicken? You can't even microwave it."

She'd also completely forgotten about the new potatoes, which would take at least a half hour to cook through. Abigail wondered if she hadn't subconsciously chosen dishes that would delay—if not derail—the date.

"Neither Dr. Freud nor Dr. Walter can bail you out of this."

With her dinner menu rapidly falling apart, Abigail had to face the oven. It was as if she was squaring off with her past. Her stomach seized into a knot. She unwrapped the chicken, rinsed it, then lumped it into a dinged roasting dish, realizing belatedly that she didn't have anything with which to season or garnish the bird.

"Garnish is low on the totem pole of your problems today."

The oven was right at the top. It was decades old, as was the refrigerator. Like the rest of the house, the cottage's kitchen hadn't been renovated in aeons. Though the painting and refurbishing Abigail had done when she arrived were cosmetic improvements, the appliances were relics, which made the oven more intimidating, its age compromising its reliability.

She set the knob for 350 and warily stepped aside, waiting to hear the sound of the gas switching on. There was nothing. Abigail stared intently at her watch, gauging the passing seconds. Two minutes. Five minutes. Eight.

Clock ticking, she couldn't stand there and continue to monitor the oven the way she would have liked. In one swift motion, she flung open the oven, threw in the chicken, and slammed the door shut. Her hands were shaking. They wouldn't stop.

"You did it," Abigail told herself. "It's done. Okay, not *done* done."

She filled a pot with water for the potatoes, put it on the stovetop, and flicked on the burner. Except it wouldn't light.

"Come on, play along," she pleaded, but the burner refused.

Abigail was emotionally maxed out. The notion of lighting a match and igniting the burner set her heart pounding. With the heat compounding her anxiety, she feared she might faint.

"Scratch the potatoes."

Since there was no time for a bath, she blotted her face with a paper towel, then hurried upstairs to change, swapping her tank top for a milky blue T-shirt. It was too muggy for pants and she didn't have any dressier options than the shorts she had on.

"Not much of an improvement," Abigail pronounced, putting on a lavender-scented deodorant that would have to stand in for perfume. Though it smelled sweet, she could still detect the tangy odor of bug spray under the floral bouquet. She dashed into the bathroom to brush her teeth and was almost finished getting ready when the toilet suddenly stopped up again.

"Not now. Please not now," she begged, pumping the plunger. But she couldn't unclog the toilet. Meaning there was no place to go to the bathroom. Again.

Abigail flew downstairs, reasoning with herself to keep from panicking. "Maybe he won't have to go. There's always outside if he does. No, you can't tell a guest to go to the bathroom outside. What are you thinking?"

The minute hand on her watch was crawling ever closer to twelve. Abigail sprinted into the kitchen to check on the chicken. She tentatively opened the door and discovered that the oven had never heated up. The air inside was the same temperature as the rest of the kitchen—hot, yet not hot enough to cook a chicken.

"No, no, no! Why is this happening?"

This series of calamities struck Abigail as more than happenstance. She hadn't had trouble with the stove in months. Then again, she hadn't really used it, so it could have been broken the entire time. The toilet and the telephone were a different story. She used them every day. Worry began slinking around in her mind. Was Mr. Jasper up to his old tricks? Had too much talk about the *Bishop's Mistress* prompted him to make his presence known again?

No chance to speculate. Tim's convertible rolled to a stop behind her station wagon, the gravel crunching beneath his tires. Abigail had no shoes on, a nonoperational toilet, and nothing to serve besides salad dressing and brownies.

This was your brilliant idea. Adios, comfort zone. Bon jour, embarrassment.

Braced to be shamed, she swung open the front door.

A bottle of wine under his arm, Tim mounted the front stoop, saying, "Wow, this lighthouse is amazing. Oh, wait. Am I early? I can sit in the car if—"

His perplexed look took a second for Abigail to translate, then she realized that her being underdressed and barefoot had caused him to think he'd caught her at an inopportune time. Which he had.

"There are far worse things than being early," she said, motioning him inside.

And you're about to hear a slew of them.

Abigail could smell Tim's cologne as he glided by her. He'd changed clothes, swapping the polo he'd been wearing for a button-down, the cuffs rolled, showing off his muscular forearms.

"Fantastic house," he declared, admiring the interior of the cottage. "These antiques are extraordinary. Are you a collector?"

"They're not mine," Abigail answered offhandedly, still mentally ironing out how she would tell him dinner was a no-go.

Tim was studying the pieces as closely as Duncan had. "Really? These aren't the sorts of items that fall off a truck."

Catching her error, Abigail corrected herself. "They're part of the property. Historically accurate furniture from the original dwelling."

"You hit the lease lottery. Last time I rented a place, all it came with was a dirty futon and an empty keg the last tenants left behind."

That's a step up from what I got.

When she took over the caretaker's cottage, no one had lived there in almost twenty years. The cottage was filthy, it reeked of mildew, and every surface was coated in a thick blanket of dust. Flophouses had more refined furnishings. The cottage had come a long way.

"Yours or not, I think these antiques look . . . pretty. Was that not masculine enough? I am talking about antiques excessively, aren't I? That's not exactly macho or alpha male-y."

Tim's considerate words about the cottage filed the edge off her nervousness. His obvious desire to make a good impression didn't hurt either.

"*Pretty* is perfectly acceptable," Abigail said with a smile. "Thank you."

"I wasn't sure what you were making, so I brought red wine. Should I have picked up white?"

"About that," she began. "I had an oven malfunction, there's sand in the salad, and the ice cream might be rancid."

"Uh, give that to me again."

She went on to describe how supper got derailed, careful not to let on about her broken toilet. Much to her relief, Tim took the news in stride.

"Yeah, none of that sounds very appetizing, and I'd prefer not to get ptomaine poisoning on our first date. Let's not rush. I'm much more of a third-date-food-poisoning kinda guy."

That got a laugh out of Abigail. She hadn't laughed in a while.

"Listen, it seems as though you've had a rough day. How about we head into town for a bite? My treat."

Tim's easygoing manner was a welcome change from the demands she'd been fielding. Unlike everybody else, he wasn't making her feel awful about her attitude or forcing her into bizarre chores. Abigail had basically dared herself to go on this date, and, despite the rocky start, she didn't feel right declining his invitation.

"I'll get my purse."

"Shoes might not hurt either."

She'd forgotten she wasn't wearing any. "I'll take that under advisement."

Abigail headed up to her bedroom. After sliding on a pair of sandals and grabbing her handbag, she sneaked a quick peek in the bathroom mirror to smooth her frazzled hair.

"I can't believe this guy wants to go out with you."

Willing to believe it or not, Abigail was about to go on an actual date, and that left her conflicted. One part of her felt as if she was insulting Paul's memory. Another part reminded her that he'd saved her from the fire for a reason. As their house had burned, he'd chosen to carry her out first, before their son. He wanted her to live. But she hadn't been. She'd been only existing. If anybody could elucidate the subtle differences between the two definitions, it was Abigail.

"Do you want seafood, seafood, or seafood?" she asked, bounding down the staircase. "I doubt we'll have much else in the way of choices."

From the steps, she saw Tim peering into the basement. Abigail stopped mid-stride.

He quickly shut the door, saying, "I was looking for the bathroom. That definitely wasn't it."

"We should get going," she told him. "If we want to get a table, that is."

A loud *bump* resounded from the top of the lighthouse, similar to the noises Abigail had experienced when she initially moved in.

Unnerved, Tim asked, "What was that?"

"Nothing," Abigail maintained. "Nothing at all."

Grok [grok]—*v.*, grokked, grokking. *Slang*—*v.t.* 1. to understand thoroughly and intuitively. v.i. 2. to communicate sympathetically. [coined by Robert A. Heinlein in the science-fiction novel *Stranger in a Strange Land* (1961)]

◆　　◆　　◆

Evening had fallen. The temperature hadn't. Chapel Isle's town square was teeming with vacationers listening to live music put on by street performers and fanning themselves as they waited in lengthy queues outside a series of restaurants Abigail hadn't even known existed.

"Huh," Tim said, assessing the lines that spilled over from the sidewalks. "I thought you said there wasn't anywhere to eat on the island."

"There wasn't."

She took a closer look at the eateries dotting the square. They'd been closed since the previous summer. Abigail had passed the storefronts regularly but they had all been shut down until recently. Most bore nautical names like Saltwater Grill, Bisque, and The Crab Shanty, and they were all bustling. Blue and white colored lights twinkled over the restaurants' awnings as the aroma of chowder and French fries floated in the humid night air. Once the shock wore off, Abigail was excited to see so many new additions to a town she thought she knew by heart.

"I'll check how long the wait will be," Tim offered.

"Okay," she replied, fingers crossed propitiously.

He returned shortly afterward to report that the wait was an hour at the first restaurant, forty-five minutes at the second, more than two hours at another, and the last place was accepting reservations for only after ten p.m.

"Maybe I shouldn't move to Chapel Isle," Tim sighed. "I may never eat again if I do."

Abigail would have gladly conceded defeat and brought this disastrous date to an end, except she could tell Tim was starving, and she was getting hungry too. Given that Tim had been such a good sport about the dinner debacle, Abigail suggested they try the Kozy Kettle, though she was loath to go there with him in tow. That was sure to set the rumor mill spinning.

"I'm warning you, don't expect five-star service and sorbet to cleanse your palate."

"First you call me 'sir,' as if I'm over the hill. Next you take me for a snob. I was raised in a rough section of New Jersey. It wasn't exactly a hub of fine dining."

Tim's admission put her at ease. Albeit only slightly.

The Kozy Kettle was jammed, same as the other restaurants. However, there was a lone booth available in the rear. Amid the mix of islanders and tourists, Abigail hoped to steal back to the table unnoticed. Then Denny Meloch stopped her in her tracks.

"Hey, Abby! Haven't seen you here in ages. It's like old times."

Evidently he had forgotten that during their last meeting at the Kozy Kettle, she'd landed him in a punching match with Nat Rhone.

"You gettin' supper?"

"We are," Tim informed him, positioning himself at Abigail's side, bottle of wine displayed in his hand.

Crestfallen, Denny asked, "You came together? On a date?"

It was an awkward moment made worse when Denny's father, George Meloch, glanced over at Abigail from his usual spot at the counter and his face instantly hardened into a rigid glare. George whispered something to Merle Braithwaite, who was seated on his left, then to Sheriff Larner on his right. All three men turned to look at her, so she hastened Tim to the booth. Abigail was about to sit with her back to the room, out of sight from prying eyes, when Tim insisted she take the side with the view into the café.

Every bit the gentleman, he told her, "You shouldn't have to face a wall."

"How . . . chivalrous. Thanks."

"This place is quaint." He dusted off the seat before sitting.

"That's a charitable description. Yes, the menu is limited and your elbows will stick to the tabletop, but what they serve can't put you in the hospital, as opposed to what I was about to put on a platter."

"Food is food," Tim reassured her. "There's nothing to be ashamed of, Abigail."

She wasn't convinced. Denny had joined his father at the counter, and Ruth had appeared from the kitchen. Abigail could see Denny mouthing something to Ruth. The other men weighed in afterward. It was as if Abigail was watching a silent movie, and she got the gist of the conversation because Ruth was standing on tiptoe trying to discern who she was sharing a booth with.

"What sounds good to you?" Tim was skimming a copy of the café's single-page, double-sided menu. Dried ketchup was flecked across its laminated surface.

Going home, Abigail thought.

What she said was, "I could really go for a burger."

"Me too. Well, now that we have that settled, we can get down to the important stuff—where you're from, what you do, your hobbies, favorite color. Spare no detail."

"I, um . . ."

Abigail could think of several aspects and tidbits worth omitting from the backstory of her life. She was contemplating how to edit her history into first-date-appropriate content when Nat Rhone burst into the café, shouting for Sheriff Larner.

"Damn it, Caleb. Did you turn down your police radio? Clint Wertz has been trying to raise you for the last ten minutes."

He rushed over and said something in Larner's ear that sent him bolting from his seat. Merle and George followed suit. Denny got up from his stool, confused.

"What? What happened?"

Remembering that Clint was a volunteer firefighter, Abigail jumped to her feet to see what the fuss was about, unaware that Tim was trailing her to the counter.

"Nat, what's wrong?"

"There's a fire at Pamlico Shores Beach. And it's no bonfire."

Nat noticed Tim beside Abigail and put two and two together, which added up to an expression Abigail couldn't read. Was he mad that she was with another man, or something else entirely? She was too preoccupied with the fact that there was a fire to tell the difference.

While Nat and the rest of the local men hurried out of the café, Ruth announced to the startled tourists that there was nothing to worry about. "It's a routine situation, folks. The volunteer squad's got it covered."

That didn't do much to stanch the concern of the diners, Tim included. "Where is this fire in relation to the homes and community at large?"

Other patrons seconded his question.

"Routine?" a vacationer asked. "I came for fireworks, not actual fires."

"This *is* an island," another asserted. "We have nowhere to go besides the ocean if it spreads."

"Don't put your flippers on yet," Ruth told them. "Pamlico Shores Beach is at the far northeast end of the island. Only thing over there is a swamp, so everybody's safe."

Her efforts fell on deaf ears. Most customers began decamping for their rental houses, leaving their meals unfinished. Assurances aside, Abigail sensed Ruth was unsettled by the fire too.

"Some dinner," Abigail said. "Or lack thereof. I'm really sorry, Tim."

"It's not your fault." He rubbed her shoulder warmly, an exchange Ruth noted while busing the abandoned tables. "If you'll excuse me, I have to run to the men's room before we head out."

"Sure. No problem."

Abigail was relieved he was going here. That way there was no chance he'd ask to use the bathroom when he dropped her off at home.

"Hubba-hubba." Ruth sidled up next to Abigail and bumped her with her hip. "Call the weather service. There's the reason for our heat wave. That man is *H-O-T* hot!"

"More like he's going to get me in hot water. By tomorrow morning, gossip will have spread at Mach speed and everyone in town will have us married off. For the record, I went out with him only because Merle told me to."

"What? Merle Braithwaite is your pimp?"

"No, he told me to get out of my comfort zone."

"Honey, I'd let that man o' yours in my comfort zone anytime he damn well pleased. He looks good enough to put on a plate and sop up with a biscuit."

"Ruth, I'm not interested. Seriously. I'm not ready. I'm not—"

"Opening your mind to the possibilities?" she asked as Tim exited the men's room. "Suit yourself."

He grabbed the bottle of wine off the table where they'd left it then motioned to Ruth. "Say, would you like this? We didn't get a chance to drink it."

"Aren't you the sweetest thing? Don't mind if I do." Ruth batted her eyes at him.

"Good night," Abigail crooned, quickly escorting Tim out of the Kozy Kettle before Ruth could start making lewd gestures.

"Get home safe," she called after them.

Safe was a word Abigail had grappled with for nearly a year. She wasn't sure how to feel safe anymore. This sudden fire reminded her of that.

*   *   *

Once she and Tim reached his convertible, he opened the car door for her. Abigail started to get in, then hesitated.

"This might be too much to ask, especially since I've put you on an involuntary hunger strike, but would you mind driving me to Pamlico Shores Beach?"

"Where the fire is?"

"I want to be sure they put it out."

Tim hemmed his lips. "I don't know, Abigail. The police and firemen have enough to handle. We shouldn't get in their way."

She knew he was right.

He rubbed her shoulder again. "But if it'll make you feel better, we'll drive by."

Heading northeast, they traversed the winding main road that bisected Chapel Isle. Tim's was the only car on the road. News must have traveled fast. People were already steering clear of that section of the island.

Up ahead, the road was blocked by fire trucks as well as police cars. From a distance, Abigail and Tim could see the flames burning yellow and white against the black sky. A lifeguard shack was ablaze. The conflagration had spread into the dune grass. Sprays of water glinted in the firelight as the squad wrangled hoses over the sandy ridge that fronted the waterline. Abigail couldn't help but tumble back into her memory of the night she'd lost her family. It took every ounce of her concentration not to cry.

"Abigail, are you okay?"

"Sometimes I think I am, then . . ."

Tears in her eyes, she began to tell him how Paul and Justin had died. When she was finished, she sighed, "You said, 'Spare no detail.'"

Tim took her hand and held it. "I couldn't be more sorry."

Neither could Abigail. That was the problem. She was so full of sorrow it left no room for anything else. Not even her.

She slid her hand away from Tim's. "Thanks. Oh, and my favorite color is magenta."

"Magenta. Got it." He tapped the side of his head, mentally filing the detail, then said, "You ready to go home?"

Feeling exposed and exhausted, Abigail wanted nothing more than to shift the spotlight off her past and head back to the lighthouse.

"Ready."

When they got to the caretaker's cottage, Tim walked her to the door. "Do I get a second chance?"

Abigail thought she ought to ask herself that too. Did she deserve another crack at life, another opportunity to uncover what the world had in store? Maybe Ruth was right. Abigail had been closed off for months, and it hadn't brought her any peace. Could it hurt to give open-mindedness—and Tim—another shot?

"Admittedly, most of the problems tonight were my fault. Which means you're entitled to a do-over."

And so am I.

"Looking forward to it." Tim gave her a soft kiss on the cheek, then got back in his car and drove off.

As she stood on her front stoop watching his taillights vanish into the darkness, she remembered how Paul used to kiss her on the forehead. He was more than six feet, almost a foot taller than Abigail, and the top of her head was easier for him to reach. That became their thing. She would tip her chin and he would lower his.

"Eskimos have Eskimo kisses. Butterflies have butterfly kisses. And we have the 'short-tall kiss,'" Paul used to joke. "I don't think we can patent it. But I'm looking into a trademark."

Abigail hadn't been kissed since she said good night to Paul the evening he died. He'd stayed up to finish some work in the study while she called it an early evening. She'd stood on the bottom step of the stairway, still inches shorter than him despite the boost from the riser, and he'd pressed his lips to her skin. There were so many things she missed about him. The tally was endless. Abigail added Paul's "short-tall kisses" to the inventory.

Upon unlocking the front door, Abigail instantly recalled one of the reasons she and Tim had left. The toilet.

She mounted the stairs, shouting, half to the moody plumbing, half to the ghost, "I will not stand for this. Not my toilet. My only toilet!"

Abigail hadn't "spoken" directly to Wesley Jasper in aeons. Barking orders at him, whether he was there or not, was proof the heat was getting to her.

Armed for combat, she was about to cram the plunger into the basin when she noted that the water level was at its regular height. She pressed the handle and the toilet flushed normally. Abigail didn't know how to take that. Was it a fluke, or was Wesley Jasper angry about something, angry enough to temporarily disable the pipes?

After brushing her teeth and removing her contacts, a watchful eye on the toilet for any sign of change, she undressed, then went into the bedroom, which was her crowning renovation achievement. The whitewashed furniture, baby-blue walls, and handmade quilt—which she'd folded on the end of the bed frame, because it was too steamy for blankets—were perfectly in keeping with a cozy cottage feel. The cardboard box wasn't. Only she didn't have anyplace else to put a laundry basket. Her closet was narrower than the home's refrigerator. Sadly, neither held very much. Though the cardboard box wasn't attractive, it would do.

She put on a white eyelet nightgown—another catalog purchase—which was all she could stand to wear. Even sheets were too heavy in that humidity.

Thankful the day was behind her, she crawled into bed and was fast asleep when a harsh *bang* jolted her awake. Abigail fumbled for her glasses on the nightstand, listening closely and attempting to place the noise. Moments later came another boisterous *boom*.

It wasn't upstairs.

It wasn't downstairs.

It wasn't in the lighthouse.

The sound was coming from outside.

Was that the toolshed? Did you forget to shut the door? No, you haven't opened it weeks. What else could it be?

She could argue with herself all night and not get another wink of sleep or go investigate. Neither option was appealing.

With the plunger held like a bat, Abigail glided down the stairs, mustering her courage. She grabbed a flashlight, opened the front door, then inched across the lawn, curving around to the rear of the property.

If somebody is here, they're going to see you. You glow in the dark!

Her eyelet nightgown was iridescent in the moonlight, and she imagined that she herself looked like a ghost.

The backyard was a dam of darkness, fortified by the thick heat and the din of crickets. Her flashlight cut a bright groove into the blackness. Abigail could see a few paces ahead, no farther.

The shed soon appeared in the glare of the beam. Made of wide wood planks combined with large stones from the nearby shore, it was as solid as a safe. Abigail held her breath and tested the door. The lock held tight.

Reassured, she turned to go inside, then heard another bone-rattling *bang*. Abigail jerked the flashlight in the direction of the sound. The door to the oil cellar was open, creaking in the breeze. Small as a doghouse and built into the side of the lighthouse tower, the stone cellar bore a wooden door and a padlock that had held it shut since before she'd moved in. There was no way it could be open unless the lock had been picked.

So much for feeling safe.

H

Hebetude (heb´i tōōd´, –tyōōd), *n.* the state of being dull; lethargy. [1615–25; < LL *hebetūdō* dullness, bluntness, equiv. to L *hebet–* (s. of *hebes*) dull + *–ūdō;* see –TUDE]

◆ ◆ ◆

Dawn broke, but Abigail had barely slept.

Last year, the mysterious rash of burglaries on the island had turned out to be the work of one man: Sheriff Caleb Larner. Once Abigail and Larner had struck a deal, the robberies stopped cold. From what she had heard, Larner took extra shifts and worked odd jobs to earn money to send for his daughter's medical treatments on the mainland. Talk around town was that she'd being undergoing radiation and healing well, which meant Abigail had no reason to believe Larner had tried to break into the oil cellar. That left an entire island full of locals and summer people as suspects.

Padding around the living room in her nightgown with nothing to do, Abigail came upon Lottie's box of romances. Among the tales of lonesome cowboys, tough yet tenderhearted mercenaries, and fighter pilots with chiseled pecs popping out of their bomber jackets was the story of a sultry-eyed Bedouin nomad. The cover was tattered around the ends and riddled with fissures from too many readings. A crack glanced across the upper part of the Bedouin's high cheekbone, as if a tear was poised to fall.

"Veronique De Montgrove," Abigail said, reading the author's name aloud. "That doesn't even remotely sound real." She thumbed to the opening scene. "Let's see what you've got, *Veronique.*"

The story opened in the vast desert of some far-flung region, a string of camels with hooded riders on course for a city in the distance, lights burning as beacons in the night. The wide focus of the narrator's lens soon zoomed in on the handsome Bedouin leader. Within the span of a half dozen pages, he and his tribesmen were captured by their sworn enemy, an Arab king who ruled the land with an iron fist. While imprisoned at the king's castle, the Bedouin was beguiled by a lowly yet beautiful chambermaid, who brought him extra water and was whipped for her compassion. When the Bedouin escaped from the king's dungeon, he vowed to free his beloved and take his revenge on the king. A scant twenty pages into the novel, the overwrought descriptions were flowing as fast as the ambrosia. Then the tawdry sex scenes ensued.

"I've got to hand it to you, Veronique. You work fast. But it's a little *too* early in the morning for that."

Abigail dressed, doused herself in bug spray, and went to the one place where she wouldn't be the only person awake: Merle Braithwaite's house.

Merle's motorboat was missing from the dock in back when she got there. He was out fishing, as she assumed he would be.

The cedar shakes on Merle's shingle-style home were weathered a pale gray, except in spots where he'd done recent repairs. New orange-hued shingles spotted the façade as well as the rear of the home, where Abigail went to wait on Merle's deck.

A soft, salt-tinged gust blew in from the water as the sun edged up the sky. The wind got Abigail thinking about feeling versus fact. She couldn't bottle the breeze to have validation of its presence, but she knew it was there. She couldn't say with confidence that Wesley Jasper haunted the lighthouse, but she was willing to believe he might. The broken padlock on the door to the oil cellar was evidence that *someone* had been at the cottage while she was sleeping. Beyond that, Abigail didn't have much to go on. She was hoping Merle would be able to offer some advice on the situation.

"Either you couldn't sleep or you want grouper for breakfast," Merle called out, lashing his motorboat to a piling. He scaled from the outboard onto the dock in a single step, a cooler hanging from his arm.

"I'm not hungry, but I'd take a cup of coffee."

"Then take this first." He handed her the cooler, and the weight almost made her legs buckle, though he'd carried it with ease. "Whoopsies," Merle said, grabbing it from her. "Didn't realize how heavy it was."

Abigail rubbed her shoulder. "You must think I'm stronger than I am."

"I don't think. I know."

She'd earned his respect by standing up for Nat Rhone and lasting on Chapel Isle for longer than a season, something Merle's ex-wife was unable to do. But Abigail hadn't put any effort into maintaining his hard-fought esteem, and she thought maybe she'd hurt Merle's feelings by growing distant. Despite his colossal stature, he was a softy—a *big* softy.

"Decaf or high-test?"

"The stronger the better. I'm running on fumes."

Merle put a coffeepot on to brew as Abigail pulled up a chair at his kitchen table. His ex-wife's floral décor had remained unchanged since her departure nearly twenty years ago. It was garden-motif overkill. Ruth had told Abigail that Merle refused to get rid of the rose wallpaper border, the sunflower place mats, the plastic lilies in urns, the daisy magnets on the fridge, any of it. The house was a shrine to the past. Abigail realized her house was too. Only it lacked the accessories to make that obvious.

"Did you hear Nat Rhone is thinking of moving off the island?"

Merle pushed the cooler into a corner. "Wouldn't surprise me. Fishing for a hobby is fun. Fishing for a living is hard as hell. Ain't for everybody. If Nat can't make ends meet, the man's got a right to find another line of work."

Abigail could tell he was skirting the real issue—that Nat was still grieving for Hank rather than focusing on the business.

"Think he'll be missed?"

"Dunno. Will he?"

"Not by me," she retorted, too defensive. "I meant by people in town. He's made more enemies than friends."

"True. But he stayed. Built a life here. Locals respect that, if nothing else."

"Has sticking it out earned me any points?" Abigail asked, arms crossed.

"Why? You keepin' score?"

"It feels like I'm the only one who isn't."

"You suited up and joined the team, but you've been sitting on the bench. Time to get in the game."

"Enough with the sporting analogies. I'm starting to get athlete's foot and grow hair on my chest."

"That reminds me, how was your date?"

Abigail fell back in her seat, beaten. "It put the *ass* in embarrassing."

"Going out with him again?" Merle asked, pouring her coffee.

"Probably. How's that for team spirit?"

"Want me to get my pom-poms?"

"That I'd pay to see."

He made himself a cup and joined her at the table.

Abigail pushed the sugar bowl across the table toward him. "Are you going to tell me what happened at Pamlico Shores Beach?"

As Chapel Isle's unofficial mayor, Merle always had the scoop. How he got it baffled Abigail. All she ever heard him talk about with anybody was drill bits and pressure-treated lumber. She would have liked to ask if he knew who was responsible for circulating the report that she was a widow, though she assumed he'd just make another sports comment to avoid answering.

"Details are still sketchy," Merle told her. "Someone said they saw a red SUV full o' teenyboppers around the shack earlier in the afternoon. Caleb's checking into it."

That was the same car that had whizzed by Tim and Abigail the previous day, almost running her over. The driver did seem reckless.

But Pamlico Shores Beach was also where the man in the straw hat had been going. Abigail wasn't sure if any of it was relevant or worth mentioning to Merle, especially since she had yet to tell him about the oil cellar.

When she did, he rubbed his chin thoughtfully. "The lock was picked? Not broken?"

"I didn't get out my magnifying glass, but how do you break a padlock?"

Merle shrugged, as if to say it would be well within his capabilities, strong as he was.

"Let me rephrase: How would the average person break open a steel lock?"

"They wouldn't," he admitted. "They'd pick it."

"I also had an unexpected visit from Duncan Thadlow yesterday. Usually it's Lottie who drops by unannounced."

"You didn't give him any food, did you?"

"Actually, I did. Not then. Earlier in the day. Why?"

"It's like the zoo. He's an animal you're not supposed to feed or he'll follow you home."

"You don't think he was the one who . . . ?"

"Duncan? Not a chance. Sure, he can fix damn near anything. Had a knack for taking stuff apart since he was young. So if you're asking could he have picked that lock, then yes indeedy. Would he have? I doubt it. Unless you keep cookies down there."

"But he went on and on about the *Bishop's Mistress,* the golden cups, and missing clues."

"Abby, Duncan goes on and on about *everything*. If he was obsessed with finding the shipwreck, why would he have waited this many years to go snooping in the lighthouse when he's lived on Chapel Isle his entire life? Whoever broke into the cellar thought it was connected to the rest of the caretaker's house, that it was a way in. An islander would know it wasn't."

Merle had a valid point, which put Duncan in the clear. Though it didn't lessen Abigail's concern.

"Whoever picked that lock was banking on the cellar being an entry to the basement. They were probably disappointed it wasn't."

"Are you saying this person will try to gain entry to the house again?"

"Guess I didn't have to say it. 'Cause you're already thinkin' it."

The comment reminded Abigail about seeing Tim open the door to her basement. He claimed he was looking for the bathroom. What if he wasn't?

Or what if you're just jumping to conclusions and looking for a reason not to date the guy? Doesn't that seem more logical?

"Be straight with me, Merle. Is there anything in the house a treasure hunter might be after, anything whatsoever?"

He took a sip of coffee. "There's always been talk of secret hiding places in the caretaker's cottage."

"Secret hiding places?" Abigail repeated, incredulous.

"Never noticed any myself in all the years I tended the place. Doesn't mean they ain't in there somewheres. Lottie probably excluded 'em on the list of amenities when she rented you the place."

Treasure hunters, clues, hiding spots—this wasn't what Abigail wanted to hear. It seemed better suited for one of Lottie's romance novels or a kid's cartoon than average everyday life. For her own safety as well as her sanity, Abigail decided that she had to find whatever the would-be intruder was looking for first or prove it never existed. She wasn't sure if it was public knowledge that Mr. Jasper kept ledgers or that those ledgers were stored in the basement, but if it was, people might assume they held some hint about the *Bishop's Mistress,* so she had to find a secure place for them too.

"You gonna tell Caleb about the 'break-in'?"

Because Merle wasn't privy to her arrangement with Sheriff Larner—though he'd intuited that she hammered out some kind of deal with him to help Nat Rhone—Abigail remained noncommittal. "I wouldn't want to bother him."

"Now you're thinking like an islander. Go, team."

* * *

Abigail left on the heels of Merle's comment and stood outside next to her car, debating how she should take it. If thinking like a native meant lying to the authorities, then she was going to need a helmet to play in this division. Larner would sense if she wasn't telling the truth the next time they talked. She had to forestall any run-ins with him as long as she could.

While Abigail may not have wanted to bother Sheriff Larner, Lottie had no problem bothering her. At seven a.m. on the dot, Abigail's cell phone rang.

"Rise and shine," Lottie trilled. "That woman you helped with her toaster yesterday absolutely raved about you. Raved. Said you're a whiz with electronics. And plumbing. And HVAC. Who knew? Don't go hiding your talents in a bushel basket, young lady."

"HVAC?"

"Heating, ventilation, and blabbity blah."

"Glad we're clear on the terminology," Abigail said as the line crackled.

"I have just a few teensy-weensy little errands for you today."

Abigail would have preferred to return to the caretaker's cottage and begin her hunt for the so-called secret hiding places, but Lottie starting listing numerous rental units for her to visit. Abigail soon lost count.

"Swing by the realty agency, then I'll give you a set of spare keys and the list of addresses. Oh, you're not afraid of dogs, are you?"

Static flickered and the connection dropped.

"That sounded vaguely menacing. Was she talking pit bulls or teacup Yorkies? Wait, why are you asking yourself what she means?" Abigail said, throwing her hands up. "*Lottie* doesn't even know what Lottie means."

She drove to the realty agency, but since there were no parking spaces nearby, she was forced to circle again and again until she snagged a spot.

"It isn't even eight o'clock in the morning. What are all of these cars doing here?"

Then a group of men with fishing poles went by, making for the dock.

"Mystery solved."

Chapel Isle had been founded on fishing. The island would be nothing without it. But Abigail hadn't come for that. She'd moved there because Paul had always wanted her to experience the place for herself; her experience, however, had not yet included fishing.

Abigail followed the guys with the poles toward the bay. It was the same direction as Gilquist Realty. Situated in a dollhouse-size yellow cottage overlooking the docks, the scale seemed to speak to Lottie's diminutive frame, while the array of spinning, clattering, colorful lawn ornaments filling the yard spoke to her state of mind. The men paused to stare at the flock of plastic pink flamingos that appeared to be trampling a trio of garden gnomes and a lawn jockey. One called to Abigail as she walked up the path.

"Hey, you work there?"

Grudgingly, she said, "For the time being."

"Is your boss crazy?"

"That would be an understatement."

A note was waiting for Abigail on the door to the agency. It hung beside a wooden plaque carved in the shape of an angel and inscribed *Bless This Mess*. Rain had damaged the angel's wings, making them look like a football player's shoulder pads, and the wire halo was crooked.

Abigail read the note: *Keys are in the mailbox. Here's a map and a list of complaints. If the tenant isn't home, leave a message saying you were there. PS—Don't tell anybody you're not licensed. Love, Lottie.*

The *i* of *Lottie* was dotted with a smiley face.

Seven properties were listed on the complaint sheet. Abigail was sorting through them when she got to the car and accidentally dropped the hefty set of keys on her foot. Pain shot up her leg. She thought she'd broken a toe. Abigail slid off her sandal and massaged her foot.

"Who's crazier? The boss or the employee who does what the boss says?"

The first rental unit was a beachfront property. Wetsuits hung from the railings of the two-story stucco house, and cars were parked out front. Abigail knocked on the door, but nobody answered. She checked her watch. It was quarter to nine. Perhaps the tenants were asleep.

"Wetsuits but no boards," she said. "They're out surfing." And it's too hot for the suits.

Abigail let herself in with the key. Towels were slung on the sofa, and beer cans were scattered across the blond-wood floors.

"Hello?" she called. "I'm here from the rental agency."

There was no reply.

According to the complaint sheet, the tenant's freezer wouldn't stay cold. Since she didn't have the slightest notion how to fix an icebox and the renters weren't around to press her, she grabbed a pen off the counter and looked for paper to jot a note. A pizza-box top wasn't going to cut it, so Abigail took a paper towel off the roll in the kitchen, where empty liquor bottles and dirty dishes crammed the countertop. She scribbled a message saying that a repairman would be by shortly to address the problem, then discovered that she'd been resting her arm on a sticky slick of melted Popsicles.

"I guess the freezer isn't working, or these guys are just really messy."

Abigail was peeling a Popsicle stick off her forearm when she heard a growl. A German shepherd was standing in the living room, eyes locked on her. She froze.

"Nice dog."

The shepherd advanced a step toward her.

"Want a Popsicle?"

Careful not to make any sudden movements, she gently tossed the stick to the dog, who sniffed it and began to lick the syrup contentedly. That was Abigail's opportunity to ease out of the room.

She slammed the front door behind her, cursing Lottie's name.

"Do I like dogs? I am going to kick that woman in her stunted shins when I see her."

Abigail went to the next rental unit, where the cable connection was supposedly wonky, only the tenant wasn't there either and, fortunately, they didn't have any pets. She left another note. The same was true at the bayside bungalow with the backed-up kitchen sink. A memo promising forthcoming service would have to suffice. This job wasn't actually that taxing, as long as the renters weren't around. Abigail thought she might be able to skate by without having to lift a finger.

Then she got to the address with the "funny noise" complaint. The squat one-story cinder-block unit had an inflatable kiddie pool out front and beach lounge chairs propped under the windows. A bumper sticker on the truck parked in the driveway stated *I'd Rather Be in South Carolina.*

So would I, Abigail was thinking.

"You from the realty agency?" the guy who answered the door asked, drowsily rubbing his sunburned face.

"Yes, sir."

"'Bout time. I'm hungover as hell and I can't get a minute of sleep with that racket."

"Racket?"

"There's a goddamn bird stuck in the eaves."

That was leaps and bounds out of Abigail's league.

"I'm sorry, but I'm just here to"—she scrambled to concoct a lie—"take your statement and pass it through the correct channels to facilitate the prompt, proper rectification of this issue by a trained professional."

"What?" he asked, bewildered. "They send a woman pushing a pencil to handle what I shoulda done myself two days ago?" the man huffed. "I'm not paying to have problems. I'm paying to be on vacation."

Furious, Abigail chewed her lip, but she felt like she'd been challenged.

"Of course. You're on vacation. Allow me."

Pushing past the man, she searched the ceiling, looking for a hatch that would lead to the crawl space under the roof. Toys littered the sandy tiled floors, and half-eaten bowls of children's cereal sat at the table. Abigail surmised that the man's wife had taken the kids to the beach and left her husband there to snooze off his bender.

"Where you going?" he demanded.

Outside the master bedroom, Abigail found a trapdoor to the eaves. She jumped to grab the handle, then used her weight to pull down the levered hatch. Afterward, she went and rolled open the sliding door to the backyard.

"Ten minutes and the bird will fly out. Problem solved. Enjoy your stay."

Abigail intentionally left the front door open, though she would have preferred to slam it behind her. She resented that the tourists viewed the island as a sprawling hotel where their every wish was to be catered to. Their lack of appreciation galled her.

"Now you really are thinking like an islander."

I Indagate (in´də-gāt´)—*v.t.*, -gat·ed, -gat·ing. Archaic. to in-vestigate, research. [1615–25; < L indāgātus, ptp. of indāgāre to track down, v. deriv. of indāgō ring of beaters, nets, etc., for trapping game, equiv. to ind–, by-form of *in* in– [2] (see ENDO–) + –āgō, deriv. of *agere* to drive (cf. AMBAGES)]

◆   ◆   ◆

With her duties for Lottie complete and the day half gone, Abigail returned to the lighthouse to start on her top priority: finding what the picklock was after. Having lived in and refurbished the caretaker's cottage, she'd assumed she knew the place from top to bottom. She was in for a rude awakening.

Starting in the basement would have been the prudent ap-proach. That appeared to be what the intruder was trying to gain access to, but the basement still unnerved her.

"I'll have to work up to it. Or down, as the case may be."

Beginning instead in the home's open living and dining area, Abigail went inch by inch, rapping on walls to listen for hollow spots and bouncing on floors to check whether any boards were conspicuously loose. In the kitchen, she upended drawers and in-spected the depths of the cupboards. She attempted to shimmy the relic of a refrigerator outward so she could see behind it, but it hardly budged. Abigail had to contort herself across the countertop to peer around the back. There was nothing there except a width of wall.

Upstairs, she started in the bathroom, tapping on the tiles to see if any were wobbly. Those that were had water damage to blame. Afterward, she groped the underside of the claw-foot tub, in case anything had been affixed to it. Her hand came back covered in rust flakes. Abigail checked behind the pedestal sink as well as the toilet, with no luck.

Then came the bedroom. From corner to corner, the ceiling was a seamless sheet of plaster, and the walls were unflawed except for an old nail hole where a picture once hung. The dresser held no clandestine compartments, nor did the nightstand. Abigail removed her clothes from the closet and scrutinized the inside with her flashlight. No strange niches, no faux panels, zilch.

Next was the study, a narrow alcove at the rear of the house that had served as the watch room for past lighthouse keepers. When Abigail moved in, the furnishings consisted of a flimsy cot, an elementary-school-sized desk, and a bowed bookcase. Lottie had pitched it as the perfect guest room. That would have been true if Abigail's guests were pygmies. But Abigail hadn't planned to have visitors, and she never did.

Abigail had given the cot away to Nat Rhone, who confessed he'd been sleeping on an air mattress on the floor in an apartment over Hank Scokes's garage at the time. Since Hank's suicide, Nat had taken up residence in his house, which, according to Ruth, Hank's kids were renting to him. They couldn't bear to part with their father's home, and it fell to Nat to keep it up. Hank's funeral had been held on the mainland by his family, even though there was no body. He'd thrown himself off the side of his fishing trawler, inconsolable after his wife's death. His passing was a parable to Abigail. Losing a spouse was enough to make somebody take their own life. Hank wasn't the first nor would he be the last. Although Abigail had briefly toyed with the notion, she wouldn't have been able to go through with it. She'd survived the fire for a reason.

With the cot gone and the kiddie desk sequestered in the basement, the only original piece of furniture that remained in the study was the bookcase. Stunted and nowhere near large enough for Abigail's needs, the shelves overflowed with the books that had been spared by the fire, mixed with those she'd ordered to pass the time. Extra stacks climbed the walls from the top shelf, grazing the alcove's low ceiling. More were piled on the dark-wood commander's desk, which had replaced the junior version. A few were even lingering on the stately swivel chair that accompanied the desk. Of all the books Abigail had ordered, there wasn't a single dictionary. She couldn't bring herself to buy one.

Like the furniture in the living room, the desk and chair were antiques that Abigail and Nat had rescued from the basement. She felt certain they had belonged to Wesley Jasper. Since moving the set into the study, she'd rarely used the desk other than to hold more books—less because she was afraid and more because sitting at it reminded her of her former life.

Cramped as the alcove was, Abigail quickly detected that there were no hidden cubbies or recesses. That left two locations to search: the lighthouse and the basement. Abigail chose the lighthouse. She'd spent so much effort emotionally convalescing that going to the top of the lighthouse for the view—the reason she'd leased the place to begin with—no longer held its appeal. It was high time to see what she'd been missing.

Slowly reacquainting herself with the spiral staircase, Abigail was careful not to rush. The wrought-iron steps that coiled up the interior of the lighthouse grunted and squealed an off-key tune, singing her trail to the top. A trapdoor-style opening led to the lamp room, which held the hulking, glass-enclosed lantern that had once guided ships to shore. At its base sat an oil pail. Abigail had used the pail as a litmus test to see if the ghost of Wesley Jasper was real. After hearing that Mr. Jasper liked the pail to stay in a specific spot, she'd moved it, then waited for the pail to move back. It didn't—empirical proof that either there was no ghost or the story wasn't true. That was the thing about gossip. Where the truth started and where it ended were hard to differentiate. Were these "secret hiding places" merely a rumor too?

Abigail combed the entire lighthouse turret, picking at exposed nail heads with her fingertips and pounding on the wallboards to determine if any were fakes. She attempted to pull off the plaque soldered to the base of the lamp, but it was on tight. The room was a bust, at least in regard to her search. It was, however, a success for her to revisit the turret, and Abigail vowed to come up more often.

From there, the view of the coast was mesmerizing, hypnotically calming. What caught her attention, however, was the inland panorama, something she'd barely noticed before. At that height, she could discern the town square, because the colored roofs of cars stuck in traffic looked like a patchwork quilt amid the sea of trees and greenery. Abigail hadn't ever looked inland from the turret. She'd always looked outward.

"That says a lot. You're more interested in where you aren't than where you are."

Winding down the staircase, she clutched the railing. The black wrought iron was curled tight against the whitewashed walls, making for a dizzying contrast. She'd forgotten how daunting the descent was.

"You think this is bad? Now you have to go to the basement."

Her voice echoed faintly against the conical lighthouse walls, the first phrase repeating and blurring the second.

The words *You think this is bad, you think this is bad, you think this is bad* resounded through the structure.

She couldn't ignore the irony. The death of her family had made her think things *were* bad, unfair, inequitable. Abigail could apply as many defamatory adjectives to her life as she pleased. That didn't change the reality that she had to live it.

Taking the flashlight as backup, she delved into the basement. Sandwiched between the two bare lightbulbs that bracketed the far ends of the room and the one dingy slit of a window in the middle was a wide, murky area. It was enough space to get lost in. Abigail poked around the basement's perimeter, inspecting the mortar on the walls for special grooves, then pushing on the bricks as if they'd open a special chamber. They didn't.

The gigantic water cistern wasn't something she was willing to tackle. Deep, dark, and easy to get stuck in, Abigail wouldn't brave it.

"Okay, picklock, if the secret compartment's in there, be my guest. It's all yours."

Though the basement yielded far more nooks, crannies, cracks, and crevices than she'd anticipated, most held only dust or cobwebs, not some hidden compartment. Believing every stone to have been turned, Abigail rubbed her eyes in frustration and her gaze came to rest on the crates of Wesley Jasper's leather-bound ledgers. They'd stayed right where she'd unearthed them months earlier. Abigail had carefully cleaned each ledger before returning it to its crate. She'd considered donating the collection to the island's library, but it wasn't hers to give. So there it had stayed.

Abigail briefly contemplated digging out the ledger that corresponded to the date the *Bishop's Mistress* sank, but she preferred not to tempt fate. Having a clogged toilet might be a picnic compared to what could happen next.

Positioned beside the crates was the old-timey hand-crank porcelain washer. Old sheets that had covered the antiques were swagged on top of it, as though waiting to be laundered. The sheets reminded Abigail of the Easter when she'd hidden plastic candy-filled eggs for Justin. Because it had rained that week and she couldn't put the eggs outside, Abigail had squirreled them throughout the house. Justin was only three at the time, so to ensure he'd find the treats she hadn't gotten too creative. Months later, she found a forgotten purple plastic egg under the living room sofa. The sheets had covered the antiques the way the sofa had concealed the egg, making Abigail wonder if the furniture itself could hold secret hiding spots. Happy to leave the basement, she hauled the crates full of Wesley Jasper's ledgers upstairs, then went to see if her idea held any water.

The drawers in the console and end tables were too obvious, and she'd already rifled through them looking for Lottie's phone number. The chairs and settee were unlikely, same for the dining table and chairs.

"The desk," Abigail said.

Inspired, she returned to the study and pushed aside the chair. She knelt on the floor, then knocked on the underside of the desktop as well as on the legs. Everything was solid. She removed every drawer, joggling open the ones that had swelled from the humidity. There were no concealed compartments, no false backs.

Yesterday Abigail had felt like an idiot for allowing Lottie to send her on a wild-goose chase to find a plumber. Today she'd led herself on one. She was replacing a sticky drawer when her knuckles grazed the interior tier between the drawer levels and she discovered a hollow slot.

"Wow. Seriously? This really happens? I'm having a Nancy Drew and the Hardy Boys flashback."

Abigail's favorite childhood heroines had been the bookish ladies of the Jane Austen ilk, those with the odds against them and only their brains to see them through convoluted social dramas, not the adventure-loving, teen-sleuth types like Nancy.

"What would Nancy do?" Abigail asked herself. "I think she'd want to see what was in this secret compartment."

Inside was an envelope that held a hand-drawn map. The paper was amber with age and velvet soft. From what Abigail could decipher, it wasn't a chart of the neighboring land but rather a sketchy rendering of the sea beyond the lighthouse. She was well versed in Wesley Jasper's writing style from his journals, the stiff script and unmarred margins. This was more personal. Where his descriptions of the tides and changing winds were devoid of inflection, the crude map with its dashed lines and squiggles illuminated his character. Abigail felt as if she were finally meeting the man.

Exhilarated by the find yet ever cautious, she returned the map to its slot and shut the desk drawer tightly. As Abigail stood up to stretch, she noticed a flicker of movement outside the study window.

There was somebody in her backyard.

Heart racing, she pressed her face to the glass. Whoever it was had moved out of sight below. Abigail hurtled down the stairs and was about to throw open the front door when the voice of reason weighed in.

How about calling Sheriff Larner, locking the door, and staying inside, instead of rushing into who-knows-what with who-knows-who?

The problem was, she didn't want Larner to find out about the padlock. Not yet.

Abigail skulked from window to window, hoping to catch a glimpse of the person on her property. There was no car in her driveway and no sign of anybody. Then she heard rattling through the open windows. It was coming from the oil cellar.

Ignoring her better judgment, she grabbed the only heavy thing she could find—the receiver from the rotary telephone, which she'd disconnected while attempting to fix it. Phone in hand, the cord jiggling lamely, Abigail slunk around the side of the house. As she leaned around the corner, Bert Van Dorst plowed right into her.

"Bert, what are you doing here?" she panted, frightened.

"Hey there, Abby. Merle sent me over to repair your lock." He had a toolbox. Abigail had a detached receiver. "Are you trying to make a call?"

After Bert had finished replacing the padlock, Abigail invited him in for a glass of water. As he was reading the labels on her munitions stash of bug repellent, she put the tops on the crates holding Mr. Jasper's journals to keep them out of view.

"You still unpacking?" Bert asked.

"Just a few boxes left," she lied. "Let me get you some water."

When she came back into the living room from the kitchen, Bert said, "These chemicals are heavy duty. Most of the compounds could fell a horse in higher doses. Or melt off your skin."

"As long as they keep the flies away, I'll take my chances."

They took a seat together at the dining table, and Abigail realized that while Bert had been to the cottage before, as had Nat, nobody had ever sat at the table with her.

This is your first proper houseguest, and you're serving him tap water in a glass with a Spanish galleon etched on it. Your manners have gone down the tubes.

The galleon glass was part of her mismatched set of dishware. Her mug was a beer-barrel-shaped giveaway from a restaurant called Skeeters. Each of the rental units she'd visited that day had up-to-date appliances, homey accoutrements, and, Abigail suspected, matching dishes. She was really beginning to feel gypped.

"What's wrong?" Bert asked. "You got that look."

"What look?"

"Like you're grinding a diamond out of a lump of coal in your mind."

His description wasn't far off. Abigail found herself wanting matching dishes and a complimentary toaster. If she wasn't perceived as an islander, why not get the perks of a tourist?

She pushed her beer-barrel mug aside and said, "Bert, do you know much about the layout of the Ship's Graveyard?"

"A little. In a nautical sense, a shoal—which is what the Graveyard would be classified as—is similar to a reef, a shallow formation of sand that makes it a navigational and grounding hazard at a depth of six fathoms or less. In the case of our particular shoals, they almost totally surround the east of the island, and breaking waves set up a shoreward current with a compensating countercurrent along the bottom."

"Which does what?"

"Makes 'em dangerous. In some places the sandbars are close to the surface, visible. In others, they're deep enough that they can't be seen but can rip the bottom of a boat hull to shreds." Bert took a drink of his water, as if to clean his palate after discussing the island's taboo subject. "Why do you ask?"

"Just boning up on Chapel Isle topography."

He beamed with pride. "Nice to hear you're not taking this place for granted the way so many others do. If you want to learn more, the library has sea charts."

"Sea charts, absolutely. I'm on it."

Feeling guilty for stretching the truth, Abigail offered to drive

Bert back to town. He had no car, which was why there hadn't been one in the driveway when she looked. Bert declined the ride.

"I enjoy walking," he said.

"But it's about a thousand degrees outside. I could fire pottery on my front stoop."

"Oh, no, it would have to be approximately fifteen times as hot as that to——"

"Okay, now you're walking."

While Bert headed for home, Abigail was bound for the Chapel Isle library. First she had to figure out what she was going to do with Mr. Jasper's ledgers. If the intruder was looking for something in the house, the journals couldn't stay there.

That left her car.

The station wagon had a well for a spare tire behind the backseat, so she hefted the spare out and rolled it to the shed, then filled the well and the backseats with the crates. Afterward, Abigail recalled how full her car had been when she moved to the island. Suitcases and boxes of books crammed the interior to the point that she could barely see out the rear windshield. It was precious cargo, the last remnants of the life she'd had. Mr. Jasper's ledgers were just as valuable.

As she drove to the library, Abigail was careful on the rutted roads, taking bumps and turns slowly, as if the journals could break. Once she arrived, she sat in the car for a minute, not wanting to go inside. As with Wesley Jasper's desk, the library was a reminder of what she once loved. Abigail had been purchasing books instead of checking them out from the library in an attempt to rebuild her formerly impressive collection. Going inside threatened to make her feel as if she was behind in her efforts. She drummed her fingers on the steering wheel, dawdling as the air-conditioning buffeted her face.

"What would Nancy Drew say? She'd probably call you a *pansy* or *lily-livered*. Get it together."

The same librarian Abigail had encountered the last time she was there was stationed at the front desk, her hair shorn in the same close-cropped cut, as if having it a centimeter longer would have been a nuisance. Her harsh demeanor completed the stereotypical picture of a strict librarian. It was as if she'd accepted the cliché and run with it. Though there wasn't a pigeonhole for lexicographers per se, Abigail with her scholarly nature and glasses had often been typecast too. She rather enjoyed having people perceive her as smart without even having to say anything. But with her old profession unknown to most on the island and her glasses swapped for contacts, she couldn't lead with her look or a label other than *widow*. That was a disappointment in and of itself.

"Good afternoon," the librarian said curtly.

When Abigail had first visited, the woman refused to tell her anything about the history of the lighthouse. Abigail expected a similarly tight-lipped response this time too. The brusque greeting was an inauspicious start.

"Good afternoon. Can you tell me where I could find a nautical map of the island?"

"Those must be popular," she said, tapping her pen rhythmically against the desktop, as if the question was an inconvenience, even though there was no one else in the library. "You're the second person to ask about them today."

"Who was the first?"

"A tourist," the librarian replied dismissively.

"Can you describe this tourist?"

The librarian scowled, as if she was being asked to do something wholly outside her job parameters. "I couldn't see much of the gentleman's face. Because of his straw hat."

Certain there was a connection between the man and the attempted break-in, Abigail asked again, "And those maps are where?"

"In the back, by the periodicals," the librarian replied, apparently happy to answer when it came to something under her purview. "Any more questions, Ms. Harker?"

Great. Here's yet another stranger who knows your name.

"Nope," Abigail answered, though she had more questions than she could count.

Studying the sea charts, she couldn't make much of them. Based on the labels and landmarks she recognized, she sorted through the pile until she found one that corresponded with her section of the island and depicted the lighthouse. She wished she knew which maps the man in the straw hat had been looking at, but there was no way to tell. Abigail copied a portion of the one featuring the lighthouse by hand on scrap paper and was stuffing the drawing into her pocket when her cell phone rang, eliciting a glower from the librarian. Abigail trotted outside to answer. Lottie's name was on the caller ID.

Duty called, so the map would have to wait.

J Jussive *(jus´iv), Gram.—adj.* 1. (esp. in Semitic languages). expressing a mild command.—*n.* a jussive form, mood, case, construction, or word. [1840–50; < L *juss(us)* (ptp. of *jubēre* to command) + –IVE]

❖   ❖   ❖

Between the iffy cell reception and the brisk, hot wind, Abigail couldn't hear Lottie clearly.

"Did you say 'wasps' nest'?"

"It'll only take a minute, Abby. I need you to find out if it's a big'un or not."

"How would I judge that?"

"If it looks like a giant wad of chewing tobacco and wasps are streaming out, that's a doozy. Then I gotta call the pest guy on the mainland, see when he can come over to the island. He charges more for the big, scary ones."

Rightly so.

Abigail contemplated asking for more in the way of compensation herself. Before she could, Lottie was giving her the address.

"Honestly, Lottie, I'm not really qualified to determine the size of a—"

Lottie had already hung up.

Abigail couldn't help but think of the occasions when she'd been invited to speak at language conferences, to contribute to lexicographical academic articles, or to guest-chair study groups at local colleges: the stuffy meetings, tea sandwiches, polite chatter about new additions to Merriam-Webster. Lexicography wasn't exactly a booming industry, yet she'd carved out a laudable reputation for herself in a small community of like-minded scholars. What would her colleagues in the field say if they knew what she was doing these days?

In need of reinforcements to face a wasps' nest, Abigail stopped by Merle's hardware store. It seemed as if a tornado had touched down inside the shop. Steel bolts and washers were strewn across the floor. Scattered among the metal were brochures for lawn mowers as well as a rainbow of paint swatches. Merle was leaning heavily against the cash register, a miserable expression cemented on his face.

"What on earth . . . ?" Abigail declared as she watched an eight-year-old boy wreck a drill display while his father yammered on his cell phone, totally ignoring his son's rampage.

"This isn't earth," Merle whispered. "This is hell."

"Aren't you going to stop him? That kid is destroying your store!"

"I don't want to go to jail for squeezing the life outta that snot-nose, so no."

Unable to stand idly by a second longer, Abigail grabbed the boy by the arm right as he was about to topple a container of lug nuts.

"Stranger! Stranger! Let go of me," he shouted, squirming wildly.

Abigail dragged him over to his father. "Is this your son?"

The man had the phone mashed between his shoulder and his ear. "As long as the shipment gets there after the holiday, we're golden. Have my secretary track it. Call me when it arrives."

"Dad, this strange lady is touching me!" the boy yelled. The father finally glanced over at them.

"Do you see what your son has done to this place? It's unconscionable."

The boy wrestled his arm away from Abigail's grasp as the father half-listened to her.

"He'll clean it up," he told her, then returned to his conversation. "No, I wasn't talking to you. Go ahead."

Abigail stormed back to the register.

"See. Not worth going to prison for," Merle pronounced. "Unconscionable, eh? Doubt that word made much of a dent on either of 'em."

"Speaking of being locked up, did it cross your mind to mention that Bert would be coming over to fix the padlock? He scared the heck out of me."

"Bertram Van Dorst scared the 'heck' out of you? Now that's something you don't hear every day. The man is like a human cupcake."

"Cupcakes can be frightening if you aren't expecting them to pop up in your backyard unannounced."

"Mea culpa. Figured you'd be running one of Lottie's errands, that you'd be tickled to have the lock fixed."

"You're right," she sighed. "I *am* tickled the lock is fixed."

"You seem downright overjoyed."

"Would you be smiling if you had to go inspect a wasps' nest?"

Merle grimaced. "Eesh. Careful, Abby. Those aren't to be fooled with. Is Lottie calling the guy from the mainland to come do his thing?"

"Yes, but I'm the warm-up act. I thought I was only supposed to make notes for Franklin on what was wrong, yet somehow I keep getting roped into all the terrible, I-ought-to-have-a-hazmat-suit type of chores."

"You don't have to do this. Call Franklin and tell him you quit."

Quitting had never sat right with Abigail, no matter what the task. When she was in junior high she'd joined the lacrosse team. By the third practice, she detested the sport. She had blisters on her palms from learning how to cradle the ball but couldn't keep it in the stick's net. The ball would just plop onto the ground the instant she started to run. Her parents suggested she try soccer instead. Except she didn't want to give up. Although she'd dreaded donning the goofy pleated skirt and the gummy mouth guard and only played in a single game, where nobody passed to her, Abigail stuck out the season.

"I want the cottage repainted," she told Merle.

"Abby, they should paint the darn place regardless."

While that might have been true, she simply couldn't welsh on her deal. If she started quitting on people now, it wouldn't be long before she quit on herself too.

"Just give me some wasp spray, will you?"

"All right, my liege. Off to battle we go."

Cruising the store for necessities, they sidestepped the mess as well as the bratty boy, whose father had ordered him to stay at his side. The kid glared at Abigail for getting him in trouble. When he stuck his tongue out at her, Merle had to physically restrain Abigail.

"Summer people love to press charges," he cautioned in a singsong voice. "Focus: Wasps. Small. Annoying."

"Small and annoying, I'm with you."

"Let's get you away from this rack of hacksaws, why don't we?"

Merle began outfitting her with a battery of gadgets and products so she would be fully equipped for any maintenance issues that came at her. Once he was through, Abigail was wearing a leather tool belt stocked with everything from a staple gun and mini-drill to Drano and duct tape.

"You look like a gunslinger. Wasps, beware." Merle whistled the theme to the movie *The Good, the Bad and the Ugly*.

Abigail felt like she *was* the good, the bad, and the ugly. Armed to the teeth, she was on her way out of Merle's trashed store when she realized she'd meant to ask if he had any phone cords. Perhaps that would mend her crossed wires at home.

"I know you said you don't carry phones anymore, but do you have any cords?"

Merle thought for a second. "Don't stock 'em, but I got an old one in the back room if you want it."

"Please!"

He returned with the cord, asking, "You do TV repairs too? My cable's been going out when it rains."

"Get in line, bub."

She was sorting through her purse to pay for the part and trying not to knock the tools off her belt when she spotted the man in the straw hat strolling past the hardware-store window. Instinctively, Abigail ran after him, cord in hand.

"She's stealing," the boy hollered. "Dad, that mean stranger is stealing!"

"I am not stealing. I have a tab!" she shouted back, racing after the man, her new tool belt jangling noisily.

Abigail traced him by his hat, but he quickly immersed himself in the morass of tourists filling the town square. She kept pace, zigzagging between couples holding hands and a blockade of adolescent boys carrying boogie boards, but it was as if he knew he was being tailed and handily gave her the slip.

Sweating, Abigail paused to wipe her head with her forearm. A little girl passing by pointed and said, "She's a janitor, Mama. Like at school."

The girl's mother hustled her daughter onward.

"That's some belt."

Abigail spun around to find Tim Ulman grinning at her and sipping a lemonade slush through a straw.

"I'm, um, doing some repairs at the caretaker's house. You know, this and that."

"I hope you're being properly compensated to slave away in this heat."

"Paying me?" she scoffed, then rethought her answer, too humiliated to admit the truth. "Yeah, I'm . . . being reimbursed for my time and effort."

In a podunk, backwater, bartering kind of way.

"I'm actually taking a breather from work myself," Tim admitted. "Even though I swore I wouldn't look at a single stock price while I was here, I was giving day-trading a whirl, seeing how I'd handle working from home rather than from the office. A guy could get used to this. Statistics and numbers, those are fine by me. Pushy people and demanding bosses, them I could do without."

"You're a numbers guy?" The model-looks-meets-math-whiz-mind equation didn't compute.

He shrugged shyly. "Not in a geeky way. Okay, in a slightly geeky way. My firm originally hired me out of college for statistical analysis. I wound up on the trading floor only because I could handle the figures faster than the other new-hires. Is my being a nerd at heart a deal breaker?"

"No, no," Abigail assured him. The fact that Tim had a brain between his ears made him exponentially more handsome, if that was possible. "I'm a card-carrying member of the club myself."

"A strapping woman like you? I find that hard to believe," he teased, with a nod at her tool belt.

"Me, I'm a book dweeb. I started reading the dictionary when I was five. Memorized most of the Latin roots by my teens. While the rest of the girls in my senior class were picking their prom dresses, I was applying for an internship at Oxford University Press in England because they—"

"Publish the Oxford English Dictionary. The OED."

"A man who's facile with his acronyms." She smiled.

"I can't take too much credit. Reading a stock ticker all day long has that effect on a guy. So can we try our date 'part *deux*' this evening, after we've each finished toiling? I could camp out in front of one of the restaurants at around four, then we might actually be able to eat dinner by eight. Or we could go to my place? I'm a decent cook for a math geek."

"I was thinking the *fire*house instead of your house."

It was Thursday, bingo night at the fire station, and Abigail needed to talk to Ruth about the *Bishop's Mistress*. An avid, almost rabid player, Ruth would give Abigail only somewhat divided attention at the game, but it was better than nothing.

"It's a local custom," she clarified. "They play bingo and serve these amazing hot dogs."

"The tool belt, bingo—I'm getting a mixed message here. You're part handy hottie, part senior citizen?"

Abigail had never been called a "hottie." Not in her entire life. Though it was slang, and not even a terribly unique or elevated form of colloquial speech, she was flattered.

"Bingo is fun. For people of all ages. The whole town comes. Oh, and they have beer."

"Say no more. The beer clinched it. You're on. Wait," he said, suddenly remembering something. "I have a work call at seven. Save me a seat and I'll meet you there?"

"I'll have to defend it tooth and nail if you're late. That's how serious islanders are about their bingo."

"I'll bring shin guards. And a helmet. You sure I can't buy you a lemonade before you're back on the clock?" He shook his cup, rattling the ice.

"We have a lemonade stand?"

"Two, as a matter of fact."

Abigail had been so diverted by the horrendous traffic, the aggressive out-of-towners, and the renters' ghastly attitudes that she hadn't seen the forest for the trees. Chapel Isle was alive with activity. Seasonal businesses that had cropped up out of nowhere were thriving, and people were enjoying themselves. She seemed to be the only one who wasn't.

"I'll take a cold beer at bingo instead," Abigail told Tim, then patted her tool belt. "Off to the grind."

The address Lottie had given her was inland from the beach, a picturesque cabin with a trellis of climbing roses gracing the entry. Abigail knocked and heard footsteps. From inside, a female voice said, "Maybe it's the real estate agency."

A woman answered the door wearing a man's T-shirt over a bathing suit, the wet outline showing through. "It is, honey," she called, noting Abigail's tool belt. "Do you want to show her or should I?"

"Let me explain," Abigail interrupted. "While I am a representative of Gilquist Realty, I'm here only to make an assessment."

Confused, the woman beckoned her husband. "Honey?"

A guy with a towel around his neck ambled to the door. His

trunks had sand on the hems. The couple had obviously just gotten back from the beach.

Abigail politely started her spiel about providing an intermediate evaluation until a proper professional could be brought to the residence, but the husband cut her off toward the end.

"An assessment isn't going to do a bit of good if she gets stung. My wife is allergic to bee stings. Deathly allergic. We aren't going to wait around to see if the same is true of wasps." His frustration was rising fast. "Babe, get the phone. I'm calling the agency and telling them we're out of here. We'll find a hotel room or—"

"Okay." Abigail stopped him. Like this couple, she wanted someone to step in, man up, and help for a change. "Where is it?"

The wife stayed inside as the husband showed Abigail around to the side of the cabin. Wedged under the roof's overhang was a thick brown mass riddled with holes. Wasps were flying out of it by the dozens. The husband was careful not to get too close.

"We're afraid to open the windows," the wife yelled through the back door.

"It's hot as hell, we have no A/C, and we've got to have our windows shut in case there are holes in the screens," the husband added. "Not the most pleasant way to spend your vacation."

The nest was swarming with wasps, and all Abigail had was a can of broad-spectrum insecticide. Rather than mulling over the myriad ways she wanted to kill Lottie, Abigail had to think fast.

"I need trash bags. Lots of them. And one of those mesh laundry sachets you wash bras in," she instructed the wife. "Oh, and do you have anything with a long handle?"

Sighing, the husband said, "I see where you're going with this. I have something that might do the trick."

He reticently relinquished a prized golf putter, and his wife contributed her laundry sachet as well as a box of jumbo black trash bags.

Conjugating Latin to calm her nerves, Abigail tore openings in the bags and fitted them over her torso to cover her arms and legs.

Last, she put the mesh bag over her head, completely protecting herself from head to toe.

Trepide, trepidius, trepidissime.

Audeo, audere, ausus sum.

Commoveo, commovere, commovi, commotus.

Sheathed in layers of black plastic, she was sweating profusely and could barely see through the white mesh.

"If either of you takes a picture, I'll leave you to the wasps."

The husband, who was standing twenty feet away, promised not to. The wife agreed from her post at the door. "We swear."

A memory of standing on the back porch of her parents' house in Massachusetts as a child came to Abigail. Her father was pointing out a hornets' nest in a neighbor's tree, explaining how it had been there for months. The only reason they were able to see the nest was because winter was coming and the missing leaves had exposed it. The hornets' nest in the tree reminded Abigail of the map in the desk and the golden goblets from the *Bishop's Mistress*. Had Wesley Jasper hidden the map because he knew what was on board the ship? Or because he didn't want it to be disturbed out of deference to the sailors who'd lost their lives on it?

As the couple watched intently, Abigail approached the nest, her bug spray aimed high, as if she actually was a gunslinger. Firing a stream of liquid into the air sent the wasps into a fury. She had to stand her ground during the frenzy in order to knock the nest down from the roof with the golf club. A giant chunk of the hive smashed to the ground, then she blasted it with the spray until the remaining wasps were dead or had flown away.

From indoors, the wife was cheering. Abigail handed the husband his club, which was covered in goo.

"Thanks," he said, disgusted by the state of his putter. Afterward, he turned sincere. "My wife and I are glad you came."

Abigail shucked off the trash bags, dripping with perspiration and feeling repentant despite the couple's appreciation. Though she'd been successful, there was a sense of sadness in what Abigail had done. Ruining the insect colony seemed akin to what the tourists were doing to Chapel Isle.

"You're welcome."

Back at home, Abigail should have been getting ready for her date but couldn't concentrate. She tried reading more about the Bedouin and the slave girl. By the fifth chapter, the evil king had attempted to take her as a concubine and the girl had slapped him, earning another whipping as well as a stay in the dungeon from which her Bedouin lover had escaped. The racy seduction scene and brutal beating were more needless drama. Abigail couldn't take it. She dug Merle's old phone cord out of her purse and plugged it in, hoping it would work.

It did. So she phoned her parents.

Because they usually spoke once a week, on Sundays, her mother was taken aback by the call, immediately concerned. Although her parents hadn't been in favor of her staying on Chapel Isle and continued to hope she'd return to Boston, they remained cautiously supportive, especially Abigail's father, who'd always been her biggest champion. A respected, now-retired surgeon, he doled out moral prescriptions the way he had medical prescriptions: with the intent to help and, hopefully, to heal.

"This fellow, is he a gentleman? A scholarly man?" her father asked evenly.

"As far as I can tell."

"Then what harm can come of it? It's been almost a year, Abigail."

The fire had taken place at the end of July, and the anniversary was fast approaching. She feared the date to her core. Abigail wasn't sure how she'd handle it. Would it push her off the edge, or would it wind up being just another day—and was that worse?

She'd been staying away from Boston and putting off invitations to visit her parents at the Cape, because she didn't want to be in the state, let alone the town. when the day arrived. It would have been too much to bear. Acknowledging that the anniversary of Paul and Justin's deaths was coming soon made Abigail wonder whether she'd been hiding at home in a vain attempt to slow time. She'd been operating under the misguided belief that if she didn't participate in the world, perhaps it wouldn't catch up to her. However, it had.

"You deserve some happiness in your life again," her father told her. He reminded her that she was a good wife, a good mother, a good lexicographer, and a good decision maker. "You'll do the right thing regardless."

Except it was being *regardless* that troubled Abigail. As an adverb, the word meant *in spite of everything* or *no matter what*. As an adjective, it was defined as *indifferent*. Neither connotation sat well with her.

K Kenspeckle (ken´spek´əl) *adj. Scot and North Eng.* conspicuous; easily seen or recognized. Also, Ken´-speck´led. [1705–15; deriv. (see –<u>LE</u>) of *kenspeck* (< Scand; cf. Norw *kjennespak* quick at recognizing, lit., know–clever); see KEN]

◆　◆　◆

*It had been so long since Abigail went on a date—excluding the ca-*tastrophe the night before—that she found herself standing in front of her closet, flummoxed about what to wear.

The last time she'd been in this predicament was back when she and Paul were in grad school and living in a cramped apartment together in Boston's Back Bay. Though they were often only heading to a local pub or low-key restaurant, whatever their student budgets allowed, Abigail would spend an hour changing clothes in front of the mirror, attempting to apply mascara, or trying to get her blush not to look as if she'd come down with a rash. She usually wound up washing it all off in the end. Paul appreciated the effort nonetheless.

"No need to gild the lily," he would tell her. He liked her without makeup, without pretense, simply as she was. Abigail missed that unconditional acceptance. She hadn't realized how much.

Craving some form of company, she switched on the radio. Dr. Walter's morning show was about to be rerun. The local news station that broadcast him from the mainland didn't have enough programming to fill its airtime, so if Abigail missed the show she was sure to catch it again later that day. She was flicking through hanger after hanger in the closet, searching for something to wear, as the female host of a nature program summed up the habitation threat to the many types of egrets that called North Carolina home.

"Are we ready to say goodbye to the great egret, the snowy egret, the reddish egret, or the cattle egret? Do we want that on our consciences?" the host decried.

Abigail was thinking there was more variety in the egret population than in her entire wardrobe. Her clothes lacked any sort of flair and seemed to imitate the colors of the island: browns, sand tones, pale blues, soft greens. There wasn't a red, purple, or orange item to be had, nothing showy whatsoever. Abigail had wanted to blend in when she arrived. Now she literally did.

"This is a wake-up call," Dr. Walter shouted to open his show, then began bellowing about the topic of the day, which concerned American jobs being lost or reallocated to nations overseas.

"Have you or anybody you know gotten the ax, only to have your position taken by some schmo in another country? Is it his fault for wanting to make a wage? Should we be angry at the stranger in the strange land or at our brethren American bosses for ditching us in favor of the almighty dollar?"

While the first caller ranted about outsourcing, Abigail wished she could have outsourced her clothing. She thought of Tim and his eye-catching Mercedes compared to her ho-hum style.

Maybe you should cancel. You didn't really want to do this in the first place.

Except Abigail didn't have Tim's phone number. She contemplated bailing on bingo night to avoid him but wanted to talk to Ruth.

"You'll have to face Tim eventually."

With limited choices in apparel or excuses, Abigail opted for a sage-colored cotton blouse paired with jeans that had a paint stain she couldn't pick off the leg. She would have preferred not to wear pants given the weather, but Tim had seen her in shorts and mistaken her for not being ready. A skirt or summer dress would have been perfect, only Abigail didn't own anything that feminine, not anymore.

With her hair twisted into a loose bun and deodorant caked on to mask the smell of bug repellent, Abigail took a final glance in the bathroom mirror before leaving. She looked like she always did. Like she wasn't trying.

Abigail opened the medicine cabinet in search of something to make it seem as if she was putting forth an effort. Chapstick didn't qualify as makeup, but she did have a tinted SPF15 moisturizer that her mother had sent in a care package. She rubbed on the liquid, which promptly disappeared. The *tint* in the tinted moisturizer was barely that. It was imperceptible. The more she put on, the greasier her skin got. Between her paint-splattered pants and her oily face, she was quite a sight.

"Straight from the pages of *Vogue*," she said wryly, then shut off the bathroom light.

On her way out the door, the house phone rang. She hadn't heard it in ages and the sound gave her a start. Having just spoken to her parents, she assumed it was them again. When she picked up, there was nobody on the other end.

"Hello? Hello?"

No answer.

The phone had been working fine when she had her parents on the line, meaning it wasn't a bad connection again. Was it a wrong number? Or was the person who'd attempted to break in to her oil cellar calling to see if anybody was home?

Unnerved, Abigail closed and locked every window on the first floor. It would be a battle to reopen them, but she was willing to tolerate the fight as well as the heat in order to secure the house. She drew the curtains and turned on the lights to make it appear as if somebody was at home. That was all she could do, yet it didn't make her any less apprehensive.

*   *   *

Judging by the sea of cars surrounding the fire station, the tourists enjoyed the traditional Thursday-night bingo game as much as the residents. The traffic forced Abigail to park four blocks away on Timber Lane, a road she was thoroughly familiar with. One night last fall when she'd been doing Merle's security detail during the height of the burglary scare, she'd seen a shadowy male figure in the street. While the figure turned out to be Bert Van Dorst, the fright she'd gotten that evening stayed with her.

After Abigail had struck her agreement with Sheriff Larner, the break-ins on the island ceased. Until yesterday. She knew Larner wasn't to blame, and, as Merle had pointed out, all of the locals were well aware that the oil cellar wasn't an entry point to the caretaker's cottage. So it had to be an out-of-towner. As Abigail joined the flow of summer people on their way to the fire hall—teens eager to get to the game, couples arm in arm, parents holding their kids' hands—she appraised each of them as potential suspects.

The fire station was a two-story cinder-block stronghold fronted by glass-topped bay doors. Inside were the island's fire trucks—three short, squared-off, secondhand models, the words *Chapel Isle* repainted on them where another town's name had once been emblazoned. Abigail recognized the fleet from the night before at Pamlico Beach. She wished the lights hadn't been on downstairs in the station. Seeing the fire trucks through the bay doors spiked her anxiety.

Bingo was held in the meeting hall on the upper floor of the station. The place was packed, standing room only. Folding tables and chairs sectioned the substantial room into long rows. Children were scurrying around, eating popcorn, while the adults fortunate enough to have snagged seats fanned themselves with extra game cards. Dozens of people in one space combined with the humid weather made for one very hot room. Some of the fluorescent lights overhead were flickering, as if it was too steamy for them to stay lit.

Natives sat apart from the tourists, distinguishable by their thinly veiled irritation at the visitors horning in on their weekly game. Abigail spotted Janine Wertz at a corner table. Her husband, Clint, was at her side. Abigail had never seen the two of them together. Clint was sullenly nursing a beer, while Janine chatted with another woman at the table, clearly ignoring her husband's mood.

"Over here, hon."

Ruth hailed Abigail from a nearby table and motioned her over to the spot she'd saved. Daubers in different colors were on standby, and dozens of bingo cards papered Ruth's parcel of space. She had on a pink canvas ball cap, the brim tugged low, as if she was about to play poker rather than bingo and didn't want her opponents reading her eyes.

"I was hoping you'd come," Ruth said, delighted. "Couple o' summer people tried to bribe me for your seat. Woulda made more than I did in tips today. They wanted it something fierce. They were ready to hock their offspring."

Abigail suddenly understood why Clint Wertz was so mad. Because of the out-of-towners, there were no stools left at the back bar and he couldn't sit and drink with the rest of the volunteer firemen. He seemed more rankled by the vacationers than did Abigail.

"A whole day's worth of tips?" she asked. "Maybe you should go into business. Come early, grab up chairs, then sell seats at a profit."

"Like the mob. I could do that."

"And the hat is very gangster."

The pink cap had an emblem for the North Carolina Voters' Registration Drive on it.

"That's the vibe I was going for." Ruth handed Abigail a blue dauber, saying, "Get ready, missy. Game's about to start."

A heavyset man plodded to the microphone positioned at the front of the hall. He was wearing suspenders that hiked his pants well over his waist, exposing his socks at the bottom. Abigail recognized him as the bartender at the townie bar, the Wailin' Whale. When she'd ventured in there one night in search of Sheriff Larner, the guy in suspenders had been cordial to her, a memorable contrast to the other natives at the time. He'd even known her name, though she still didn't know his. Abigail felt a pinch of remorse about that.

"Evening, ladies and gentlemen. No doubt it's hot. But it's never too hot for bingo!"

The crowd cheered. A giant bingo board was propped against a wall alongside a metal cage for manually spinning the balls. The man in suspenders had a folding chair set up between the cage and the board so he could sit while he worked the cage, microphone, and board in tandem.

As the man began the night's inaugural game with a vigorous spin of the cage, Abigail filled Ruth in on what had been happening: the failed date with Tim, the robbery attempt, the man in the straw hat, and Nat's pending departure. Riveted, Ruth listened while marking her bingo cards on autopilot, nodding with each plot twist yet refraining from comment. She was too absorbed either in the game or in Abigail's story.

When a boy shouted out, "Bingo," Ruth put aside her dauber and crumpled her cards defiantly. "Beginner's luck."

During the break before the next round, Ruth laid out another ream of cards and huffed, "Happens every year."

"What? The summer people beating you at bingo?"

"No, the wreck divers. Sometimes it's only a handful of 'em searching for the *Bishop's Mistress*. Other seasons they come in droves. A few years back, three divers almost drowned in the Graveyard. Nearly destroyed the boat they rented in the process. That's why nobody lets their rigs to divers. And that's probably why George Meloch was being crabby the other day when I mentioned that famous treasure hunter. George was in the rescue party that saved those three guys. Refused to ever do it again." Ruth chose a different-hued dauber, priming for the next round. "Seems to me, mainland folks don't understand the meaning of the word *graveyard*. It's a sacred place, a place of rest. To us, anybody going out there to find the *Mistress* isn't a 'wreck diver' or a 'treasure hunter.' They're grave robbers."

"Then why would Nat agree to take this famous treasure hunter there if the other captains will give him flak for it?"

"He may have been here a while, Abby, but that don't make him a local."

Aware the caveat was meant for her as well, Abigail decided to tread lightly on the topic of the Ship's Graveyard and the *Bishop's Mistress* going forward.

"As for Nat leaving, can't say I'm shocked. Fishing is a tough row to hoe. He may not be cut out for it," Ruth lamented, echoing Merle.

Abigail had to wonder if she was the only person who'd be sorry to see Nat go and if that should tell her something. Then a thought sprang into her mind.

What if Nat's the one who broke into the oil cellar?

From their conversation yesterday, she'd sensed he knew what the treasure hunter was after but was downplaying it. As Ruth had reaffirmed, Nat wasn't a native. That meant he might not have been privy to the fact that the oil cellar wasn't connected to the lighthouse. Merle had told Abigail that, prior to coming to the island, Nat had been arrested for breaking into cars to steal change because he'd been penniless. More importantly, Nat said his business was in dire straits. Had hard times made him reckless enough to break into her house?

"Onto the juicy stuff," Ruth demanded. "Where's this stud muffin of yours?"

"He said he had a work call, then he'd . . ."

Abigail checked her watch and realized Tim was actually quite late. If he was ditching out on their date, she wouldn't have been offended—it wasn't as if she'd made a sterling first impression— and, moreover, she wouldn't have been too broken up about it.

"He'd what?" Ruth asked. "Be here wearing a fig leaf? Sorry, that was just wishful thinking."

"Give *me* the fig leaf. I'm roasting. I guarantee there'll be grill marks on the backs of my legs from these jeans."

"That your foxy date attire?" Ruth inquired, chagrined at Abigail's ensemble. "Sorta low on the sexy scale. You could unbutton your blouse. Show some more skin."

Ruth went after Abigail's top button, and Abigail batted her hands away.

"Hey! You wouldn't want to get injured during a game, would you?" Abigail threatened.

"Poor guy. The only action he'll get will be if you sit on his lap. 'Cause that chair you're on is prime real estate, and you two have to share or I'll auction it off to the highest bidder."

Abigail saw her chance for a segue. "I got a lot of stares when I was with Tim at the Kettle, namely from George Meloch. Any guess why?"

"Maybe he assumes you're betrothed to Denny," Ruth replied with a smirk. "Speak of the devil."

Denny was pushing through the crammed row of people seated in folding chairs, clamoring to chat with Abigail. He'd shaved his scruffy stubble and was wearing cologne. A lot of it.

"Hey, Abby," he said, patting down his hair self-consciously. "How are you? Ya hot? You need a beer? A drink? Water maybe? Don't see that guy o' yours around. He like bingo? Or is he not the bingo type?"

Denny continued to fire off questions, and the barrage made Abigail run for cover.

"I am thirsty, actually," she said, standing and scooting past Denny, who followed, undaunted, as she headed for the food stand in the rear of the hall.

"He's rich, huh?" Denny asked, dejected. "Donald Trump rich or Lotto rich?"

"I honestly don't know. And I really don't care."

His face registered the shock. "You don't care about his money?" Denny restated, encouraged, as though that gave him a chance with her.

"Let me buy you a soda," she offered, hoping he would drop the subject.

"I'm over twenty-one. I *can* drink beer," he attested, to prove he was old enough to consume alcohol and to be in the running for her attention.

"I'll take a beer too."

It was Tim. He'd come up from behind them. "But let me get it. What are you drinking?" he asked Denny. "Regular or light?"

"Shouldn't keep a lady waitin'," Denny grumbled.

"You're right. I'm sorry, Abigail. My call ran unexpectedly long. I'll make it up to you with a hot dog, if you'll let me?"

Denny quickly bowed out of the conversation. "You guys have fun," he said, shuffling away.

"We're going to try," Tim answered. "Nice kid," he added after Denny had walked off.

"Yeah, he is."

Abigail hated to see Denny sulking. She'd hurt his feelings in the past, snapping at him and accidentally implying that he wasn't smart. He might not have Bert or Lottie's lofty IQ, but he could be sharp when it came to what counted.

"You look great tonight," Tim said. "Green's your color."

Nobody had given Abigail a compliment on her appearance in longer than she could remember, at least not since Paul's passing. For her, being intelligent always came before being girlish.

"Nothing wrong with being both," Paul had told her when they began dating. "You're a Pythagorean beauty. You're as pretty as you are smart, and two equal angles mean the sides subtended by the angles are equal. Makes you an all-around catch."

"Is that a line math guys use to pick up chicks?" she'd asked.

"No, but now I may have to loan it out to my buddies."

Blushing at the memory as well as at Tim's remark, Abigail fidgeted with the collar of her shirt.

"Ah, a fellow late bloomer," he said, nodding. "I was one myself. Scrawny, bad skin, quintessential loser, that was me. You don't put stock in your looks. You didn't have to, because you had brains. To me, that makes you prettier." He elbowed her gently. "Come on, let's eat."

Abigail was intrigued but also a little put off. She'd believed she would spend the rest of her life with Paul. Everything inside her was slamming on the brakes, as if flirting with Tim went against her vows. But being a widow meant she wasn't married anymore.

"So how did the day-trading go?" Abigail inquired as they got in line. Three girls behind the counter were serving up drinks; hot dogs glistened on an open rotisserie. In the sweltering hall, the ice melted before it hit the cups, and the hot dogs were half cooked before they even touched the grill.

"Droning on about the latest stock stats doesn't make for scintillating conversation," Tim told her. "Believe me, I listen to it all day long. Who cares about the Dow? Let's talk about you. How was your day?"

This man wanted to get to know Abigail, when she didn't even know herself anymore. That was more of a compliment than anything. Tim had managed to make her smile again. However, Abigail's smile evaporated the moment the fire alarm sounded, sending everybody into a panic.

People leapt from their chairs and started huddling their children. The men from the volunteer fire squad scrambled to extricate themselves from the crowd, Clint Wertz included. He looked elated to be escaping from Janine.

"Hold tight," the man in the suspenders urged over the microphone. "The fire alarm means there's a fire somewhere else. Not here, folks. Not here."

Despite the instructions to exit in an orderly fashion, the mass egress turned into a stampede. Abigail noticed the locals hanging back, letting the tourists hurry ahead. When Tim tried to pull her toward the door, she said, "Give it a minute. It'll clear out."

As Abigail and Tim waited at the snack bar, they overheard a squad member saying the fire was by the salt marshes.

"Is that close to where we are?" Tim asked.

The marshes were a vast plain of wetlands that encompassed the southeastern quarter of the island. "No, and it's not near any homes. But it isn't as far away as the last one."

While this blaze was also in an uninhabited area, it was too close for comfort. There hadn't been a single fire since Abigail moved to the island. Now there had been two in two days. Were the summer people simply acting carelessly, or was something else going on?

L **Lethe** (lē´thē)—*n.* 1. *Classical Mythology.* a river in Hades whose water caused forgetfulness of the past in those who drank of it. 2. *(usually lowercase)* forgetfulness; oblivion. [< L < Gk, special use of lēthē forgetfulness, akin to *lanthánesthai* to forget]

◆　◆　◆

*Fire trucks wailed into the night as people gathered outside the sta-*tion. Abigail led Tim over to where Ruth was standing on a curb, away from the crowd.

"Get a load o' him," Ruth said, gesturing at Denny, who was helping to keep the tourists out of the trucks' path, then guiding everyone safely to their cars. He seemed to be in his element amid the commotion and confusion, displaying a take-charge side Abigail hadn't seen before.

"He's not half-bad at bossing people around," she commented to Ruth. "Especially for somebody who gets bossed around so much himself."

"Denny's not half bad at a lot of things. Just isn't all good at any one thing." Ruth held back any further explanation, because Tim was there.

From the few interactions Abigail had witnessed between Denny and his father, it was apparent that George Meloch wasn't a warm, fuzzy kind of dad. It was difficult to watch the friction between them, especially since Abigail's own father had been unwaveringly encouraging and proud. When she decided to become a lexicographer, he'd sent out notes to friends as if they were engagement announcements. Like her, he loved language, revered it, often saying that his knowledge of Latin was the only reason he got through medical school. Abigail believed her father was more saddened by her leaving lexicography than by her leaving Boston. They didn't talk about books anymore when they chatted on the phone. He would skirt the subject, as if not wanting to distress Abigail. Watching Denny assist in directing traffic and getting families away from the station, she realized that her father didn't discuss books anymore because it made *him* sad. She was no longer what he'd wanted her to be, at least professionally. Maybe that was also how Denny's father felt.

"It's a damn shame," Ruth sighed.

"The fire?" Tim asked.

"No, I almost had bingo on three of my cards. But, yeah, that too."

Abigail shook her head. "Has there ever been a fire in the marsh before?"

"Not that I can recall."

Logic was pecking at Abigail, seeking a satisfactory explanation. "It's a marsh. It's wet. And nobody lives there. How would a fire even get started?"

"Swamp gas. Spontaneous combustion. You got me. I'm calling it a night." Ruth departed, but not before motioning to Abigail to undo her top button.

Tim noticed her gesticulating wildly and said, "Are you all right, ma'am?"

"Just fanning myself," Ruth replied. "This heat. It's, uh, making me crazy."

Abigail rolled her eyes, but Tim seemed to buy the lie. Once Ruth was gone, he offered to walk Abigail to her car.

"Not unless you brought hiking boots. I should have left my car at home. That's how far away I'm parked."

"I could stand to stretch my legs a spell."

"A *spell*?"

"Being in the South really agrees with me. If I start uttering phrases like *I do declare* or *Well, shut my mouth,* the transformation will be complete and irrevocable. They won't let me back into New York City and you'll be stuck with me, Abigail."

"Who knew it was such a slippery slope?" she teased as they walked. Absent a breeze, the night air was close. Abigail thought she vaguely smelled smoke. That put her on edge.

"Speaking of phrases, they say *the third time's a charm*. I'd like to see you again if you'll let me. If only to make sure you get a decent meal. I'm turning into the male equivalent of a diet pill."

"Most women would thank you for that."

"But you're not most women, are you?" Tim looked at her seriously. "How do you feel about this new fire? Are you—"

"Okay. I'm okay." Abigail cut him off abruptly. She didn't want to hash out her feelings. Not with Tim or herself.

During Abigail's visit home for Christmas, her mother had suggested she see a therapist to cope with her grief, but the idea was loaded, however well intentioned. She'd argued that Abigail wouldn't be able to find a qualified therapist on the island, which was incentive to move back home to Boston. Abigail had no interest in therapy—not because she didn't think she needed it but because she wasn't sure she'd be able to stand it. As a person who chose her words artfully, with full knowledge of their every nuance, she was not capable of compacting her emotions into words for someone to dissect and analyze. *Sorrow* was too broad. *Melancholy* too poetic. *Depression* too loaded. Lingo such as *survivor's guilt* and *repressed anger* was so superficial and oversimplified that she refused to entertain it.

Language had failed Abigail. There weren't enough words in the entire English dictionary to encompass the range of feelings she'd faced. After years as their faithful advocate and guardian, she was angry at words for not coming to her rescue when she needed them most.

"Tim, I didn't mean to be short with you. It's a touchy topic."

"No, I overstepped my bounds. I'm the one who should be apologizing." He dug his hands into his pockets.

"Look, give me a call. We'll reschedule."

He brightened. "I will if you give me your number. Home, cell, license plate—I'll take any of them. Let me get my PDA." Tim patted his pockets and came up empty. "It's probably in the car. Or at the house. Or in my other shorts. All right, let's do this the old-fashioned way."

"As in a pen and paper?"

"I was thinking I'd memorize it. If I can't keep ten digits in my head, I should probably drop the day-trading."

"Good, because I don't have a pen or a piece of paper."

"A word junkie without a pad and pen? What if you hear some verb you've never encountered before? Or an esoteric adjective?"

From the mundane to the obsolete, there were very few words unfamiliar to Abigail. She used to search out rare terms the way a biologist would a new species. That had been a point of pride for most of her life.

"On Chapel Isle?"

"Why not? You said it yourself. This place is quirky. Maybe there's some heretofore unknown noun that originated on the island, just waiting to be discovered."

Abigail gave him a skeptical look. "You mean like the Sasquatch of the English language? Well, let me know if you hear this mythical word, because I certainly haven't."

"For you, I'll keep my ears open."

They reached Abigail's station wagon on Timber Lane. The cars that had been parked at either end of hers were gone, but the lights were on in the nearby houses. When last she'd been there, all the rental units were dark inside and locked up tight. Seeing the street in a different way convinced Abigail that she could see the whole island differently if she'd try.

"I'm ready for those digits," Tim declared, opening the car door for her.

Abigail said her home phone number twice, then he repeated it back to her perfectly.

"There. It's spot-welded into my brain."

"This from the man who can't remember what he did with his phone."

Tim laughed and gave her a hug, which was uncomfortable at first. By the time it began to feel good, it was over.

"I'll call you," he told her.

Abigail got into her car, glad she'd gotten that new phone cord. Because she genuinely did want Tim to call.

Returning to the lighthouse, Abigail was on alert for anything unusual. The lights were still lit, and from outside she could make out the silhouette of the wingback chairs. Otherwise, the interior was shrouded behind the drapes.

She unlocked the door. Inside, the temperature was staggering. Windows closed, bulbs burning, the house had become an oven. Abigail ran around shutting off the lamps, then opened and closed the door like a bellows to bring in some fresh air. Nothing she did put a dent in the solid block of heat that had coagulated in the caretaker's cottage.

Be happy the heat is the only thing that's different since you left.

If the phone had rung in her absence, she couldn't tell. She didn't have an answering machine because the rotary model phone had no receptacle to connect one. That evening, Abigail was thankful it didn't. If she'd heard another hang-up, she would have gotten scared.

With the lights off, she had to feel her way upstairs to change for bed. It was even hotter on the second floor. Abigail put her clothes away and sorted what needed to go into the hamper by smell rather than sight.

Sniffing the shirts, she said, "Oh, boy. I have *got* to go to the laundromat."

Then she found her hand-drawn map from the library crumpled in the pocket of her shorts.

"I'd forgotten about you."

She headed into the study to compare it to the secret map she'd uncovered in the desk. Though it would add to the heat, Abigail turned on the light. When she did, the desk drawer in which she'd found the map was ajar. Except she'd made certain to shut it tight after finding the hidden compartment.

Was this Wesley Jasper's doing? Or the intruder's?

Abigail yanked open the drawer to check that the map was still there. It was. She was relieved but still mystified.

Summoning reason, she paced the study. "Either the ghost opened the drawer or—" Abigail stopped dead. "The person who picked the lock on the oil-cellar door also picked the lock on the front door."

But they didn't find the map, she reminded herself.

Furious at herself, Abigail started to mentally backtrack. Though she was reluctant to admit it, the first thing that popped into her head was the way she'd seen Tim peering into her basement. What would have simply seemed nosy under normal circumstances was downright suspicious after the incident with the oil cellar. Then Tim was late to the bingo game, which would have given him ample time to raid her house. He could have faked not having her phone number to throw her off the scent.

"Presuming the man is an accomplished criminal and an expert liar."

His compliments and keen interest in her suddenly seemed so contrived that her cheeks burned with hurt and humiliation.

"Fast car, fast talker. You should have known better than to think a guy that handsome would be into you, *Abigail*."

It was what Tim had been calling her. Not *Abby,* like everybody else. Her real name didn't even feel right on her anymore, because of him.

Shaken, she re-dressed, preparing to head into town to talk to Sheriff Larner. She'd protected his secret these many months and hoped she could confide in him.

"It was his bright idea that you go out with the guy," Abigail fumed.

And you went along with it, she thought. *So who's more to blame?*

In lexicography, checking and verifying the authenticity of sources was the cornerstone of the profession. Etymology couldn't be taken for granted. Tracing a word through its various incarnations, back through time to its origin, wasn't only necessary, it was fundamental. Were it not for the diligent work of lexicographers who held themselves to the highest standards, the dictionary wouldn't even exist. Yet Abigail had thrown her years of training aside and taken advice from a lawman who'd broken the law—in her own home, no less. The logic of her actions eluded her. Between the heat and the open drawer, it was easier to be angry than to figure it out.

"I am finally going to give Caleb Larner the dressing-down he deserves."

A bulky brick building in a corner of the square served as the island's sheriff station. Abigail went in expecting to see Larner at the desk and instead found his deputy, Ted Ornsey, with his feet up, a fan blowing right at him while he threw pencils into the particleboard ceiling tiles. There were more than a dozen dangling above his head.

Abigail cleared her throat and Ted jerked his feet down off the desk, straightening up.

"How may I help —oh, hey, Ms. Harker."

"At ease, Ted."

"Thought you were a tourist." He got up on his chair and pulled the pencils out of the ceiling. "I'm supposed to be on my best behavior case any of 'em come in, but it's dead as a doornail. Fire musta spooked folks. No stolen bikes or purses. No loud parties. No missing kids. Wait, that didn't come out right."

"I get the idea."

"Worst part is, our backup guy, Larry, is down with the summer flu. So it's only Caleb and me. I'd prefer to be out there with him, looking for who set the fire, 'cept somebody has to hold down the fort."

"Set the fire? You believe it was arson?"

"Guys on the fire squad figured the blaze started 'cause someone flicked a cigarette from a car window into the salt marsh. But the 'point of origin,'" he said, making air quotes with his fingers, "suggests otherwise. That fire was intentional. Can't say much more. Ongoing investigation and such."

Ted had said enough for Abigail.

After Paul and Justin's passing, fire had been transformed into a serious phobia for her. She recalled only bits and pieces of the actual blaze. Paul had carried her, barely conscious, out of the burning house. What Abigail did remember were the dreams she'd had at the hospital in the days and weeks that followed. In them, she was the one trapped inside as the roof collapsed and the walls folded in on themselves, flames barring her path as she frantically tried to escape. She would wake up choking, as if she'd been inhaling smoke. Her lungs didn't seem to know the difference between dream and reality. Between the fires on the island and the broken padlock, Abigail was feeling extraordinarily vulnerable, and the fear was all too real.

En route back to her car, she passed the Wailin' Whale. Remembering that Merle said Larner often went there even when he was on the clock, Abigail decided to stop in. It was a long shot, but she was desperate.

Dim lighting, saloon-style doors, and the glow of the jukebox gave the Wailin' Whale the feel of a honky-tonk bar circa three decades ago. The cracked-vinyl booths and scuffed pool table that was short a couple of cues told a tale of too many customers and too many bar fights over the years.

"Fancy seeing you here."

Nat Rhone was at the bar, swirling an empty shot glass on the wood countertop. His slur said he'd had more than his fill.

The bartender waved Abigail over as if she were his savior. "Ms. Harker, join us. Nat was just talking about you."

"Really?" she said.

Nat shot him a dirty look that sent the man in suspenders loping off to serve another patron.

"What's he like, this Mr. Mercedes? You two seem . . . close." Nat downed the last few drops in his glass.

"Close? I hardly know the man," she said offhandedly. Which was Abigail's whole problem. Tim was practically a stranger to her.

"Is he funny?" Nat asked, his tone razor sharp.

"Sort of."

"Smart?"

"I suppose," Abigail replied, trying to be blasé as she bobbed and weaved to avoid Nat's verbal punches. The booze had brought out his nasty side.

"Don't know much about a guy who you let in your house," he sneered.

Stunned, she was about to ask Nat how he knew that. Then Abigail realized the only way he could have was if he'd seen Tim coming or going from the property. That meant he'd been there last night. The same night the oil cellar had been broken into.

"I'd keep an eye on him," he warned.

Abigail was thinking she'd be wise to keep an eye on Nat.

"I saw him tonight right in front of the bar, talking on his cell. He was saying, 'I love you, I love you. You have to believe that.' And a bunch of other mushy crap. Thought you oughta hear about it. One friend to another."

The term *friend* bruised Abigail, but she was too busy piecing together the timeline to let it ache.

"What time?"

"What time what?" Nat said thickly.

"What time did you see Tim here?"

He bridled at her interest. "Boy, he's got you hook, line, and sinker."

"Was it six, seven?"

"Seven. I think. It's not my job to keep your boyfriend's schedule."

If Nat had spotted Tim talking on his cell when he was supposed to be at bingo with her, then Tim couldn't have broken into her house. Any relief that news delivered was washed aside by the fact that Tim *was* being lovey-dovey with somebody else—at least according to Nat, whom Abigail was no longer convinced she should trust.

"I'll buy you a drink," Nat offered. "Do you good."

Abigail was getting sick of people telling her what was good for her. Getting out more, dating, drinking—none of it was what she wanted. Everybody on Chapel Isle knew her name. That didn't mean they knew her.

"No thanks," she told Nat, grabbing her purse to go. "I never liked alcohol much. It makes people do and *say* things they might regret."

M Misprize (mis prīz′), *v.t.*, to despise; undervalue; slight; scorn. [1300–50; ME *misprise* < MF *mesprisier*, equiv. to *mes–* MIS– [1] + *prisier* to PRIZE [2]]

◆ ◆ ◆

Abigail wasn't two steps outside the Wailin' Whale when she came face-to-face with Tim Ulman. He was sweating, frazzled, and wearing different clothes than when she'd seen him a few short hours ago. He'd gone from a polo and freshly ironed khakis to a rumpled T-shirt and nylon shorts.

"Hey, um, hi," he said, attempting to pull himself together.

In light of what Nat had just told her, Abigail struggled to remain civil. "Tim, what are you doing here?"

"Don't hold this against me." He hung his head, resigned. "I can't find my PDA. Not to seem like a slave to the damn thing, but it's got my whole life on it. I've looked everywhere—in the car, around the house—so I thought I must have dropped it someplace. I've been searching the square for the last ten minutes."

"Maybe you lost it after you were here whispering sweet nothings into the phone."

Speaking of losing it . . .

Abigail was cringing inside. Though she was fully aware of how paranoid she sounded, she couldn't help herself. What Nat said had really gotten under her skin.

"Sweet nothings?" It took a moment for Tim to figure out what she was referring to. "I was talking to my daughter."

"Your . . . ?"

"She's five."

Of all the embarrassments Abigail had suffered in front of Tim—this was by far the worst.

"We can't even get through a first date. How was I supposed to drop the bombshell that I have a child and am going through an ugly custody battle with my ex? She hates the idea of me moving away, because she doesn't want to ship her kid off to what she calls 'the boondocks' when it's my weekend for visitation. My ex and I fought tonight, then afterward she put my daughter on. I was just telling her that things would be okay no matter whether I live on Chapel Isle, stay in the city, or am all the way in Iceland."

Abigail felt like a jerk. A big one. For behaving the way she had and for believing Nat without an iota of proof.

"What are *you* doing here?" Tim asked.

"About that . . ." she began.

Thinking she had truly misjudged him, Abigail owned up to the trouble she'd been having at the lighthouse, careful to edit the extent of what had transpired as well as any reference to the ghost of Wesley Jasper.

"Broken plumbing, searing hot weather, and a wannabe burglar have made me one very unhappy camper. Or perhaps *unhinged* camper is more like it."

"No, I totally get it," Tim said in earnest. "I'm going berserk on account of a measly phone. But you, you're entitled to be freaked out. This is serious. What did Sheriff Larner say?"

"I haven't exactly told him."

"Uh-uh, you've got to report this." Tim started marching her toward the sheriff's station. "Tell him the whole—"

Abigail spun around, slipping out of his grasp, and put her hands up to stop him. "I can't."

"Why not? Badge, gun, that's what a sheriff is for."

"You aren't from here, Tim. You don't understand how this works."

You realize you're paraphrasing every local who's ever said you don't "get" Chapel Isle, right?

The message finally sunk in and Merle's sporting analogies hit home. The island was the game, the people its players. If Abigail didn't memorize the rules backward and forward, she was bound to lose. And she was still in the process of committing the playbook to memory.

Tim folded his arms. "Okay, then explain it to me."

"That would take too long. Days, months, decades even. Suffice it to say, Larner will find out when he needs to."

"You're telling me your safety and privacy have been invaded, except you won't inform the sole law-enforcement authority on the island? In Jersey, we'd call that a damn stupid thing to do. Seeing as we're in the South, I'll have to go with *plum crazy*."

"Each would be a fitting description."

"Then stay with me. I have a guest room. Four actually. And a couch. You can have your pick."

"You have *four* guest rooms? You could be running a bed-and-breakfast."

"If I included breakfast, would you take me up on the offer?"

While Abigail appreciated the invitation, she declined. The ghost hadn't scared her off. A real live person wasn't going to either.

"I have to hand it to you. You're braver than I'd be."

Tim was leaning close to her. He ran his thumb under her chin. Abigail's brain began scrolling through reactions.

He's in your personal space. He's touching you. He's . . . Uh-oh. This man is about to kiss you.

Without warning, the door to the Wailin' Whale was flung open and slammed against the frame. The bartender and another burly man hauled Nat Rhone outside by his arms.

"What've I told you about starting fights, Nat? I ban you from here and you'll have no place else to go. Remember that next time you wanna take a swing at somebody in my bar."

Nat wrestled with the men as they pinned him to the hood of his truck. He stopped the instant he saw Abigail and Tim to-gether in the square. His expression was awash with another inscrutable emotion. The men eased their grip on him as he ceased to fight.

Abigail hurried to catch the bartender before he could return inside. Tim tried to hold her back gently by the arm, but she broke free, asking, "What's going on?"

"When he drinks, Nat Rhone is as useless as a back pocket on a shirt. Unless you want a pay-per-view-worthy boxing match, that is." The bartender wiped sweat from his forehead with the heel of his hand. "He was trash-talkin' another captain. Something to do with the Graveyard. Don't forget what I said about fightin'," he shouted at Nat.

"Yeah, yeah, yeah."

Aggravated, the bartender and his buddy retreated into the Wailin' Whale, as Nat was climbing into the cab of his truck. He was in no condition to drive.

"Where do you think you're going?" She went and nimbly swiped the car keys from him.

"Home."

Nat held his hand out, a silent command to return the keys. He didn't blink, bullying her with the might of his stare.

"I can give you a lift." Tim came up to Abigail's side. "Couple beers too many. Happens to all of us. I don't mind."

Abigail could tell Nat did. She stepped between them before Nat had the chance to do something dumb.

"No, I'll take him. There aren't many streetlights on the island, and the roads can be tricky at night. It's easy to get lost."

"Yup, get lost," Nat echoed archly.

"My car. Now," she told him, pointing.

"Yes, ma'am." Nat saluted her and winked at Tim, whose jaw was visibly flexing.

"I'll call you, Abigail," Tim said, landing the last dig as they walked away.

It wasn't that she hadn't wanted to hear Tim say that. She hadn't wanted Nat to hear him say it.

* * *

The car ride across the island was tense. Wasted as he was, Nat continued to needle her about Tim, rooting out opportunities to insult him.

"Guys actually dress like that? Straight guys?" he asked, rubbing his chin in mock curiosity.

"I'm not the right person to ask about fashion."

"Were those hair plugs?"

Anger roiling in her chest, Abigail decided not to let Nat bait her. She turned the tables on him.

"Are you trying to get run off the island? There isn't a surfeit of people who like you here to begin with. Why alienate the few who do?"

"This isn't a popularity contest."

"Lucky for you."

They each fixed their gaze straight ahead at the windshield, agreeing on silence if nothing else. Clumps of brush grew from the culvert running alongside the road, glowing a dazzling green in Abigail's headlights. Overhead, stars dotted the sky, which brightened with the occasional burst of heat lightning.

The northwest section of the island where Nat lived was filled with fellow islanders' homes rather than rentals. The houses weren't large or flashy, mainly ranch-style ramblers and Cape Cods that the salt air had aged prematurely, most set far back from the street. From somewhere, wind chimes were tinkling.

"Why would you argue with a fellow captain?" Abigail asked, breaking the cease-fire. "Aren't you guys brothers in arms, so to speak?"

"You think being a fisherman is, what? The same as being in a fraternity?"

"There does seem to be a significant amount of drinking." She thought it was a decent comeback. Nat just snorted in displeasure.

"Ah, I get it. You were *that* girl. The one in the sorority who only went for the big man on campus."

"Do I look like the sort of person they'd let into a sorority?"

"Actually, yeah," Nat declared. "You do."

For a second, she thought he meant it as a compliment. Having been the typical bookworm, Abigail believed that sorority girls embodied what it meant to be pretty, bubbly, and popular. Then she caught a whiff of his disdain.

"Oh, you meant I'm snobby and shallow, is that it?"

"You stay at the lighthouse, haven't tried to make friends, don't deign to hang out with any of us townies."

The word *deign* had an etymological pedigree stemming from the Old French *deignier* and the Latin *dignus,* meaning worthy; the term *dignity* shared the origins. It wasn't the sort of verb the average drunk bandied about in casual conversation. That was what threw her about Nat. Abigail knew next to nothing about his background, education, hobbies—none of it—other than the low points in his life. But any curiosity his use of language had sparked was overshadowed by his jab at her.

"Ruth told me you're not technically a townie, because you're not from here. So you don't count," she retorted.

Nat turned away, as if her comment was a slug in the gut. "Oh, and you're special because you've got fancy degrees and awards for your work."

Abigail's mouth almost fell open. Anyone might assume she had an advanced education. The award was different.

She'd been part of a team that earned honors for the translation of an especially challenging version of a Malaysian dictionary, a little-known fact that wasn't highly publicized. The only way Nat would have found that out was if he'd searched for information on the Internet. Why was he snooping around on the Web for details about her? What else had he learned?

"These people," Nat went on. "They talk about me, think they know me, what I've been through. They don't. And they won't miss me when I'm gone. Which is fine by me."

They pulled up to Hank Scokes's house, and Abigail put the car in park. She wished she could have told Nat that she understood his past and how he'd lost his parents, except Merle had sworn her to secrecy. She almost wanted to tell him she'd miss him, to make him feel better, only after tonight she wasn't sure she would.

The house was dark. Nat hadn't left a light on outside, so Abigail had to grope her way around the front end of her station wagon to help him from the car.

"I'm fine. I'm fine," he protested, even as he stumbled.

She caught him and guided him to the front steps. Abigail remembered the night she'd seen Nat come to Hank's aid at the Wailin' Whale. He had practically carried Hank to his truck. Now Abigail was using every ounce of her strength to hold Nat upright and get him indoors before he collapsed.

"You have my keys to the door," he told her.

"Right. Which one is it?"

"Can't tell. It's dark."

She was about to start trying each of the keys in the set when it dawned on her that Nat was pulling her leg. Abigail shoved the key ring at him, saying, "Give me a break."

Grinning because he'd almost gotten one over on her, Nat slowly plucked the correct one from the bunch and unlocked the door.

A wan glow illuminated the living room, radiating from a small bulb above the stove in the kitchen. Fishing gear was shoved into every corner, and the old plaid sofa and worn recliner seemed untouched. Hank's family pictures dotted the paneled walls. The inside of his house felt similar to Merle Braithwaite's home. It was a shrine to the previous occupant. Only here, a shroud of mourning pervaded the entire place, as though the light in the kitchen couldn't shine any brighter because of it.

"Home sweet home." Nat tossed the keys on the sofa. Too plastered to censor himself, he said, "Everybody in town assumes I'm renting it or that I bought it from Hank's kids at a cut-rate price, but he willed it to me." He patted the recliner lovingly.

Even Abigail had heard Nat was renting the house. From Ruth.
You believed the gossip. So did Ruth. And she's a native.

That was one of the reasons Sheriff Larner and others hung on
to their suspicions about him, Abigail realized. They didn't have the
full picture. How could they? Nat wouldn't tell them.

"Come on. Let's get you to bed."

She expected him to make some vulgar remark, except Nat had
lost all his steam as well as his swagger; his eyelids were heavy. Abigail trailed him to a back bedroom, noting that he'd passed what
was formerly the master, where an oak four-poster queen-sized bed
sat. Instead, Nat plunked down in a guest bedroom on a half-made
single mattress. The room held another one just like it, a dresser,
and little else. She wondered why he'd relegated himself to what
was clearly a guest room, then decided that Nat probably didn't feel
comfortable sleeping in his best friend's bed. Abigail removed his
boots and pulled a chenille coverlet over him, as if he was a slum-
bering child rather than somebody she'd briefly entertained feelings
for.

"Thank you," he said, drowsy. "For this and for the thing with
Larner too. I know what you did. I've known the entire time."

With that, Nat fell fast asleep, as if he'd stayed awake only to express that final, parting phrase. Taken aback by the revelation that
he'd been aware of her deal with Sheriff Larner from the very beginning, Abigail bolted from the home, nearly tripping over Hank's
old fishing poles in her haste.

How did Nat know?

On the ride back to the lighthouse, Abigail's head was spinning. The
entire day had been an emotional roller coaster: the fire, the intruder, the news about Tim, the revelations from Nat. It was too
much for her to process. The logical side of her brain was on over-
load.

Nat's admission got her thinking about the town's constantly
churning rumor mill. Was everyone aware of what she'd done for

him? Abigail doubted it, or else she'd already have caught wind of it, the way she had when news of her widowhood hit the circuit. So why hadn't Nat offered his condolences, like Denny, or intimated sympathy, like Lottie and Janine? In a place as small as Chapel Isle, Nat would have heard the same chatter as the rest of the locals. Was it out of deference, ambivalence, or something different altogether? Then it occurred to her that if he'd searched the Internet for her by name, he easily could have found out about the fire. Which meant he might have been the one who told people she was a widow.

Abigail also couldn't understand how Nat knew Tim had visited her house. Nat had seen her with bags of groceries earlier yesterday and later with Tim at the Kozy Kettle. Neither incident would directly indicate that Tim had been at her home. The conclusion rattled her. Nat was either watching her or he was watching her house.

Her thoughts in a tangle, she had to force herself to concentrate on the road, even though it was late and the streets were deserted—so deserted, in fact, that she couldn't miss the red SUV parked on the side of the street. It was the same red SUV that had almost run her over and had been spotted near the site of the first fire. Slowing, she looked closely. There were shadows moving inside.

Without thinking, Abigail screeched to a stop on the sandy asphalt, jumped from her car, stomped over to the SUV, and rapped on the driver's-side window, through which she could see a teenage boy and girl making out.

"Hey! Hey!" Abigail pounded on the glass.

Red-faced, the boy rolled down his window as the girl cowered, hiding behind her hands.

"What?" he asked, acting tough.

"Don't 'what' me, young man. Were you two at Pamlico Shores Beach yesterday? Were you at the lifeguard's shack? Answer me."

Her intensity frightened the girl into answering first. "Yeah, it was us, okay. But we didn't mean to."

"Shut up," the boy hissed, then fell silent as Abigail glared him into submission. Nat would have been proud. She'd been taught by the master of menacing stares.

The girl seemed to shrink into her seat. "We figured it'd be cool—go to the shack, bring some food, light some candles. Romantic, you know? We forgot to put out all the candles before we left. We're, like, really sorry." She elbowed the boy.

"Yeah, we're totally sorry." He wouldn't meet Abigail's eyes.

Abigail shook her head, disgusted. "Your contrition is thoroughly insincere."

"Huh?" The boy squinted at her.

"Never mind. What about the second fire? Were you two having some romantic soirée on the marshes?"

"No way." The boy was firm. "That wasn't us."

"Swear to God it wasn't," the girl added. "I was grounded for staying out late last night. You can ask my parents."

It was the boy's turn to elbow her. "Are you going to tell them it was us?" he asked Abigail.

"Who? Your parents? No. However, I am going to tell the sheriff."

The boy sighed, scowling at his date. "Man."

"I'll say it was a couple of teenagers who ride around in a red SUV. That means if you were to not drive this car anymore, then the sheriff wouldn't know it was you."

Two birds, one stone, Abigail thought. *Or, rather, one SUV.*

She would no longer run the risk of being creamed on the sidewalks and she could keep the lovebirds out of hot water, recompense for scaring them into talking.

"Not drive my car? Are you kidding?" the boy asked, as if it was his only hold on freedom, adulthood, and a reasonably fun vacation.

The girl smacked his arm to get him to wise up.

"Your call, genius. I see this SUV again and you're toast."

The boy rolled up his window and took off, his tires spitting sand. Abigail returned to her station wagon, astonished by her own actions. As she sat in the driver's seat, her heart finally settled into a normal pace, which kept time with the steady rhythm of frogs and crickets outside. The haze of uncertainty about what Nat had said had driven her to act irrationally, to demand answers from a pair of kids because she couldn't get any from him. Although Abigail was convinced the dopey teenagers were telling the truth, she wished she didn't believe them. Because if they were being honest, then there really was an arsonist on the loose.

Once home, Abigail reinspected the caretaker's cottage top to bottom. Everything was as she'd left it. After double-checking the locks on the windows, she dragged the heavy wingback chair to block the front door as an additional precautionary measure.

"If someone does try to get in, they'll have to push over the chair. Which should wake me up."

At least, you hope it will.

Absent any other rational options, Abigail decided to do something that wasn't rational.

"Um, Mr. Jasper, would you mind keeping an eye on the house? And me? If that's not asking too much."

It was, however, asking a lot in the broader sense. She was requesting a favor from a ghost. Abigail should have questioned her decision or, at a minimum, her sanity, but she'd had enough questions and answers for the day. She went to bed, somewhat safe in the knowledge that if the wingback chair didn't protect her, perhaps Mr. Jasper would.

N **Nisus** (nī´ses). *n., pl.* –sus. an effort or striving toward a particular goal or attainment; impulse. [1690–1700; < L *nīsus* act of planting the feet, effort, equiv. to *nīt(ī)* to support or exert oneself + *-tus* suffix of v. action, with *tt* > *s*]

◆   ◆   ◆

A piercing noise roused Abigail from a restless sleep. Fortunately, it wasn't her wingback "security measure" being tripped. It was her cell phone beeping on the nightstand, indicating she had a new voice-mail message.

Abigail suspected it was Lottie with another litany of errands and decided the message could wait, especially since she hadn't heard a peep from Franklin about her request to have the caretaker's cottage repainted.

That's presuming he isn't running some con game, like Lottie would, she thought.

Engaging in hand-to-hand combat with everything from wasps' nests to clogged toilets had taxed Abigail mentally and physically. She hadn't exerted herself this much since she'd moved in and started renovating the house. The most exercise she'd gotten lately was mowing the lawn, and she hadn't even kept up with that given how steamy it had been. She made a mental note to ask Franklin to throw in a new lawn mower too.

Since her boundaries were being tested by the intruder, by Tim, by Nat, and even by Lottie with her overbearing requests, Abigail chose to regain ground for herself and do what *she* wanted that day.

First on her agenda was comparing the map she'd copied at the library to the one she'd found in the desk.

Abigail had never been much of an artist, and it showed when she tried to make heads or tails of the two maps laid side by side on the dining-room table. While her version was an unskilled rendering of a real map, with the lighthouse, shoreline, and seawall unmistakable, Mr. Jasper's was a random compilation of scraggly lines. Nothing was jelling, not the symbols she assumed were trees nor the hash marks she pegged as the meadow beyond the lighthouse. She turned the maps upside down and sideways, yet there was no discernible match.

"Did I copy the wrong one?"

Then she recalled the man in the straw hat saying how he'd brought the incorrect type of map to the island, how his covered too much ground to provide a realistic scale. There was a possibility the same was true of these maps and that the size was off. Duncan Thadlow had gone on and on about how well he knew the local waters. If Merle was right—which he usually was—and Duncan had nothing to do with the break-in, he might be able to decipher the maps. However, a visit to Duncan's house would require some sort of confection to curry his goodwill.

Abigail went into the kitchen, fully aware that her cabinets held little besides jars of peanut butter, unused cookware, and chipped crockery. But the groceries she'd bought for her dinner with Tim were still languishing in the fridge, including the brownies she was going to serve à la mode, before the ice cream had melted in the car.

She pulled off a corner of a brownie to sample. The extreme sweetness combined with the flavor of toothpaste from having just brushed her teeth was awful. She poured herself a glass of water from the tap and gargled to get rid of the taste, wondering if it was possible to get a spontaneous cavity.

"Duncan will probably love these."

As Abigail was putting a couple of brownie squares in tinfoil, the memory of what Paul had called "Pot Luck Night" sprang to mind. In grad school, before either of them had a decent-paying job, they would often wind up with only odds and ends in the cupboards, so the challenge was to concoct an interesting meal utilizing what they had. Paul hadn't come from money, and Abigail had declined her parents' financial support. She wanted to make something of herself on her own. Once Paul came along and she wasn't struggling alone but rather in tandem, she reconsidered. To Abigail's surprise, he encouraged her not to take handouts from her folks. He wasn't proud. He was confident they would get by on their own. Paul's faith restored hers, and his upbeat take on the paltry state of provisions in the refrigerator made Abigail feel like they could have a feast if they simply put their heads together. One time they'd split a box of frozen chipped beef on toast, with Jell-O for dessert. On another occasion it was powdered chicken noodle soup and Tater Tots. Paul would toss a napkin over his forearm and serve their entrées as if he was a waiter at a posh restaurant, doing a bad French accent as the garnish.

"*Ze* special, *madame.* It is *très magnifique.*"

That was Paul. Always able to turn a glass half empty into a glass half full, even if it was with leftovers. The memory forced Abigail to take a hard look at her proverbial "glass." The upside was that the intruder hadn't damaged anything, hurt her, or found the map.

"My glass may be half full, only I think it's a shot glass."

With the brownies wrapped in foil like a present, Abigail drove to Duncan's house. Though it wasn't yet nine in the morning, she had a feeling he'd be awake. Muggy as it was, sleeping in didn't seem possible. Judging by the congested streets, the vacationers couldn't manage to sleep late either.

Abigail pulled into Duncan's driveway and parked beside a humongous corroded ship's anchor. It looked as if it had come off the *Titanic,* and she wondered how it had gotten on land, let alone that far back onto the property. She heard the sound of hammering coming from a shed by the dock. There she found Duncan fussing with the engine to an outboard motorboat.

"Knock, knock. I have brownies."

Duncan shook his head. "You're going to get my missus fretting. Pretty lady keeps showering me with food. That can't be good." He peeled back the foil. "Homemade?"

"I'm afraid not. Cooking isn't my forte."

"No problemo. What with as many preservatives as I eat, I'll be jetting around in the old-age home on one o' them scooters, fit as a fiddle at the ripe age of a hundred five."

Abigail couldn't determine which image she was more uncomfortable with: that of Duncan bending over with his pants half down or the one of him speeding around a nursing home with no hair and no teeth.

"This isn't about your toilet again, is it?" he asked, his mouth full of brownie.

"No, no, the toilet is fixed. For the most part. When it wants to be. As I understand it, you're a bit of a conspiracy theorist, so this might be right up your alley."

"Ooh, I'm all ears." He glanced down at his large belly and corrected himself. "Well, not *all* ears."

She proceeded to spill the beans about the map, the broken padlock, and the intruder, while Duncan devoured the rest of the brownies, held rapt by her story.

"Good grief, Abby. That's a mouthful. And I'd know. How can I help?"

She retrieved the maps from the pocket of her shorts. "What do these look like to you?"

"You found it, didn't you? The secret hiding place?" Duncan did a little jig, elated. "This is big, Abby. People will be downright thrilled. They might even make you an honorary islander!"

That was a big deal to Abigail. Politeness hadn't worked. Neither had avoidance. If all it took to get the locals to warm to her was finding an enigmatic scrap of paper, she would have been hunting for it since day one.

Duncan smoothed the maps out on his workbench and studied them.

"A real live treasure map. I'll be damned. Wesley Jasper has done Blackbeard proud."

"The pirate?"

"Ms. Abby, you're living smack in the middle of the swashbuckling motherland. Outer Banks was where Blackbeard made his name, sailing the waters, plundering hapless ships, then slipping back out to sea with their booty. And he was renowned for burying his treasure. He would take a chest ashore with one sailor and always return alone. It was said the ghost of the sailor was left to guard the treasure in case anybody came to steal it."

Terrific. More ghosts.

Abigail couldn't understand the appeal of pirates. They were the thieves of the ocean, marauders who looted and terrorized people for pleasure. To her, there wasn't anything fantastical about them. They were common crooks. How did the bad guys become the heroes? Was it easier to romanticize the past the further away it got, to color it up as something it wasn't while artfully editing the unsavory parts? She had to ask herself if she was guilty of doing the same with her own past.

"Legend has it, Chapel Isle is where Blackbeard was killed," Duncan continued, growing more animated as he recounted the tale. "Had a bounty on him and was hunted down, then cornered in one of our very own inlets. He and his crew fought back. Boarded the ship of the men who were after him. They got to dueling with swords, but in the end, Blackbeard had his head lopped off. It's said the captain who caught him hung it on the prow of his ship as a trophy and a warning to other pirates that they'd meet the same fate."

"Live by the sword."

"Aw, Ms. Abby, where's your sense of adventure? Life is like an action movie. You take away the action and all that's left is talking, not living. Pirates appeal to the piece of us that prefers to *do* rather than just *think*. That so terrible?"

In her world, it was. *Doing* without *thinking* was antithetical to Abigail's nature. Then again, that was what had gotten her to move to Chapel Isle.

"Let's have a gander at these markings on the maps," Duncan said, excited.

"I copied the second one from a sea chart at the library," she explained.

"I see that, but you forgot the important part."

He took a pencil and extended the dotted lines she'd transcribed from the library's map, making the old and new maps look nearly identical.

"What is that you drew?"

"The end of the Ship's Graveyard. You'd be familiar with it only if you'd sailed there." He tapped his fingers on the workbench, scrutinizing the revised map. "If I'm reading this right, old Mr. Jasper's map shows the *Bishop's Mistress* sinking in the southern tip of the Graveyard. Most dangerous section. Been down there so long, though, that the tides might have moved the wreckage, possibly outside the shoals." Duncan circled where Mr. Jasper had indicated the ship's original location, then put an arrow and an *X* where the *Bishop's Mistress* had likely migrated.

"I guess if you wanted to find her yourself, now you could. You would be a very rich man, richer than Blackbeard."

"Not me," Duncan assured her. "Some things should be left where they lie."

As a Chapel Isle native, Duncan seemed duty-bound to honor the sailors who went down with their ships. What those ships carried didn't hold a candle to the memory of the men who sailed them. Abigail could respect that.

"About this intruder of yours: What are you gonna do to keep him out?"

"What can I do?"

"Allow me to give you a short lesson in the art of booby-trap construction."

While Abigail was doubtful that Duncan had a firm handle on the definition of *short,* she was open to hearing him out. Merle had told her how clever Duncan was with anything mechanical, and as far-fetched as booby traps sounded, she was up for whatever would make her feel safe. After receiving a crash course in home protection, she wrote out a list of what she needed to buy, on the back of her hand-drawn map.

"Duncan, have you ever implemented any of these booby traps, or is this purely theoretical?"

"The first airplane was theoretical until the Wright Brothers flew it."

"What is it with you islanders and your evasive answers?"

He simply shrugged.

"My point exactly."

"Thing is, booby traps are all well and good, but if this intruder is after the map and he learns that we know where the *Mistress* is, he won't need it. All he'll need is—"

"Me or you."

It was a sobering thought. Suddenly Abigail's cell phone rang, jarring her and Duncan. Lottie's number flashed on the caller ID. Abigail could hear Lottie hollering before she put her ear to the receiver.

"I was worried sick," Lottie shouted. "Sick."

Duncan tried to tiptoe away, as if Lottie had physically entered the shed to yell at Abigail.

"Worried about what, Lottie? Me?"

"Well, of course you, dear. You haven't been answering your phone, and you never replied to my voice mail."

"I told you. My cell reception is the pits."

"You shouldn't lie to Lottie," Duncan whispered.

Abigail covered the receiver with her hand. "She lies to me constantly!"

"I know, except then you're sinking to her level."

"I'm about to booby-trap my own house. What level do you think I'm on?"

"Abby, who in heaven's name are you talking to?" Lottie demanded.

"Nobody. You were saying?"

Lottie informed her that a tenant had called five times, adamant that someone check on his rental unit immediately.

"He claims his stove is acting hinky."

Of all things, Abigail lamented silently.

"I can't get a repairman on such short notice. You need to go over and act like you're sorta fixing things."

"How, pray tell, am I supposed to do that?" Abigail asked, her dread rapidly ratcheting up.

"Make him feel better. Ply your feminine wiles if you have to."

Her landlord was practically prostituting her to the renters. This wasn't what Abigail had signed on for, and she put her foot down.

"Sure, I'll get right on that, Lottie. If you get me a new lawn mower. Thomas Edison had a nicer one than I do."

Duncan interrupted, saying, "Point of fact, Thomas Edison didn't—"

Abigail shushed him as Lottie hemmed and hawed.

"You drive a hard bargain," Lottie said, halfheartedly agreeing to her terms.

Not hard enough.

Once Abigail had hung up, Duncan asked, "Lottie willin' to spring for the mower?"

"Willing? That's debatable. But she agreed."

He squeezed her shoulder. "You're getting the hang of it here, Abby."

If lying, manipulating people, and learning to rig her house with homemade snares was considered *adapting,* then Abigail couldn't fathom what would happen once she was fully acclimated to life on Chapel Isle.

The address Lottie gave her was close to town. It was a bungalow with Spanish moss dripping from the trees and enshrouding the house. The unit was near neither the beach nor the bay, making it undesirable by vacation standards.

"A bum location and your stove's shot. Poor tourist. I feel your pain."

Angst over having to face another oven prickled along Abigail's spine, making her breathe fast. After getting no answer to her knocks, she used the spare on the set of keys Lottie had given her. The home's interior was dusky, despite the white stucco walls and pale linoleum floors. Duffel bags and reinforced equipment cases were piled on the couch. A lot of them, as of yet unpacked.

"I'm with the rental agency," she called out. "Here to check your oven."

Her voice resonated through the empty bungalow.

"It appears I won't have to fall back on my feminine wiles after all."

Though the Formica counters and almond-colored fridge made the kitchen appear outmoded, it was futuristic compared to Abigail's. The gas range was almond, too, a far newer model than hers. That didn't make it any more appealing to her.

Shoulders tense, she tested each of the burners. None of them lit. And she didn't smell gas. That was broken enough for her. Abigail wasn't going to deal with the oven itself. The sweat running down the sides of her face was more from nerves than from heat. Every fiber of her being was crying out for her to leave.

"My job here is done," she declared, eager to go.

Then she spotted a straw hat hanging from a chair. It was the same hat the man she'd chased around the town square had been wearing. Abigail couldn't believe her luck.

Keen to uncover more about him, she started poking through the house, searching for clues about his identity. History books lay on the dinette table, scuba gear was stacked in the hall, and more maps of the local waters were in the bedroom. There were notes on them marking areas in the Ship's Graveyard where the *Bishop's Mistress* could conceivably be.

"Aha. My suspicions were correct. Nancy Drew would definitely give me a high five."

That was when Abigail heard the front door to the bungalow creak open.

She darted through the rear of the house, out of the bedroom, and past the bathroom, arriving in the kitchen in the nick of time.

"Who are you?" the man asked, as he entered and found her hovering over the stove, peering at the burners as if analyzing them for a microscopic flaw.

Without his trademark hat on, the man's face was visible in full. The wrinkles around his eyes and mouth seemed to come from too much sun rather than too much smiling. He wore a chambray button-down short-sleeved shirt, exposing sinewy, muscled forearms. Abigail realized that she had initially misjudged his age. This man wasn't as old as she'd first thought. The weathered skin was a veil covering a hale man.

"Oh, hi there!" she replied, far too cheerfully. "I'm here to inspect your oven. You're having trouble with it, I understand."

The man was eyeing her, guarded, and Abigail wasn't bearing up well under the pressure.

"You're with the rental company or the repair company?"

"The former. There's a repairman on the way, though. Sir," she added, her voice pinched as she anxiously wiped the sweat from her cheek.

"Then what are you doing here?"

"Preliminary, um . . . checking, uh . . . passing by. Well, we'll be in touch."

Abigail beat a hasty retreat from the house, and when she glanced over her shoulder, the man was watching her from between the blinds in the window.

Once she was in the car, Abigail turned out her pockets to make sure she had both of the maps. Much to her relief, she did. Because she was convinced she'd just come face-to-face with her intruder.

Objurgate (ob´jer gāt´, eb jûr´gāt), *v.t.*, -gat-ed, -gat-ing. to reproach or denounce vehemently; upbraid harshly; berate sharply. [1610–20; < L *objūrgātus*, ptp. of *objūrgāre* to rebuke, equiv. to *ob-* + OB- + *jūrgāre, jurigāre* to rebuke, equiv. to *jūr-* (s. of *jūs*) law + *-ig-*, comb. form of *agere* to drive, do + *-ātus* -ATE]

❖   ❖   ❖

Following her fateful run-in, Abigail made tracks for Weller's Market to buy the requisite items for putting Duncan's booby traps into place. The store was as packed as it had been when she went to stock up before the hurricane last fall, every aisle jammed with shoppers pushing full carts.

"Why on earth are all of these people here in the middle of the afternoon?"

"Because the day after tomorrow is the Fourth of July," a voice replied.

It was Bert Van Dorst, and he'd given her a start. Somehow he was always around when Abigail was talking to herself and thought nobody was listening, as if he were her conscience personified.

"What are you doing here, Bert?"

"Shopping," he stated, holding up a jug of bleach.

"I swear I'm going to put a bell on you."

"Sorry."

"No, it's me. I'm cranky because——" Abigail stopped herself from divulging anything about the man in the straw hat. "Of the heat."

"Wouldn't be summer without it," Bert sighed.

It was the sort of comment Paul would have made, factual yet oblique. There were the obvious voids left by her husband's death—his presence, his laugh, his touch—then there were the wisps of character she missed, like his ability to say a great deal without saying much.

Abigail had always been so infatuated with language that misusing even a syllable was a waste. Failing to employ the appropriate verbiage was squandering a prized resource. Yet words also had the ability to thwart her, as they had at the man's bungalow, where she faltered when explaining why she was there. Paul would have asked him straight out what he was up to. Not in a confrontational manner, but to get at the truth. His natural curiosity was transparent, and no one could have mistaken his interest for accusation. Where Paul had been direct, Abigail relied on the precision of words to explicate her feelings and intentions. Unfortunately, her poor choices had done just that. Now the man in the straw hat was as suspicious of her as she was of him.

"You going to the fireworks, Abby?" Bert asked.

"Fireworks? Um, when are they?"

She'd been lost in thought, debating whether to tell Sheriff Larner that she'd been snooping through one of Lottie's tenant's personal possessions and had deduced that he might be her intruder.

"The day after tomorrow," Bert reminded her, perplexed.

"Right, right."

"I've been helping the fire department with safety arrangements, what with the concern over the blazes the last two nights. Bad business, that. We haven't had a marsh fire in a dog's age. Between you and me," he said in her ear, "makes us islanders dislike the summer people even more. We're accustomed to the noise, the parties, the trash. But setting a fire, that's cruel."

Abigail thought of the kids in the red SUV while she watched the tourists steadily strip the market's shelves of food, paper plates, and soft drinks, blissfully ignorant of their reputation among the locals. She considered mentioning her theory about the man in the straw hat when she told Larner about the lovebirds, though she worried the sheriff already had too much on his hands. If Abigail told him about the man, she'd have to divulge the location of the *Bishop's Mistress* too. While Duncan Thadlow believed that would elevate her to local-hero status, Abigail had a hunch Larner wouldn't take it that way.

"Uh, Abby?"

"Yes, Bert?" she replied, still mulling over her next move.

"What exactly are you trying to cook?"

Her shopping cart was full of canned soda, dry beans, and twine. Abigail waffled on how to reply. Acknowledging what she was doing would make her seem more unstable than she already appeared, except Bert was the ideal person to recruit for her mission to booby-trap the caretaker's cottage.

"Promise you won't tell anybody?"

Bert thought for a second. It seemed that on Chapel Isle, a promise was a serious commitment, not to be entered into lightly. Abigail had trusted Ruth and Merle not to say anything about her being a widow, but the secret got out nonetheless. If Merle's sporting analogy about the "home team" and the "visitors" was true, Abigail was more like the mascot, dancing on the sidelines and watching the game rather than participating. The regulations didn't seem to apply to her.

"I promise," Bert finally said in earnest.

She walked him to a quiet corner near the deli section and gave him the play-by-play on the intruder, judiciously skipping certain details.

"I could be overreacting. It was probably kids trying to sneak in to see the lighthouse," Abigail suggested, masking what she truly believed.

"Or it was somebody looking for clues about where the *Bishop's Mistress* sank."

"Damn it, Bert! How did you know that?" she shouted, attracting attention. A guy sorting through cold cuts pushed his cart away from them with a nervous glance. "Why won't anyone ever give me the full story on the lighthouse where *I* live?" she complained in a softer tone.

"Folks are used to the break-ins. Happens every year."

"*Every* year?"

Abigail imagined herself prancing around in a Chapel Isle mascot's suit, then getting tackled.

"They say there's some secret hidden chamber," Bert began. "And whoever 'they' are, they've said it enough that the rumor has made its way into a bunch of treasure-hunting books. People regularly attempt to get into the caretaker's house. 'Specially come summer. Caleb Larner wanted to erect a fence with barbed wire surrounding the place after last summer, when a couple drunk college kids nearly broke down the front door."

"Barbed wire?" Abigail massaged her temples, as if to erase what she'd just heard.

"Lottie didn't—"

"Tell me? Of course she didn't mention that the lighthouse was a seasonal hotspot for treasure-obsessed wreck divers willing to break the law. Why would she? She's Lottie!"

"Is that lady mad, Mommy?" a girl asked as her mother poked through the packages of steak and beef tenderloin. The woman took her daughter's hand and led her to a different aisle.

Infuriated at being conned yet again, Abigail dragged Bert to the checkout counter, saying, "That's it. You have to help me with these booby traps. I need your scientific expertise."

Flattered, he replied, "It would be my honor, Abby. Only . . ."

"What?"

"One condition. You have to come to the laundromat with me first to settle . . . an issue."

"What sort of *issue*?"

Two female tourists were embroiled in a rollicking hissy fit at the laundromat when Abigail and Bert arrived. Bedding, towels, T-shirts, and undergarments were strewn everywhere. A petite blonde in a tennis skirt was about to lunge at the throat of a tall, tan brunette. The sound of their bickering reverberated off the rows of metal washers and dryers.

"Holy sheets," Abigail whispered, afraid the women might notice and turn their rage on her. "Bert, what is going on?"

"The big one left a black dress in the little one's white load. Turned everything gray. I went to Weller's for bleach."

He handed her the bottle, a token to go make peace.

"Me?"

"They're scary."

"They are not. They're upset. About laundry. You, of all people, should identify with that."

"Sooner we get this settled, sooner we get to your booby traps."

"Not you too, Bert?" Abigail had unwittingly entered into another one of Chapel Isle's favor-for-a-favor deals. "Fine. I can handle this. Woman to woman to woman."

Terrific. You've gone from island mascot to referee.

Abigail crossed herself and entered the fray.

"That's the stupidest thing I've ever heard," the brunette shouted. "Why would I intentionally ruin your laundry? I don't even know you."

"So you're admitting that you're careless," the blonde spat back.

"Now that I see how you're behaving, I wish I had left that dress in there on purpose."

"Ladies, ladies," Abigail announced. "I have the answer to all of your problems." She held up the bottle of bleach.

The blonde ignored her. "Careless and a bitch."

"What did you call me?" the brunette demanded.

"Whoa, whoa," Abigail said, getting between the women. She was holding out the hefty bleach bottle like a shield when the brunette swung at the blonde. The blonde put up her arm to defend heself and connected with the bottle instead, sending it soaring into Abigail's jaw. The argument came to a grinding halt.

Abigail clutched her face, the bottle dropped to the ground

with a thud, and the feuding women scattered, abandoning their laundry and leaving Abigail dumbfounded, her cheek swelling quickly.

"Well," Bert stated, as he scooped the bleach bottle off the ground and set it gently on a sorting table. "Might be a good time to get you home."

At the caretaker's cottage, Abigail sat down to ice her cheek as Bert penitently carried in the supplies. Although the ice was refreshing in the heat, her jaw felt out of whack and she was having trouble talking to direct him where to put the grocery bags. The more the bruise on her face bloomed, the less space there was in her mouth for her tongue.

"Least you know you can take a punch," Bert said as a consolation.

"Yup, got that mystery cleared up," she lisped.

He set out the various products on the dining-room table, including a six-pack of soda, a bag of dried beans, twine, masking tape, and baby powder.

"You want to drink these soda pops?" he asked.

"Nope. Dump 'em."

After Bert poured the contents down the drain, they started to fill the empty cans with pinto beans and tape the lids shut, per Duncan's instructions.

Bert shook one of the cans; beans rattled loudly inside. "Let me to do a test run."

He opened the front door halfway, carefully set his can on the interior side of the knob, then lightly twisted the exterior side. The can immediately fell to the floor with a clatter.

"Duncan knew what he was talking about," Abigail remarked.

"He usually does. Ready for the windows?"

Using twine and every spoon from the kitchen drawer, she and Bert rigged them so if anybody were to attempt to lift the panes from outside, the silverware would clang together, announcing the intrusion. They went from window to window, closing the sashes that Abigail had worked so hard to open.

"It's going to get hot in here. Fast," Bert warned. "Factoring in the humidity and time of day, the lack of air circulation will increase the ambient temperature by a ratio of—"

"Don't give me the statistics," she said. Or at least she tried to. *Statistics* was an incredibly hard word to pronounce given her current condition. "It's the heat or the intruder. I'll take the heat."

Once they'd finished the downstairs windows, they were almost out of spoons.

"We don't have to do upstairs," Bert assured her.

"Are you just saying that so I won't get flambéed staying in a house with all the windows shut?"

"The probability that an intruder would go to the effort to bring a ladder—"

Abigail gave him a cautioning look before he could spout more numerical data.

"Seems remote. You should address the basement window, though."

"But it's tiny, Bert. Minuscule. Who could even fit through there?"

"Don't want to find out, do ya?"

The basement was cool compared to the main floor yet still daunting by virtue of its darkness.

Get used to it, she told herself. *You may have to sleep down here.*

Bert examined the slit of a window that sat at the base of the cottage's foundation.

"Hmm . . . this one opens inward from a hinge on the top." He began mumbling to himself, doing mental calculations. "I'll be right back," he told her, and went upstairs.

"Super. I'll be here. Hanging out. Alone. Just me and my bruise."

Abigail stood in the dark basement, swinging her arms impatiently.

"Isn't this a fine mess we're in, Mr. Jasper? Spoons on the windows. Soda cans on the door. Doubted you'd ever see the day . . ."

Stop talking to him. Stop saying "we." There is no "we." And there is no Mr. Jasper.

Abigail half-expected Bert to reappear, having heard every word she'd lisped aloud. Except he didn't. Her conscience incarnate was nowhere to be found.

Minutes later, Bert lumbered down the basement steps, wielding three knives and the roll of masking tape.

"We're upgrading from spoons?"

"Call it a modification of Duncan's original premise." Bert securely taped the knives to the bottom of the window with the sharpened tips pointing up at the sill, saying, "This is where a person would put their hands if they were looking in or climbing down."

"Remind me not to get on your bad side."

"Don't get on my bad side," he said plainly.

"Thanks. Now all I need is a drawbridge, a moat, and some alligators."

"I could build you a perimeter motion sensor. Would take time, though. I'd have to order the optics, the hardware, wiring."

"This is plenty, Bert. I'm good."

Only she wasn't. Abigail's jaw ached, the heat was stifling, and her house was one giant snare. Duncan's booby traps were a success. Yet she felt like a failure.

"Oh, we forgot the baby powder," Bert observed.

"I'm sure that's so I don't get chafed patting myself on the back for doing this."

He seemed confused. "I think it's to sprinkle on the floor in order to detect if anybody has walked inside."

"Sarcasm, Bert."

"Ah. Hard to tell with your lisp."

Abigail drove Bert back to the laundromat and let him off by the entrance. He blotted his face with a handkerchief, preparing to leave the air-conditioned safety of her car for the blast furnace that was the outdoors.

"Hope those ladies don't come back wanting their laundry," he said, gazing through the windshield with trepidation.

"If they do, you know where to find me," she joked, then turned serious. "Please don't tell anybody about . . . any of this."

"A promise is a promise. I won't say anything. But maybe you should talk to Caleb Larner."

"And have him cite me for vandalizing Lottie's property and public endangerment due to knives taped to windowsills?"

"More sarcasm?"

"Took a stab at it."

"Was that a pun?"

"A lame one. I *was* bonked on the noggin."

"Think about telling Caleb, Abby. Please. I could give you numbers and data and statistics, but odds are, the intruder will make another run at getting into the caretaker's cottage. If it isn't the same guy, it'll be some other tourist."

There it is again, your conscience in the form of a man with an underbite.

Telling Sheriff Larner would be the appropriate thing to do. Only what if it was Mr. Jasper who'd opened the drawer in the study? The broken padlock was real; the drawer being ajar was arguable. Larner would posit that she'd left it open herself and forgotten. He'd reason the circumstances away. Why, she had to wonder, hadn't she?

"Okay, Bert. I'll consider it."

Abigail watched him toddle into the laundromat and was about to head home when her cell phone rang. It was a number she didn't recognize. She answered and Tim was on the other end of the line.

"I'm calling from a pay phone," he explained. "I still can't find my cell, but I wanted to see if you'd be up for dinner tonight."

Between the state of her house and the state of her face, Abigail was about to decline, and Tim must have sensed it.

"Listen, maybe I came on too strong. The stuff about my daughter, then me trying to pressure you to go to the police—it was a lot. I overstepped my bounds. I was pushy and aggressive and a pain in the ass. I'm from New Jersey. That's how we show we care. Dinner at my place? I'll cook. A nonpushy, nonaggressive, really delicious meal? Whadaya say?"

The cogent side of Abigail's brain advised her that it wasn't wise to get together with him. From the rearview mirror, she could see that she looked atrocious. Sweat glistened around her hairline, and the purplish bruise was slowly migrating up her face toward her eye and down around her bottom lip. On top of that, she had a speech impediment that made conversation uncomfortable. She didn't need to have dinner with Tim. But she wanted to have dinner with Tim.

"What time?" she sighed.

They agreed on seven o'clock and Abigail hung up, a smile wavering on her face.

"Not one of my better decisions," she said with a wince. "Then again, I do have spoons hanging from my windows. Par for the course."

Hungry, Abigail swung by the Kozy Kettle for something soft to eat as well as some sympathy from Ruth and another ice pack for her cheek.

"Jesus, Mary, and Joseph," Ruth shrieked upon seeing her. "You look like Farrah Fawcett in *The Burning Bed*."

"Is that a book?" Abigail asked.

"No, it's a TV movie that we will discuss later. When we talk about you getting a TV. But first . . ." Ruth ladled ice from a glass of water into napkins and gave it to Abigail to hold on her face. "I could get you a slab of meat to put on it, like they did on *The Brady Bunch*. Is that reference lost on you too?"

"Pretty much."

"We'll stick with the ice."

Thankfully, the café was empty save for George Meloch, who was in his usual spot at the end of the counter with the John Deere twins. He took note of Abigail's injury, pursed his lips, then made for the door as soon as Abigail sat down, as if he couldn't stand to be anywhere near her.

"Did I do something to offend him?"

"Could be. George isn't nice even to his friends, so it's hard to tell. Now, about this big honkin' bruise?"

Abigail regaled her with every gory detail of the rumble in the laundromat, which Ruth lapped up.

"Women arguing and cussing each other. A bona fide Chapel Isle catfight. It's like *Dynasty* without the big 1980s hair and the sparkly clothes."

"I'll take your word for it. Mind if I order a milk shake? I'm having dinner with Tim again tonight. Or should I say *endeavoring* to have dinner. Since I doubt I'll be able to chew in a very ladylike manner, I figure I'd better have a bite to eat beforehand."

"Another date with Señor Sexy, eh?"

"Please don't call him that. Otherwise I'll picture him dressed in a ripped shirt or a loincloth, like the men on the covers of Lottie's romance novels. She leaves them on my doorstep the way cats leave dead birds for their owners."

"Aw, she likes you," Ruth said wryly. "Maybe you won't have to 'picture' anything after tonight."

"Yes, because a welt of this magnitude really says: *Come hither, big boy.*"

"I'm putting extra ice cream in your shake. Help you turn that frown upside down."

"You're a saint. A sassy, sassy saint. So what did you mean last night when you said Denny wasn't good at any specific thing?"

Ruth's demeanor mellowed. Gone was the sass. It was replaced by the sort of resignation Abigail was all too familiar with.

"George sent him to a bunch of trade schools. Auto mechanics, plumbing, computers. Tried to put him on the right path. Get him away from the island. Denny kept flunking out, probably on purpose. He wanted to be like his dad, drive the ferry, stay here. His father wanted more for him. What parent doesn't?"

She switched on the blender, which was too loud to talk over—an excuse not to discuss the topic any further. Abigail sat there thinking that it was a natural instinct to want to protect your child, to seek out the best for them. Remembering what that felt like with Justin gave her a twinge worse than the pain in her cheek.

The blender went silent and Ruth said, "Way I look at it, hon, what you want and what you get, they're rarely the same. I wish I was a natural blonde. That ain't in the cards. I wish cookies had the same amount o' calories as rice cakes. Not gonna happen. Best to start liking what you have. Whether you wanted it or not."

P Punctilious (pungk til´ē əs), *adj.* extremely attentive to punctilios; strict or exact in the observance of the formalities or amenities of conduct or actions. [1625–35; punc-tili(o) + –OUS].

◆   ◆   ◆

Sunshine glared off the cars that filled the town square. Someone was taking too long to pull out of a parking spot, causing a jam that backed up traffic for blocks. The honking horns were the audible equivalent of the harsh light beating down from on high. Abigail wished she had earplugs as well as a pair of sunglasses, like the rest of the tourists on foot, who were bumping her and getting in her way as she crossed the square. They were as much of a nuisance as the black flies that buzzed around her milk shake. Sipping through a straw was easy on her swollen tongue, but it hurt her cheek.

Although being mired in the crowd had her feeling boxed in, the idea of being home, surrounded by her trip wires and traps, certainly wasn't freeing. With no place else to go, Abigail opted to visit Merle, who was standing at the counter, politely ringing purchases for summer people when she walked into his store. In spite of his towering stature, he seemed somehow shorter to Abigail that day, as if the heat, the tourists, and the holiday rush had physically taken a toll on him.

"Doing your civic duty, I see." The lisp made it sound as if Abigail's mouth was full of marbles.

"My, my, my." Merle shook his head at the sight of her battered face. "Is that what you were doing too?"

"Bert already told you?"

"Gave me the blow-by-blow."

"Hilarious."

"He also mentioned visiting your house for a spell today. Or, rather, it slipped out in the course of him telling me how you got clocked with a bottle of fabric softener while being a rodeo clown for two ladies bare-knuckling over their whites and darks."

"It was bleach."

"My mistake."

"No, mine. Did Bert happen to say why he came over?"

Abigail was praying he hadn't broken his promise.

"Nope. Why? He throwing his hat in the ring to become one of your male suitors?"

"Hardly. We were just catching up."

"Uh-huh." Merle was unconvinced. "Not gonna spill the beans?"

In a panic, she flashed to the pinto beans she and Bert had filled the empty soda cans with. Had he told Merle?

"It's a figure of speech, Abby. Thought you'd be familiar with that one."

Relieved, she forced a laugh. "Sure. Of course. I'm a little slow today. Being hit in the head has that effect."

"You ever talk to Caleb Larner about the broken padlock? He oughta be in the loop on this. Can't help what he hasn't heard about."

"The way news travels across this island, it's a minor miracle he hasn't gotten wind of it already."

"I'll take that as a no."

A customer approached the register, and Merle promptly rang up the purchases. For him, that was snappy service. To Abigail, it was a sign of his disapproval that she hadn't gone to the sheriff.

"Okay, okay," she acquiesced. "I'll go see Larner."

"Either that head injury is working wonders on your stubbornness or my guilt skills are ninja good."

"Both."

"But first can I pick my paint colors for the caretaker's cottage?

You can bill Franklin. Lottie's been running me around Chapel Isle like a lunatic, and I haven't seen a single plumber or handyman. Not once."

"That's because you're Lottie's new 'handyman.' Word on the street is there ain't nothing you can't fix."

She wanted to ask Merle what other gossip was floating around about her, but she'd been playing her cards close to the vest, so Merle would too. Abigail was aware she'd hurt him by not visiting much over the past months, except she didn't know how to make it up to him. Though she'd bungled her way through numerous repairs for renters, Abigail couldn't figure out how to fix what she had done to Merle.

"He really is a guilt ninja," she mumbled.

"What was that, Abby?"

"Yellow, taupe, gold, or mocha. I was talking about paint colors," she lied, quickly flicking through color samples.

Beside the paint display was a rack of brochures for lawn mowers. There were sleek red power mowers with souped-up engines and riding mowers the size of compact cars. The type that caught her eye was a lightweight, quiet model that looked like she wouldn't pull a muscle pushing it across the large collar of lawn surrounding the lighthouse.

"Ask Franklin to order me this too." Abigail tapped the brochure to indicate her choice. "I've earned it."

Unfortunately, she didn't come off quite as self-assured due to the lisp.

"Guess we each have people we need to talk to," Merle replied.

Abigail traversed the town square with every intention of going directly to the sheriff's station.

She wound up at her car instead.

Guilt was no longer a foreign tongue to her. She was fluent in every dialect of it, knew the lingo, had the patois down pat. That rendered Merle's goading effective only to a point. Abigail was desperate not to be seen as needy, although she understood that was a contradiction in terms. Going to the police wouldn't be a sign of weakness under conventional circumstances, but her life at a potentially haunted lighthouse that tourists regularly attempted to break in to didn't qualify as conventional.

Abigail had another reason for skipping the sheriff's station. She didn't want to hear any more about the fires. Larner's deputy, Ted Ornsey, had implied the last one was arson. Unless the guilty party had been caught, Abigail couldn't undergo another update on the matter.

She returned to the caretaker's cottage with mowers on her mind. Even in the strangling humidity, she didn't want to be cooped up inside, with spoons tinkling in the windows and a soda can on the doorknob, counting the minutes until she had to go to Tim's house.

"The lawn could stand to be cut," she reasoned. "Yard work. With a head injury. In the heat. Brilliant."

After drenching herself in bug repellent, Abigail trotted the old rusty mower out of the shed and started in on the overgrown grass, recalling how she'd done this when she first moved into the caretaker's cottage, how proud she had been of herself. Pushing the mower's dull blades over the lawn now, she saw the task for what it was: a coping mechanism, one of many that had become crutches. Had she really been healing from the loss of her family or avoiding the issue by busying herself with inconsequential things?

The afternoon sun beat down and a dense wind blew in off the water, thick with warm dampness. It coursed through the ankle-high grass, as if to slow Abigail down. She refused to let it.

Presuming she had been averting her pain, was the full brunt of it waiting around the corner for her? Abigail had spent so much time trying *not* to feel anything that the grief had to have gone somewhere. As she thrust the lawn mower back and forth, Abigail brooded over when the real misery might arrive and if it would blow in like a breeze or hit with gale force.

She was battling through a divot-riddled section of the backyard when she paused to wipe sweat from her face with the bottom of her T-shirt. The corner of her mouth stung where the bottle of bleach had split her lip.

"If I didn't already hate going to do laundry . . ."

Then she saw a shadow dart past the kitchen window.

Her first thought: *the intruder.*

Her second: *the booby traps.*

But Abigail hadn't left the soda can on the doorknob, because she wasn't inside. And she wouldn't have heard the chime of the spoons, because she was out in the yard. Abigail had been so wrapped up in mowing the lawn that somebody could have paraded right through the front door without her even noticing.

"I have had it! This is my house. Even if I am just renting it."

She jogged to the shed, grabbed the heaviest shovel she could get her hands on, and marched around to the front door, which she hurled open, shovel brandished like a sword.

"Whoever you are, get out here. Now!" she ordered, fighting the lisp to speak clearly and with conviction.

There was no noise—not a voice, not a footstep, not a floorboard creaking, not a peep.

Abigail went room by room. The living and dining area was clear. She flitted her head into the kitchen. Empty.

Throwing open the door to the lighthouse, she peeked inside. The stairs stood alone in the tower. Nobody could have gotten from the kitchen to the top of the turret in the short amount of time it had taken her to enter the cottage from outside. She would have caught them climbing the steps if they were there. That left the second floor and the basement.

"Maybe you should have gone to the sheriff's station after all."

The top of the staircase ended on a landing that was the equivalent of a blind alley. Her footfalls on the stairs would give her away to anyone waiting up there, so she took the steps two at a time, resting on the ones that didn't squeak, then sprang across the landing into the hall. From there Abigail could see into the bedroom, bathroom, and study. Each was undisturbed. Blazing hot but untouched.

You should check the bedroom closet. But my clothes barely fit in it—

how could anybody hide there? Do you want somebody to jump out in the
middle of the night? Stop procrastinating and go check.

She tiptoed into the bedroom and whipped open the closet
door, shovel gripped aloft. Inside, her clothes were on their hang-
ers, swinging from the surge of air. A couple of pairs of shoes sat on
the floor.

"Which leaves the ever-popular basement."

No matter how she played it, Abigail would be at a disadvantage
going down there. The lighting was terrible and the stairs were
open-construction. An intruder could grab her ankles from between the steps and send her tumbling. She needed a strategy.

Abigail crept downstairs to the living room and set the shovel in
a corner. In spite of the humidity, a few floorboards whined when
she walked on them. If there was somebody in the basement, they
could track her movements by sound, so she sidled over and quietly
locked the basement door, then hauled the wingback chair over to
face it.

She sat, watched, listened, and waited. A minute passed. Then
five. Then ten. Nobody was in the house but her.

"Then who did I see?"

Logic kicked in, positing sensible explanations. Perhaps it was a
trick of light on the windowpane. She'd been sweating, hot, exhausted. She'd also sustained a blow to her skull. Yet Abigail could
have sworn she'd seen someone.

But the only person it might have been wasn't exactly a person.

If you really did catch a glimpse of the ghost of Wesley Jasper, is that
more or less frightening than an actual intruder?

Abigail was on the fence. She *had* asked Mr. Jasper to protect the
house. Maybe he was fulfilling her request.

Abigail decided to get ready for her date. Sweaty from yard work,
she ran a bath and searched for a book to read in the tub. The task
was made difficult by the fact that the books she'd ordered wound
up reminding her of either Paul or Justin. Her tastes in reading

were broad enough that she was open to almost any subject, but the science tomes had too much statistical information in them. That was Paul's turf. Ditto for the biology and geology books that would reference animals or dinosaurs Justin had loved. Trains, trucks, and cars were also her son's favorites, so that removed a whole gamut of titles from consideration. Engineering and architecture hit close to Paul's interests, making them off-limits as well. A text on the Franco-Prussian War was safe ground; same for a biography of Genghis Khan. While she was learning a lot about random threads in history—she'd devoured each book twice—Abigail wasn't luxu-riating in reading the way she used to.

Fiction was especially risky. The stories often featured charac-ters contending with love and loss. The plots could be too realistic, too similar to the drama Abigail herself had undergone. Though Lottie's romance novels were laden with love and loss as well, they were such theatrical exaggerations that they felt safe. From sailors on Spanish galleons to Roman gladiators, from runaway Russian princesses to Mayan priestesses, none of it applied to real life. At least, not Abigail's.

"That means you're up at bat, my Bedouin buddy."

She sank into the cool bathwater, rejoining the tale where she'd left off. The chambermaid had escaped the clutches of her besotted master, the cruel king, and fled in search of her lover. Enraged, the king sent his henchmen after her, forcing the chambermaid to go undercover dressed in boy's clothes to pass as a eunuch servant. Amid the chases on camelback, the sandstorms, and the verdant desert oases, Abigail found herself relaxing.

That was until she noticed her watch, which lay on a towel be-side the tub.

While the ravishing female lead from the novel was disguising her beauty in manly rags, Abigail was racking her brain on how she could disguise her conspicuous bruise. She put the book down, drained the tub, and got to business. After toweling dry her hair, she picked through her medicine cabinet. There was aspirin, eyedrops, contact solution, toothpaste, lip balm, floss, and the tinted SPF15 moisturizer. Never the "girly" type, Abigail started to think that being on Chapel Isle was making her even less feminine than she had been to begin with.

"The sole cosmetic you own is tinted moisturizer," she scolded, doing her best to cover the bluish flesh around her mouth with what little makeup she had. "And you didn't even buy it yourself. On top of that, you've become the town handy*man*. Not very womanly."

She grabbed an aspirin and gulped it down with water from the tap.

"Please work, please work, please work," she chanted, willing the medication to kick in quickly.

Afraid she was losing her feminine side altogether, Abigail wanted to try harder on this date with Tim. Too bad her wardrobe wasn't cooperating. The cleanest pair of pants she had were the jeans she'd just been wearing. Given the grass stains, they weren't *that* clean. A trip to the laundromat was in order, but after getting decked on the premises, Abigail was in no hurry to return.

She switched tops ten times, alternating between the four clean, somewhat decent shirts she had, then settled on a navy cotton blouse.

"To match my bruise."

Her khaki pants would have looked better had they been ironed, but she was swimming in the waistband anyway. Pressing them wouldn't make them fit. Plus, she didn't own an iron. Abigail slid her feet into sandals, wishing she could paint her toenails to distinguish herself as a woman.

"Too bad calamine lotion can't double as polish."

After parting her hair, Abigail ran a comb through the wet ends to smooth them. The visage that met her in the mirror was disappointing—not unattractive, even with the bruise, but simply not what she remembered.

Halfway out of the house, she heard a *bump* from upstairs.

Was it a sign of dissension from Wesley Jasper, or the tetchy pipes settling after her bath?

Abigail went back inside and tested the spoons on the windows to make sure they held firm. Even though she wouldn't be there to hear them, perhaps they might act as a deterrent to any would-be burglars. It was a long shot.

"If that was you, Mr. Jasper, keep an eye on the place, will you?" she hollered.

Your femininity is slipping and apparently your sanity is following suit.

Since there was no reply, Abigail headed outside, slid the key in the door, and locked it tight behind her.

 **Quale** (kwä′lē, –lā, kwä′lē), *n., pl.* –li–a (–lē ə). *Philosophy.* 1. a quality, as bitterness, regarded as an independent object. 2. a sense–datum or feeling having a distinctive quality. [1665–75; < L *quāle,* neut. sing. of *quālis* of what sort]

❖　❖　❖

Riding across the island, Abigail cranked the air-conditioning to help dry her hair and examined her bruise in the visor mirror. The tinted moisturizer had left a whitish film on her skin. Instead of concealing the discoloration, it had caked up in a way that accentuated it. She tried wiping the cream off while she drove, which hurt like crazy, so she pulled over and gently dabbed it away with the underside of her shirt. She was back at square one. No makeup and now her face ached.

Abigail reread the address Tim had given her when he called. "This sounds vaguely familiar."

When she pulled up to the location, she knew why. The house Tim was renting was down the road from one of Lottie's properties that Abigail had inspected for Merle last fall, only Tim's was twice the size. Sitting high on large pilings, the angular contemporary home shouted *money.* It was the biggest stunner on a block full of magnificent, magazine-worthy homes.

Wow was the only word she could come up with. And it was the right one.

Abigail parked beside Tim's Mercedes, under the pilings. The last few days of driving on Chapel Isle's sandy streets had left telltale dust rings around the wheel wells of the pristine convertible coupe. Though Abigail was accustomed to her station wagon being covered in grit, Tim's grandiose place made her self-conscious about the dirt on her car, her clothes, her looks, everything.

She was about to take a final glance in the mirror and stopped herself.

"Nothing has changed in the last five minutes. Your bruise didn't disappear. Your hair isn't magically perfect. Your clothes are your clothes. If Tim doesn't like you because of them, that's his loss."

That was what her parents had always told her, a variation on the old adage about people appreciating you for you. In elementary school, Abigail had been advanced a year ahead of the rest of her class, creating an awkward gap between friends from her grade and her new classmates. She could recall her mother loading her textbooks into her backpack the morning of her first day in the next grade and counseling her on how anybody who didn't want to be her friend was missing out by not getting to know her. It was an abstract concept for a fourth-grader to comprehend, especially since Abigail had felt as if *she* was the one who was really losing.

As she sat in her sand-spattered car beside Tim's expensive convertible, Abigail realized that it wasn't his approval she was fretting over. It was her own. The person she saw in the mirror was a shell of the one she remembered. If her mother's maxim was true and Abigail didn't like herself, was it her own loss?

She took a deep breath, got out of the car, and rang Tim's doorbell. From inside, Abigail heard the rush of footsteps.

Tim opened the door, panting and saying, "I should have rented a smaller house. I'm getting a cardio workout from—" He saw the bruise and froze. "Abigail. My God, what happened?"

"I, uh, got hit."

"By . . . ?"

"A bottle of bleach."

Confused, he asked, "Do I want to know the details?"

"Probably not."

"Is the other guy in worse shape than you are?"

"No. But she'll be wearing gray clothes for a while."

"Would it be pandering if I told you that you looked pretty anyhow?"

"Pander away."

Tim welcomed her inside, where Abigail couldn't help but marvel at the spacious home. This wasn't one of Lottie's units—that was for certain.

The king from the romance novel would be right at home here, she mused, as Tim gave her the tour.

Each guest room was outfitted with big beds, overflowing with plump pillows and high-thread-count sheets. The bathrooms were mini-spas unto themselves. Abigail lost count of how many they passed. Plasma televisions, granite countertops, designer furniture, a hot tub on the roof deck—this didn't smack of a rental.

"Do you mind if I ask which agency you're leasing from?"

Abigail was thinking she should go work for them.

"I'm actually subletting from a friend who owns several properties up and down the coast."

"Of the Outer Banks?"

"Of the Eastern Seaboard."

"Oh," Abigail said, too abruptly. She understood that Tim was comfortable financially but hadn't a clue about the elite circles he ran in.

He shifted the conversation abruptly from the house to dinner. "I hope you brought your appetite."

"Yeah, theoretically." She gestured at her swollen face.

Tim chuckled as he led her through a barrel-vaulted hallway lined with art. "Only you would be *theoretically* hungry. I think I can change that to a definitive *yes*."

The home's cavernous kitchen was state of the art. The cabinets were custom, and a sheet of marble the size of Abigail's study spanned the center island. A hulking glass-front refrigerator acted as a display case for racks of chilled fresh produce. Copper pots were bubbling on the six-burner stove, and something smelled delicious.

"I went with flounder," Tim said. "It's my homage to Chapel Isle."

"Oh, did you catch it here?"

"I bought it here," he admitted bashfully. "Not rugged enough? Should I have said I yanked it from the ocean with my bare hands?"

"I probably would have believed you if you did."

"That's kind."

"What? You told me people from New Jersey were tough."

Tim popped the cork on a bottle of wine and poured each of them a glass. "What should we toast to?"

Abigail couldn't come up with anything worth raising a glass for. No more black flies? A toilet that functioned properly? The absence of spoons on her windows? The departure of flocks of tourists? She groped for something positive to say.

"The birth of our nation?"

For a second, Tim was lost. "Oh, because the Fourth of July is a day away?"

She shrugged, thinking, *That's what you get for winging it.*

"How about to new friends?" he suggested.

"I'll second that."

Abigail clinked her glass against his and carefully tasted her drink. When the wine hit the split in her lip, it burned so intensely that she seized up at the pain, nearly dropping the glass.

"Are you all right?"

She shook her head.

"Was it the wine? Has it gone bad?"

Abigail shook her head again.

"Was it your mouth? Did it sting?"

She nodded emphatically.

After the shock to her system, Abigail needed a moment to recover. If a sip of alcohol almost had her down for the count, how was she going to chew an entire meal? The night was already beginning to go off the rails.

"This may be gauche," she lisped, "but do you have a straw?"

"Excellent question." Tim glanced around at the multitude of cabinets. "I might." He doggedly hunted through the cupboards, opening door after door. "This is good, getting familiar with what's here. Bread maker. Wasn't aware I had that. Waffle maker. Ditto. Ice cream maker. At this rate, I'll never have to leave the house for food again."

Where Abigail's cupboards held misfit measuring cups, warped spatulas, pans permanently blackened by char, and oddball cutlery—minus all spoons and four knives—Tim's were stocked with lemon zesters, garlic presses, a panoply of spices, and a mandoline. Even his dishware made her feel insecure.

"Aha." He'd finally found a straw, which he plopped into her glass. "I do this with my daughter. She's allowed to have milk in a wineglass when we go out to dinner together. Or a martini glass. Or a margarita glass. It's silly, but it's a thing we do."

"That's sweet." Abigail wanted to tread lightly after her accusations last evening. "Say, did you ever find your phone?"

"No, and to be perfectly honest, it's ruining my vacation. I can't seem to relax about it."

"You do hear what you're saying?"

"Yes, and that's why I came here. It's why I needed a vacation. To stop focusing on what's unimportant and figure out what is. It's not easy to stop being the way you are, cold turkey, even if you don't respect certain aspects of your behavior."

Abigail could empathize.

Tim downed some of his wine. "Losing my cell phone proves that. Don't you think we'd be freer without the trappings of regular life?"

"Regular life? First of all, that's an oxymoron. Secondly, take a look around. It's not as if you have it bad, buster. I could live comfortably in your powder room."

"I don't mean to sound arrogant or ungrateful. But maybe I have been."

She took her cell phone out of her purse and put it on the

counter as a truce. "Look, I'd be unhappy if I lost my cell phone too. Even though it barely works and has terrible reception. We're human. We get used to things being a certain way. When they change, we have to change too."

"I knew there was a reason I liked you."

"Well, it's not for my cooking skills."

"It's because you see the world for what it is. That's a unique quality."

Tim was close to her, gazing into her eyes, and suddenly the moment was too intimate for Abigail.

"Have you tried calling the number?" she blurted, backpedaling a step.

"The *number?*"

"Your cell phone. What if it's just lying somewhere in the east wing of this colossal mansion? I could try calling you from mine."

"Uh, sure," he said, a bit thrown. "Smart idea."

Tim recited his number to her and Abigail dialed, saying, "We have to fan out to hear it."

"Fan out? Like a reconnaissance mission? For my phone?" he asked, amused.

She waved him on and together they roamed from room to room, listening. The house was silent. In the screening room, she noticed Tim squelching a grin.

"What's so funny? I'm going to get shin splints walking the mile back to the kitchen; meanwhile, you're cracking up."

"I already tried calling my cell from the house's line," he confessed. "I wanted to make sure you had my number in your phone. Now you don't have an excuse not to call me."

Abigail was as charmed as she was embarrassed for not realizing what he was doing sooner.

"How will you know if I've called if you haven't found your phone yet?"

"It'll turn up," Tim said with a smile.

◆   ◆   ◆

Together they set dishes out on the lengthy kitchen table, which was flanked by leather chairs. A row of scented candles glowed in a modern centerpiece. Tim shut the laptop that was sitting at the end, closing an open stock-trading page. Abigail hadn't seen a computer in months, aside from the large, clunky models at the island's public library. She'd lost hers in the fire and never replaced it. Looking at Tim's wafer-thin laptop, she couldn't decide if she missed the access computers afforded her or if she merely longed for her old one because it was a sliver of her former reality.

"Dinner will be ready in few minutes. Have a seat."

Tim pulled out a chair for her, but when she went to sit down, something pinched her thigh, sending her bounding to her feet. It was her cell phone, poking through from her pocket. Abigail rested it on the chair next to her.

"You can put your phone on the table. Elbows too. I don't mind," Tim told her. "We don't have to be all formal and proper. If we did, we'd be 'supping' in the dining room. That table seats sixteen."

"So were you raised formal and proper?" she asked.

"Far from it. Jersey is Jersey. Manhattan may be only across the river, but the fancy city stuff might as well have been a million miles away from where I grew up. I started working on Wall Street because of proximity, not passion. A hefty paycheck can keep you in a job long past your interest in the occupation."

Although lexicography wasn't a growth industry, and did not pay particularly well, Abigail had chosen it because language meant so much to her. Hearing Tim talk about his job, she realized she'd been fortunate. Most people were in his shoes, not hers.

"Once I leave work, I won't be able to afford a place like this if I move here." Tim opened the oven to peek at the food, then began slicing bread off a fresh loaf for them to snack on. "But I'd be fine with much more humble accommodations. As well as a much more humble life. Live simply, the way you do."

His comment hit a nerve with Abigail. She hadn't chosen Chapel Isle out of boredom or a desire for a change of pace. She'd come for much more serious reasons.

Aware of his mistake, Tim hurried to apologize. "That was totally insensitive. Abigail, I'm really so—"

Her cell phone rang, cutting him off and rattling against the
table. She was happy for the interruption, but she prayed it wasn't
Lottie calling at such a late hour with some hideous chore.

It wasn't. It was Merle.

"Abby, are you home? Are you at the lighthouse?" His tone was
grave.

"No, why?"

"Listen to me. Caleb called me to find you. There's a fire close to
the lighthouse. Very close. The police and the fire department are on
their—"

Before Merle could finish his sentence, Abigail grabbed her
purse and broke for the door, running at a full clip. Tim gave chase.
She flew down his front steps and jumped into her car with him calling after her, shouting questions.

"Abigail, what is it? What's going on?"

Unable to stop her, Tim got into the car with Abigail, pleading
with her to tell him what was wrong.

"This can't be happening," she muttered. "It can't. I just mowed
the lawn, damn it!"

She threw her station wagon into reverse, peeled out, and
gunned the engine, hurtling through the network of narrow sandy
lanes as she frantically conjugated Latin verbs.

Custodio, custodire, custodivi, custoditus.

Munio, munire, munivi, munitus.

Defendo, defendere, defendi, defensus.

Abigail was driving dangerously fast on the dark, poorly lit
roads, careening around sharp corners and taking turns hard.

Tim braced himself against the dash and the car door, saying, "If
you don't tell me what the matter is, Abigail, I'm going to pull this
car over myself. You're scaring me and you're going to get us killed."

She didn't need to explain. They arrived at the lighthouse to discover the island's entire fire brigade battling a blaze in the field
across from the caretaker's cottage, a stone's throw from her door.

Abigail screeched to a stop behind the fire trucks and launched out of the car, sprinting toward the lighthouse.

Sheriff Larner grabbed her before she could get too close.

"It's okay, Abby. They have it contained. It's okay."

Larner had to physically restrain her because she was in a blind panic, flailing and struggling and screaming to be let go. Memories of the night she lost Paul and Justin flooded back. Between the smoke and the adrenaline, she managed to ask a single question.

"How?"

It was the same question she'd asked when she awoke in the hospital after her house had burned to the ground.

Except Abigail couldn't hear Larner's answer. Because everything had gone black.

R Redargue (ri där´gyoo), *v.t.,* –gued, –gu–ing. *Archaic.* to prove wrong or invalid; disprove; refute. [1350–1400; ME *redarguen* to rebuke (< OF *redargüer*) < L *redar–guere,* equiv. to *red–* + *arguere* to argue]

❖   ❖   ❖

Abigail awoke, groggy, sore, her vision blurred by her dry contacts. At first, she thought she was at a hospital. But the sunlight shining through the lace curtains onto the blue shag carpet told her she wasn't.

As her eyes cleared, it was obvious she was at Ruth's house. The ranch home's low roof seemed to hover inches from Abigail's nose, and the oak-paneled walls were squeezing in on her. Head thrumming, she tried to sit up and collapsed backward in a heap.

"Knock, knock," Ruth said from the doorway. She came in and sat beside Abigail on the bed, offering her a diet soda along with a plate of Fig Newtons. "You gave us a real fright, hon. You'll be fine, though. Nothing a bit of rest won't cure."

"What happened? How did I get here?"

"You passed out. Caleb brought you over. Thought you'd prefer my digs to the urgent-care center. They'd just give you some juice, then give you the boot. I, however, have cookies. They're better for your health. That's an unwritten fact."

"What about the fire? The lighthouse?"

"Caput and safe. Here. Eat."

Abigail propped herself into a sitting position and nibbled on a cookie. Her whole body ached, making her mouth seem pain-free by contrast. She could still smell smoke in her hair.

"Your fella, Tim, he came along with Caleb last night," Ruth continued. "Asked to stay, only I wouldn't let him. Doubted you'd want him seeing you . . . this lovely."

With constellations of bug bites dotting her skin, a bruised face, and a grimy layer of soot coating her clothes, Abigail was a sight to behold.

"Thanks for running interference."

"You've already gotten calls. I feel like I'm the town switchboard operator."

"On my cell?"

"No, on my phone. Merle, Bert, Denny, and Franklin have checked in to see how you're recovering. And Lottie said to tell you to hurry and get on the mend, 'cause she has a renter with a busted screen door."

"Nice."

Ruth stole a cookie off the plate, adding, "Nat came by."

"He did?"

"'Cept Tim was here, so he took off. Told me to say, 'Feel better.'"

Abigail couldn't decide how to interpret that. Was Nat merely returning the favor for the other night's alcohol-fueled farce, or was he keeping tabs on her?

"I'd like to feel better, except I feel like I was broadsided by a truck."

"I've got something for that. It's called aspirin. Not as tasty as Fig Newtons yet equally medicinal."

While Ruth went to retrieve the pills, Abigail attempted to stand. She tottered and had to steady herself against the bed.

"First day with your new feet," she mumbled, echoing what her father often said when she was a kid.

As a child, Abigail had been tall for her age, skinny too. Growing into her body that fast had rendered her clumsy and uncoordinated. She could literally trip over her own toes. Her parents had called it her "foal phase," because she wobbled like a newborn horse. Abigail didn't mind the comparison. Horses were inelegant at first, but they grew up to be graceful. She'd hoped that she might harbor the same potential.

Abigail's first instinct was to phone her folks and tell them what had happened at the lighthouse. But that would only make them entreat her more ardently to move back home.

You can't tell your own parents about the fire. You can't tell the sheriff about the intruder. You can't tell Nat you heard about his past. You have more can'ts *than* cans.

The notion that she'd been heavily editing her life depending on the person she talked to wasn't lost on Abigail. She could have told Paul anything. She didn't have anybody should could be that open with anymore. The void made her heart seem hollow.

As she leaned over to get her shoes, Abigail heard a rustling noise. She reached into her pocket and withdraw the original map from Mr. Jasper's desk, the one showing the location of the *Bishop's Mistress,* which she'd taken to show Duncan Thadlow. She'd forgotten the maps were in that pair of pants. When she fished for the hand-drawn version copied from the map at the library, it wasn't there.

Worry palpitated in her chest. She was shoving on her shoes when Ruth returned with the aspirin. Abigail downed a couple of pills with a swig of diet soda, then frenetically got out her cell.

"Lordy, what's gotten into you, Abby?"

"What is Sheriff Larner's phone number?'

"911."

"No, his personal number."

"Darlin', you wanna say why you need it?" she asked seriously.

"Even if I did, I couldn't."

Abigail paced the path in front of Ruth's house. The dewy early-morning air was a balm for her cramped muscles, the warmth loosening the tautness. A breeze cooled her sweat-glazed skin, as if to remind her that the heat wasn't permanent. It would pass.

The homes across the road from Ruth's were carbon copies of hers—same shingles, same attached garages, same pebbles covering the driveways. The only differences were the planters outside or the colors of the shutters. All of the cars were older models, with bumper stickers from the local school sporting teams, fishing racks affixed to the roofs. The scene gave Abigail the impression that things didn't change on Chapel Isle. Yet they had. Bert Van Dorst said there hadn't been a fire on the island in ages. She feared she'd somehow brought it with her.

Sheriff Larner rode up in his patrol car, rolled down the passenger window, and said, "Come on. I'll take you home."

The air inside his cruiser was chilled, as was his demeanor. Even with his trademark shades on, Abigail got the impression Larner was having trouble making eye contact with her. She must have looked as awful as she felt.

"Thank you for coming and for last night," Abigail began. "I don't remember much."

"Maybe best you don't."

"I have something to tell you. Some *things,* plural, actually."

"It's never good when a woman says that," Larner sighed.

While he drove her across the island to the caretaker's cottage, Abigail unloaded everything about him—the break-ins, the man in the straw hat, and the missing map. With each sentence, it was as though Abigail was siphoning cement from inside her mind. Ridding herself of the weight was a relief.

"That's quite a story," Larner said when she was through.

"Story? You think I'm making this up? We have to get in touch with Duncan to confirm he's okay."

"That's assuming somebody found your version of the map and that this somebody even knew what it was. There was a huge fire right outside your house, remember? You may well have dropped the map there. Meaning it's ash. Or ground into the dirt road. Or up in smoke. You got a sharp head on your shoulders. Use it."

What struck her as an insult sank in as sound advice. She was so rattled that making sense of the situation was the mental equivalent of doing an endless math equation. Paul would have rolled up his sleeves and tried to figure it out. She just wanted to quit—quit thinking, quit worrying, and quit living in a place that was causing her this many problems.

"Abby, I gotta ask why you waited to bring this information to my attention. I am the sheriff on this island."

She answered his question with a question. "Did you ever tell Nat about our deal?"

"Me? God, never. I swear. Wouldn't be wise for me or you if I did."

Then how, Abigail wondered once again, did Nat know? The matter would have to be set aside for the time being. The map and the blaze by the lighthouse completely trumped it.

"Was the fire intentional, like the one in the marsh?"

"You considering a job in law enforcement? Because you're grilling me when it should be the other way around."

"I'll stop being evasive if you will."

"Fine. Yes, I believe it was arson. Three's too many to be a coincidence."

"Um, two. Technically."

Abigail admitted to badgering the teens from the red SUV into owning up to accidentally starting the first fire at the lifeguard shack at Pamlico Shore's Beach.

"Excellent police work." From Larner, it was as much a compliment as a reprimand. "Don't do it again or I might have to deputize you. I'm going to need all hands on deck what with tomorrow being the Fourth of July and us having a firebug here who might want to get in on the act."

"Denny, ask Denny!" Abigail exclaimed. "He can handle it. Trust me."

Larner laughed off the suggestion, as if he didn't trust her judgment about Denny or about what she'd told him.

"He's a decent kid. But not cop material."

"You didn't see him at bingo after the second fire. If it weren't for him, the summer people would have been running one another over in the streets."

"You angling to save everyone on Chapel Isle a person at a time? Is this social work to you?"

"Save them?" Abigail bristled. "Is it charity to care about a person's welfare, or is it common kindness?"

"Except you're trying to help people you barely know."

"Funny. That sounds like your job description."

She'd pegged him on that count. Peeved, Larner drove in silence until they reached the lighthouse. A blackened swath of the field across the road from the caretaker's cottage marred the landscape. The sight of it caused Abigail to catch her breath. She couldn't cry in front of Larner. She wouldn't allow herself to.

"Thanks for the lift," she grumbled, exiting the patrol car.

Before she could slam the door, he said, "Abby, I only meant it's harder to lend a hand to somebody who won't take it when you offer."

She understood that Larner was talking about her as well as Denny.

She slammed the door anyway.

After sitting on her front stoop for close to an hour and staring at the charred span of grass that bordered her property, Abigail finally stopped crying.

If by some fluke she'd dropped the map nearby, she had to find it.

"That's a big *if*."

Abigail combed the road, which had turned to mud from all the water the fire fighters needed to quell the blaze. There was no hint of the map or paper of any kind. Using the toe of her shoe, she raked the grass, scouring section by section. Every burned bush filled her with remorse. The scorched grass made her eyes well with sorrow. This wasn't remotely what her house had looked like after it burned. It felt the same nonetheless.

She returned to the cottage, grateful it was still standing, and switched on the radio for company. Dr. Walter's show was on. One of his callers was fuming about redacted government documents.

"Mark my words, they're keeping things from us," the man declared, paranoia bubbling in his tone. "From the Vietnam War to them alien landings at Roswell, they are covering their butts. Public records blacked out and as full o' holes as Swiss cheese. No way to make heads or tails of them. That's the way they want it."

This discussion was right up Duncan Thadlow's alley. Even though Larner had dismissed her apprehension, Abigail was still worried about Duncan and whether he was all right.

"And who are 'they'?" Dr. Walter asked, affecting ignorance to rile the caller.

"Rogue factions of the government. These are the guys who make the 'men in black' seem like schoolgirls. They don't want us to know who they are."

"And yet you do."

"Everybody does," the caller spouted incredulously. "It's a public secret!"

A public secret. It was another oxymoron, like *normal life*. Abigail's widowhood was a public secret, and it had neither the freeing effect of being widely acknowledged nor the comfort of being confidential. That made her even angrier at Sheriff Larner. He knew her circumstances yet had the gall to suggest she wasn't open enough.

"I'm damned if I do and damned if I don't."

Listening to the caller rant about officials backtracking to conceal their transgressions reminded her of how Tim had retraced his steps on the hunt for his missing cell phone. Abigail could do the same. She went up to the study and replaced Mr. Jasper's original map in its hiding spot, reasoning that if the intruder didn't find it the first time, he might not take a second shot—or, at the very least, he might not check the desk again. Abigail was positive she had the map after she met the man in the straw hat at his bungalow; her next stop had been Weller's Market. Which was right where she was headed.

◆ ◆ ◆

The market was bustling and miraculously the shelves were full again, as if yesterday's run on food hadn't occurred. Abigail scanned the store floors and found nothing except the occasional squashed grape. She went to the register to ask if anybody had turned in a map. Janine Wertz was there ringing up a customer.

"Like this?" Janine held out the glossy promotional map the checkout girl had offered Abigail when she mistook her for a tourist.

"No, a smaller one. On a scrap of paper."

"All's we have in the lost-and-found bin is a Frisbee and a kid's retainer. And I'm the one who sweeps up around here, so if it was on the floor, I'd 'a seen it."

Abigail was crestfallen. She'd been crossing her fingers that she'd dropped the map at the market.

"Thanks anyway," she said, and was about to leave when Janine touched her arm.

"I hope you're okay. Heard you weren't, after the . . . well, you get my meaning."

The small gesture seemed to take a lot for Janine. Abigail appreciated it more than she could express. Janine might not like her, but at least she cared, as did others on the island.

Maybe being cared about was more important than being liked.

S Solecism (sol´ə sɪz´ əm, sō´lə-), *n.* 1. a nonstandard or un-grammatical usage, as *unflammable* and *they was.* 2. a breach of good manners or etiquette. 3. any error, impropriety, or inconsistency. [1570–80; < L *soloecismus* < Gk *soloikismós,* equiv. to *sóloik(os)* (*Sólo(i)* a city in Cilicia where a corrupt form of Attic Greek was spoken + *-ikos* -ic) + *-ismos* -ism]

◆ ◆ ◆

As Abigail walked out of Weller's Market, her mind swamped with thoughts of where the map could be, she nearly crashed into Nat Rhone.

Surprised to see him, she sputtered for a minute. "I heard, uh, you . . . I'm feeling better, thanks."

Except talking to Nat wasn't having that effect.

He scrutinized her face. "That bruise come from you collapsing at the fire?"

She'd practically forgotten about the welt, because the rest of her body hurt so badly.

"No, and frankly I'm shocked everyone in town hasn't already heard the mortifying story of my laundromat boxing match. It wasn't ten rounds. Just one. Me versus a bottle of Clorox. I lost."

"News to me."

Was he kidding? Fisticuffs had broken out in the island's lone laundromat. Abigail presumed that would rank as all-points-bulletin material.

"Apparently, a girl-fight isn't the gossip golden nugget I assumed it would be."

"You want people talking about you?"

Not a minute into the conversation and he's antagonizing you. Don't you ever learn?

"That's not what—never mind. How are *you* feeling?" she asked, trying to recover ground in the skirmish that passed for conversation.

"Great, I'm great."

Nat appeared to not want to discuss what had happened at Hank's house. His response reminded Abigail of how she answered people. Equivocally. Was she as transparent as he was? She hoped not.

"What about that shipwreck-hunter guy? How are you two faring?"

And why were you looking me up on the Internet? Were you at my house? Were you the one who broke in?

She couldn't ask the questions shrieking in her head, and Nat was unwilling to answer even the ones she could pose.

"No pay dirt yet. Doesn't matter. I get my money for the hours whether he finds something or not."

"But you said you'd strike it rich if he did discover the wreck."

"Did I?"

Abigail thought he was testing her to determine what she recalled, to discover what she might give away. This was her chance to catch him in a lie.

"Perhaps I misunderstood. The way I took it was that if this treasure hunter found the *Bishop's Mistress,* you'd get a percentage. That's decent incentive. To put in the hours, I mean."

A grin played at the corner of Nat's lips. "Hanging on my every word, were you?"

"What? No."

He'd easily sidestepped her trap, then made his exit, saying, "Keep your nose clean, bruiser."

Nat strode away as she seethed inside. What was it about him that made her feel so off kilter and not herself? Abigail felt a sudden prick behind her knee. It was another mammoth black fly. She swatted it away. That was two stings in rapid succession—one from Nat, one from the bug.

Although he hadn't revealed anything to her, the conversation sparked a hunch. Merle had told her that only an islander would know that the oil cellar wasn't a passage into the lighthouse. Nat wasn't a native. Merle also said Nat did jail time for breaking into cars as a teen. Maybe Nat was the one who'd picked the padlock.

She knew money was tight for him and business was waning, which was why he was considering moving. So having a map to take the treasure hunter—or himself—straight to the sunken *Bishop's Mistress* would solve his problems. Abigail had to retrieve that map.

"Back to the scene of your prizefight," she said to herself.

She peered into the laundromat to see if the coast was clear. Thankfully, there were no shouting matches or slugfests in progress, just an elderly man folding his towels.

"All quiet on the laundry front."

Abigail got on her hands and knees to peek under the washers and dryers. She scooted down the line of machines, chin hovering above the floor. There were dust bunnies and crinkled sheets of fabric softener along with a few nickels. No map.

"Whatcha doing down there, Abby?"

It was Bert.

Of course, she thought, her rump high in the air. *Right in time to catch you in another unflattering situation.*

Abigail got up and dusted herself off. "I'm searching for that map I told you about. I lost it. You didn't see it here, did you?"

"No, ma'am. You worried somebody else did?"

"Unfortunately, I am. What about Duncan Thadlow? Has he been in town today?"

"Haven't run into him."

She rested her weight on the laundromat's sorting table, both physically and emotionally exhausted.

"After last night, shouldn't you be taking it easy?" Bert asked.

"How can I rest when that fire was set on purpose? What if the location was purposeful as well? What if the intruder is upping the ante and trying to frighten me out of the caretaker's cottage? Or maybe it's just a giant coincidence. I'm too exhausted to tell the difference."

"Coincidence isn't a scientifically sound explanation. For anything."

This time Abigail got it, though she wished she hadn't.

"Caleb's on the case," Bert assured her. "He called in some arson specialist from the mainland. But the investigator can't get here until after the holiday, so we've moved the island's fireworks supply. It's under lock and key at the fire station for security. Never had to do that before. Kinda sad."

Abigail couldn't agree more. She'd had to do a whole host of things she never imagined herself doing, and many of them, such as putting her own home on lockdown, were truly disheartening. Logic dictated that the intruder and the arsonist could be one and the same or two totally different people. Either way, they were causing a crisis for Abigail. It was a predicament she couldn't allow to become any worse.

Upon leaving the laundromat, Abigail spotted Nat sitting in his truck on the other side of the street. She even caught him looking at her. It was a peculiar moment, one neither she nor Bert would have deemed a coincidence.

Is he following me?

Abigail put her hand up in an awkward wave. Nat nodded, then pulled away.

"As if today couldn't get any stranger."

She continued retracing her steps by returning to the Kozy Kettle, where she'd gone for a milk shake. Ruth was in the middle of the lunch rush and hardly had a second to talk. Every seat was spoken for, the counter was full, and tourists were in line for to-go orders. The fans chugged in the corners, as if the heat was overwhelming them too.

"You hanging in, hon?"

"I could use a Fig Newton. Or an aspirin. Or a lobotomy."

"Ma'am?" a female diner said, interrupting to get Ruth's attention. Her wet hair was pushed back with her shades. "This sandwich has no tomatoes. I ordered tomatoes."

"I do apologize," Ruth sang sweetly. "I'm gonna fix that for you, darlin'. And I'll whip you up another shake, Abby. Ice cream is aloe vera for the soul."

"Oh, and can I use some of your bug spray?" Abigail asked in a softer tone. "I think the black flies have developed an immunity to mine. A horrifying thought."

Ruth handed her the can of bug repellent from under the counter. "Got it right here. Next to the salt," she said, eyeing the woman who'd complained about the missing tomatoes.

While Abigail waited for her milk shake, she covertly searched the café for her mislaid map. She snooped around and nonchalantly searched under tables as well as the stools at the counter.

"Do you mind?" a man in a polo shirt remarked as she sneaked a look at his feet.

"Uh, nice golf shoes."

Caught, Abigail scuttled away toward the bathrooms, tracing the lines in the linoleum floor with her gaze. Stooped over, all she saw were grains of sand and a stray packet of sweetener.

What are you looking for, Mommy?

It was Justin's voice in her head, real enough that Abigail almost turned to see if he was there. He'd asked her that a few days before the fire, when she was in her bedroom, groping the carpet because she had dropped an earring. He got down on the ground with her, mimicking the way she rubbed the carpet with her fingers.

"Why do you need it?" he'd asked.

"Because it's part of a set, sweetie. I want to keep the set together."

"Okay, Mommy. We'll find it," Justin had told her.

The bell over the door to the café rang and yanked Abigail back into the present. She was no longer part of a set. The anguish of that shadowed her everywhere.

"You lose a contact or are ya looking for spare change?"

It was Duncan, and he was staring at her quizzically as he chewed a candy bar.

Overjoyed that he was alive and well, Abigail threw her arms around him, kissing him squarely on the cheek.

"You really are going to get me in hot water with the missus."

Once she explained what had ensued with the fire and the map, Duncan understood her elation.

"Jeez, Caleb's probably right," he said, crumpling the candy wrapper. "Map might well be gone. Important thing is you have the original and it's safe, right?"

"Absolutely. And thanks again for those suggestions about"—she glanced around to make sure nobody was listening—"the booby traps."

"You thought I was near about off my rocker, didn'tcha?"

"If by that you mean I thought you were crazy, then yes. A little."

"Gotta be a little crazy to live on Chapel Isle." He cast his eye across the crowded café. "In the summer, that is," he said with a wink.

Duncan took off, leaving Abigail to contemplate the definition of insanity. The word was the direct offspring of the Latin *insanitas*. While it meant, quite literally, the condition of being insane, the connotation was grave. *Lunacy* denoted derangement, whereas *mania* hinted at excitability. *Madness* implied violence; *dementia*, mental deterioration. Abigail didn't feel deranged, excited, angry, or in decline. But between the open desk drawer and the shadow in the kitchen, she wasn't a bastion of sanity either.

"Hon, your milk shake's ready," Ruth called.

Abigail went to the counter, but when she tried to pay, Ruth wouldn't let her.

"Then consider it a tip."

Ruth held up the ten-dollar bill, loudly announcing, "A tip for me? Why, thank you, kind lady," as if Abigail was a stranger.

"Very discreet."

"Sometimes you have to spell things out for people," Ruth whispered, then went to take her next order.

Abigail would have appreciated an explanation herself. *Explicate, elucidate, enlighten, expound*—she'd have taken any form of transitive verb that would clarify her confusion over the fires, the trespasser, or the island. The mountains of doubt were adding to her headache.

Through the front window of the Kozy Kettle, Abigail could see tourists going about their day, enjoying the sun, the ocean air, and the idyllic town setting. That was what she'd come to do too. Confused or not, Abigail swore that nobody—living *or* formerly alive— was going to run her off Chapel Isle.

T Teen (tēn), *n.* 1. *Archaic.* suffering; grief. 2. *Obsolete.* injury; harm. [bef. 1000; ME *tene,* OE *tēona;* c. OFris *tiona,* OS *tiono,* ON *tjōn*]

◆ ◆ ◆

The mid-afternoon sun was centered in the sky, shining fiercely. Passing clouds were a temporary pardon. Where was the wind that steered them onward so fast? Because Abigail definitely didn't feel it.

Guzzling her liquid lunch, she hiked to her car, which was parked on the outskirts of the town square—close compared to prior spots. As she dug for her keys in her purse, she caught sight of Nat Rhone a second time. He was idling across the street, acting as if he hadn't been staring at her.

Now Abigail didn't wave. She just wondered what was going on. Once he realized that she'd seen him, he cut into traffic, then made a quick turn.

Suspicion welled in her mind. Could Nat be tracking her movements in order to make sure she wasn't at the lighthouse? Was the man in the straw hat rifling through the caretaker's cottage while Nat acted as lookout?

She was rushing to unlock her station wagon when her cell phone rang. Lottie's number was on the screen. Abigail deliberated whether to answer or not. By the fifth ring, she couldn't hold out any longer. It was as if Lottie could prod her without even speaking.

"Abby, these tenants are driving me to drink," Lottie squealed.

"And I'm not talking about a wine spritzer here and there. I mean peach schnapps. The hard stuff."

Lottie's liquor-riddled invective lasted as long as it took for Abigail to speed back to the lighthouse. She'd been peppering in "Aha's" and "Oh, no's" to feign that she was listening. Yet she wasn't. All she heard was her heart drumming in her ears until she came to a bucking stop outside the lighthouse.

There was no car and no indication that anyone was on the property.

Cell phone pressed to her ear, Abigail ran around the perimeter of the cottage, then pounded up the front steps as Lottie continued to ramble, static causing her voice to cut out intermittently due to the poor reception. Inside, the spoons hanging from the windows swayed in the draft caused by Abigail flinging open the door. The only thing in her house was bottled-up heat.

"I'm busier than a one-legged man in a butt-kicking contest," Lottie huffed. "And I'm about to lose my mind."

Me too, Abigail thought.

"Twenty-seven calls from these ingrate renters. Since this morning. Lord have mercy, Abby, you don't want to see me lose my mind. It is *not* pretty."

Unable to imagine what Lottie would be like if she *wasn't* in her right mind, Abigail assented to help her with the latest rental fiasco. Perhaps working would wash away the pall of anxiety that hung over her after the mad dash home. What was worse, she'd inflicted it on herself. Paranoia had gotten a foothold in her head, and Abigail had to recapture a semblance of control.

"I'll do it, Lottie."

A gasp of relief was audible over the static. "You're an angel, Abby Harker. An angel sent to earth on stick-thin legs instead of wings."

"I beg your pardon? Stick-thin?"

"Take it as a compliment. I'd give my spleen to be your size."

"The spleen is the most expendable organ in the human body."

"Of course. What good would it do me to be skinny and missing a useful one? You have to think these things through, precious."

"You're right, Lottie. I do need to think things through."

Logic and emotions didn't coexist amicably for her. Either Abigail was entrenched in reason, unable to connect with her feelings, or she was skating on impulse and sentiment without employing her wits. As she sat on her front stoop, catching her breath, a puff of wind blew in from the water and across the lawn, shivering the grass as it glanced along her skin. Abigail suddenly grasped that life—like a soft breeze or a strong gust—had to be felt in order to know it was real, not simply analyzed and cataloged.

"Well, put my finger in a socket and call me shocked," Lottie laughed. "I never, not in a million, gazillion years, figured I would hear you say I was right about anything."

"Why? I can admit when I'm wrong," Abigail countered.

"Sure, I believe you. Only because you just did."

The address Lottie gave Abigail was for a quaint cottage with gingerbread molding, spindled railings on the porch, and a stone bird fountain out front. Beach bags with the last name *Peterson* monogrammed on them lay on the porch, some full of beach toys, others towels. A note on the door read: *Screen door broken. Please fix.*

"How am I supposed to do that?" Abigail mumbled, careful not to alert the renters to her arrival.

The screen in the doorframe looked as if it had been kicked through. The mesh didn't need to be repaired. It had to be replaced. That was well outside her limited skill set, so it was back to Merle's hardware store for guidance and supplies.

This time her parking spot was even farther from the square, and Abigail was officially frustrated. She tromped in to the store in a sour mood to discover the place completely empty. No customers and no Merle.

Abigail went around to the rear of the building and found him sitting at the picnic table he kept there for cleaning fish. Merle's head was down, his massive shoulders hunched low. He appeared lost in thought. She cleared her throat to make her presence known.

"Oh, hey there, Abby. You feeling better?"

"I'm hanging in. Are you?"

"Eh." He shrugged.

"Is it the tourists?"

"Naw," he said, waving away the notion.

"Black flies?"

"Nope."

"Global warming?"

"Come to think of it, that does irk me. Truth is, it's the anniversary of my divorce."

Abigail sat down next to him.

"My ex, she loved the Fourth of July," he said wistfully. "She'd decorate the house. Bake red, white, and blue cupcakes using food coloring. Wanted to be first to the beach to get the best spot for watching fireworks. Holidays are always hard after . . . well, you understand. 'Cept this'un gets me the worst."

Abigail more than understood. Thanksgiving and Christmas had been agonizing for her. She'd gone home to see her parents and was miserable the entire trip. She expected to see Paul walking in with the turkey on a platter, ready to carve. Or to have Justin tugging at her pant leg, asking for an extra helping of dessert. Their absence was tangible in every passing second and every molecule of air.

Adding to the anguish were the pictures her parents had up. They were on the mantel, the piano, the walls. Because Abigail had lost everything in the fire, she had no photographs left of her husband or son. Her wedding album, baby pictures, family photos, and even the snapshots in her wallet were obliterated. Before she'd left for Chapel Isle, her mother offered to make copies for her. Abigail declined. She didn't need photographs to remember her family. Their faces were seared into her memory forever.

The fact that her husband's and son's deaths didn't coincide with any major holiday was a blessing. Abigail couldn't fathom watching people celebrating while she was in mourning. Then again, that was what she'd experienced every day since her family's death—a sense that everybody else was going on with their lives, except her.

Not wanting to pester Merle, Abigail tried to excuse herself. "I can come back later."

"No, no," he replied, perking up. "What are you in for? Propane? Welding torch? Jackhammer? I'm clean outta chain saws."

"I'm here for something far more tame. And not flammable. Mesh screening material. Do you carry that?"

"Yup."

"And do you happen to know how to install it?"

"Lucky for you, I do."

Merle detailed how to replace the screen in the frame. However, without the exact measurements—something Abigail hadn't thought to jot down—she was going to have to take a large piece and cut it to fit on site.

"This baby'll do the job." He handed her a pair of heavy-duty shears.

Its blades looked ominously sharp. Abigail held the shears as if wielding a loaded gun. "Do I need a permit?"

"No, you need to not cut your pinkie off. Saw a guy do it once. They stitched it back on, but still. You've had a rough week as it is."

"Note to self: Don't cut off finger. Got it."

He gave her a roll of mesh screening material, which she bundled under her arm, as well as a pair of work gloves.

"These should lower your risk of injury."

Abigail slid on the gloves. They were twice the size of her hand and flopped around her wrist while sagging at the fingertips.

"Or increase it," she said, flapping the gloves to show how loose they were.

"It's high praise," Merle told her.

"What?"

"Lottie working you the way she does. Means she trusts you. It takes a lot for an islander to put their faith in someone who isn't from here."

Abigail was especially touched because she sensed Merle was talking about his own faith in her as well.

"Then a woman in my position," she declared, motioning toward her bruised face and body with the oversized gloves, "shouldn't turn down flattery."

Merle smiled, and Abigail was convinced that, for a change, she'd helped him as much as he had helped her.

Tourists parted to let Abigail pass as she carted the roll of mesh down the street, gloves stuffed in the waistband of her shorts, shears held away from her body as if they might bite her.

This is more like it, she thought. *Make way for the crazy lady with the humongous scissors.*

She was adjusting her purse to prevent it from falling off her shoulder when out of the corner of her eye she spied Nat Rhone in his truck yet again. He was double-parked halfway down the block from the hardware store. Caught for a third time, Nat threw the engine into gear and took off. She'd barely seen him in months, then she'd run into him multiple times in a single day. That was a stretch, even for a place as small as Chapel Isle. Abigail was becoming a conspiracy theorist herself.

"Don't jump to conclusions," she warned under her breath. "He's probably . . ."

Unable to come up with a motive, Abigail let the sentence peter out. Attempting to guess Nat's intentions was an exercise in futility. She'd had enough of those activities as it was.

When Abigail returned to the gingerbread rental, the family occupying the unit was outside, loading their car with beach chairs and their monogrammed bags.

"You must be here about the door," the wife said happily. "I'm June. You are?"

"Abigail."

This woman was the first tenant to ask her name. That took Abigail by surprise. No one seemed to care who she was. It was a welcome sign of common courtesy.

"We're so sorry," June continued. "We'll pay for the damage. Somebody got a little excited about his new raft."

Two boys scampered to her side and she rubbed the smaller one's hair.

"This is Scott and this is Todd," June said, introducing the older then the younger child.

"It was a naccidan," Todd said.

"Accident," their father corrected him gently as he stowed a beach umbrella in the trunk.

"We're about to leave. We'll be out of your way," June told Abigail.

Thank goodness.

But the boys saw the heavy shears and Scott yelled, "Ooh, what's that? Scissors? Can I see?"

So close, yet so far.

As the mother of a boy, Abigail should have anticipated the power of a scary-looking tool on the kids.

"Sizers," Todd shouted. "Sizers!"

"Scissors," June said, enunciating. "And, no, you cannot. If this nice lady doesn't mind, you may watch. No touching, though."

"Um . . ."

Abigail wasn't keen on having an audience for her first screen performance.

"I hope that's okay," June said in her ear. "It's positive for them to see a woman working with tools. Undermines stereotypes. Reinforces equality. That sort of thing."

Impressed by June's progressive attitude, Abigail agreed on the spot. "Of course. You guys can be my assistants."

The boys clapped, and, fortunately for her, their parents went inside.

"We'll be packing the rest of the food if you need us," the father added. "And you," he said, singling out Scott. "*Assisting* means being polite and keeping an eye on your brother."

"Yes, sir," the boy answered, his excitement notching down a note.

"It also means you get to be head assistant," Abigail whispered on the sly.

A grin blossomed on his face. That in and of itself was a gift to her. While Abigail wasn't quite sure where to start with the screen door, she acted as if she'd done it dozens of times before.

"Sizers, sizers!" Todd cheered.

She resisted the urge to correct him as his parents had, and she let him enjoy chanting the new word, even if he was saying it wrong. Muddling onward, Abigail measured and snipped and had the kids pitch in by holding down the corners of the mesh with towels to protect their hands. They loved participating.

"What's this black stuff called?" Scott inquired.

"Mesh. Only it's special. This is super-duper mesh."

It was a tongue twister Todd couldn't pronounce.

"It keeps the bugs out?" Scott asked.

"Precisely."

"I have a bug bite. Wanna see?"

Abigail successfully snapped the last portion of the screen into place and said playfully, "A bug bite? Is it big?"

Scott proudly showed her a red lump on his leg.

"That *is* a big one. Do you want to see my bug bites?"

He and his brother were in boyish awe of the many welts Abigail bore, as if they were trophies.

"Buggy," Todd said, mimicking them.

"Yes, it was a buggy," Abigail agreed as their mother came to the door. "You said it right."

"Perfect," June gushed upon seeing the repair. "We were about to get mosquito netting to sleep under because of all the insects getting in. And thanks for letting them watch. Did you have fun, boys?"

They each nodded emphatically.

"Time for the beach. Say bye-bye to the nice lady and go put your suits on."

They waved as they ran inside the house. Abigail waved back. Then the door shut, the new screen blurring them from view.

"They're good kids," she said, collecting the clippings and remnants of mesh.

"We try. You were great with them. You'll make a terrific mom someday."

Abigail's heart sank. She didn't know what to say. *Thank you* would have been appropriate. However, the phrase refused to form in her mouth.

"Do I pay you or . . . ?"

"The agency will send a bill."

The woman's remark about being a mother reverberated in Abigail's brain as she sat in her car, ordering herself not to cry. She put her face squarely in front of the air-conditioning vents to dry the tears that threatened to fall.

Don't. Don't. Don't.

Abigail had been a capable, loving mother and could be again if she chose to. Yet the concept hadn't surfaced in her mind until that very moment. She could remarry, have more children, reembrace life, start over. Except she wasn't able to. The only thing stopping her was her. That was what had reduced her to tears.

U

Unaneled (un´ə nēld), *adj. Archaic.* not having received extreme unction. [1595–1605 *un* + aneled]

◆   ◆   ◆

Tim was sitting on Abigail's front steps holding a beautiful bouquet of flowers when she returned to the lighthouse. Although touched, she immediately wished her hands weren't covered with black stains from the metal screening material, her clothes weren't rumpled, and her hair wasn't in such an unsightly tangle.

"Great timing," she griped, getting out of the car. Then louder she said, "What a lovely surprise, Tim. Thank you."

He handed her the flowers. "After last night, it was the least I could do. Should I have gotten a vase or do you have one?"

Abigail had to come up with an excuse on the fly. She couldn't let Tim into the house to put the flowers in water. Not with the spoon situation.

"Yes, indeed, I do. It's in the shed."

"You keep your vases in the shed?"

Now what are you going to say, smarty-pants?

"I . . . was going to put them in this big, rustic watering can. It has an amazing patina. Cottage chic."

"Sounds pretty."

"To match the flowers."

Nice save.

"I came by your friend Ruth's house with the sheriff, but she's very protective. She told me to 'scram.' Literally. I felt badly that I hadn't had a chance to check on you sooner. I got hit with another long work call, still can't find the phone, blah, blah, blah."

"Yes, Ruth is a woman who doesn't mince words. Sorry about that. Say, what happened to your hand?"

Abigail had been so fixated on how dirty hers were that she didn't notice the bandage on Tim's right palm.

"Oh, that? Not my finest hour. When I got home from attempting to visit you at Ruth's, I was putting away the asparagus that went with the flounder we didn't get to eat and I dropped the platter, then cut myself cleaning up the broken pieces. Five-second rule applies," he joked. "I'm sure the food is still edible. I could bring the leftovers by tonight if you're up for dinner redux."

Abigail should have been resting, as Bert suggested. Yet she was too wound up. With Nat following her around all day, having Tim in the house might make her more secure.

"I'm a decent cook," Tim added, taking one last stab at winning her over, "but an even better reheater. Gold-metal status."

Given that her house was rigged to the hilt and the oven had been acting funny, Abigail made an excuse about being booked for the rest of the afternoon and said she could be ready after eight if he wanted to come then. "Casual attire is mandatory. Ditto for wine."

"Then it's a date. Again," he said, with a sweet enthusiasm that made it hard for Abigail not to feel the same.

Flowers cradled in the crook of her arm, she watched him pull out of the driveway in his coupe, pondering whether she completely trusted him. Aside from the misunderstanding about who he'd been talking to on the phone—an error instigated by Nat—Tim hadn't done anything to make her doubt him. In fact, he had been the consummate gentleman. As Merle said, it took a lot for an islander to put their faith in a stranger. Perhaps it was a mantra Abigail should have abided by also. If not with Tim, then certainly with Nat.

"Who's been semi-stalking you for who-knows-what reason."

Abigail resented how Nat had twisted the favor she did for him with Sheriff Larner into something he was holding over her, intentionally or not. She tended to believe it was the former. Nat didn't do anything *un*intentionally.

The pact was that she'd keep quiet about Larner breaking into homes and he wouldn't let on that she was responsible for freeing Nat. But she'd been too quiet, not participating fully in the island life she'd bartered to remain a part of. Her good turn toward Nat might not have been as beneficial for her as she'd anticipated. The outcome was the same as most of their arguments: Nat won and she lost.

It was too much to mentally hash through, so Abigail laid the flowers in a mixing bowl full of water and began to dismantle her booby traps. A rerun of one of Dr. Walter's radio programs was on. She collected the soda cans full of beans while callers phoned in with opposing views on the politically charged topic of immigration.

"They need to go back to where they came from," one woman shouted.

"Then so do you," the next caller fired back. "Technically, every single American is an immigrant. Unless you're an Indian."

"Native American," Dr. Walter corrected him. "That's why they're called *native* Americans."

The phone battle raged on as Abigail unwound the twine tying the spoons to the windowpanes. In the eyes of Chapel Isle's residents, she was an immigrant. She felt more akin to a refugee, a displaced person seeking asylum.

It doesn't have to be here, though.

While unstringing the last set of spoons, Abigail vacillated about staying on the island.

"Look at what this place has reduced you to."

She surveyed her surroundings—the improvements, the paint, the furniture, the home's innate character. Compared to Lottie's other rentals, the caretaker's cottage was second-rate, if that. Could Abigail give up the house? Possibly. But did that mean she was giving up *on* the house? That didn't sit well with her.

Abigail rapped the last of the spoons against her palm. "At least I'll be able to eat yogurt again."

"You're kidding, right?" a male caller barked, his voice crackling with contempt. "These people are leeches, draining a system, not paying taxes. This country ain't a free ride. It ain't for me. Shouldn't be for them neither. Hell, most of 'em can't even speak English!"

"That's quite the vituperation," Dr. Walter noted.

"A what?" the man replied.

"Thanks for proving the point about speaking English. Next caller."

"On that note," Abigail sighed, "time to take the knives off the window."

When she opened the basement door, she heard a distinct *pop*. The noise made her jump. Once she'd caught her breath, her mind clicked into logic mode.

This house always makes noises. Except it hasn't made that kind before. Bert did disturb some of the boxes before he installed the knives. One of them could have shifted or fallen. Or there's somebody downstairs. Or it's the ghost.

"Enough," she said aloud to halt the babbling in her brain.

She had two alternatives: call Sheriff Larner or investigate the basement by herself. Although Larner now knew the score, Abigail didn't relish him seeing the knives. Even if she told him they were Bert's idea, Larner would give her that condescending look of his, which she hated. That alone was enough to sway her decision.

Abigail poked her nose into the basement, using the flashlight to brighten the path. She bent over the top stair and shone it between the steps. The light glinted on the white old-fashioned hand-crank washbasin, illuminating nothing more than rusty pipes and dust-covered boxes too small to hide behind. Tentatively taking one stair at a time, she fanned the flashlight's beam back and forth. From upstairs, she could faintly hear Dr. Walter criticizing a caller. Otherwise, there was silence.

The knives were still taped to the small basement window, though two of them were canted to the side. The tape seemed to have loosened, likely from the heat. Abigail ripped the contraption off the window sash, flinching as the row of knives sprang back at her.

"Not well executed. Emphasis on the *executed* part."

Upstairs, she discarded the tape and picked away the adhesive residue from the knives, listening as Dr. Walter berated a caller for flip-flopping on their stance about federal aid for immigrants.

"You're either for something or against it or your head's not screwed on straight. Stop being wishy-washy. There are no *three* ways about it!"

That was Abigail to a tee. She was wavering between staying on Chapel Isle or running for the hills. She couldn't choose. After months of not doing anything, making a decision seemed completely unmanageable.

"Well, Dr. Walter, I'm wishy-washy and wishy-*unwashed*."

Standing at the kitchen sink, Abigail scrubbed her filthy hands and nails until her fingertips were pruney, her sense of touch heightened. She recalled the days she'd spent poring over the dictionary as a child and remembered feeling the words under her fingers as if they were Braille rising off the page. She loved reading. But she loved reading *the dictionary* even more. Lamenting the loss of her husband and son had squeezed out room for everything else, including the activities she actually enjoyed.

The reality was that Abigail didn't really mind working for Lottie. Every errand was a new adventure, each rental unit a different can of worms. Which raised the question: Was she content and completely unaware of it?

Abigail shut off the faucet. She didn't have an answer.

With nothing to do and no desire to get ready for her date early, Abigail plodded around the house, bored. It wasn't as if there was a sexy selection of clothes waiting in her closet or a bevy of lipsticks standing by in her medicine cabinet. The preparation process hadn't done much for her spirits the first few times. Why rush it?

The metal shears and gloves lay on the dining-room table, ready to be returned. It was a sign of pure desperation if Abigail was willing to journey into town and contend for parking rather than stay at the cottage. A big, flashing neon sign.

"Where did I put my keys?"

Merle was waiting on a customer when Abigail arrived. The man wore a white tank top emblazoned with the slogan: *Chapel Isle: If the World Were to End Tomorrow, We Wouldn't Find Out for 3 Days.* His exposed shoulders were peeling from a severe sunburn and he had a cap on backward, as if he was barreling into his vacation head on, despite the consequences.

"You have any folding lawn chairs left?" the guy asked. "Need some to take to the fireworks. Adult- and kid-sized, if you got 'em."

Abigail saw how it affected Merle to hear the request.

"Right this way."

The guy's T-shirt was completely accurate, she realized. The inhabitants of Chapel Isle wouldn't know if the world had ended, nor would they care to. That was why they lived where they lived, how they lived—so they could choose how much of the world got in. For better or worse, it was an outlook Abigail shared.

Once the customer had taken off with the folding chairs slung over his burned shoulders, Abigail did something unexpected.

"Merle, would you like to watch the fireworks with me tomorrow?"

"I don't go anymore," he told her. "But thanks for asking, Abby."

"Weren't you the one who said to get out and face things?"

"You trying to use that there reverse psychology on me?"

"It's not reverse psychology. It's barely even psychology."

Merle folded his arms, adopting a stoic stance.

"Come on," Abigail pleaded. "I can't think of anybody I'd rather see them with."

"Not even what's-his-name with the spiffy car?"

"Not even what's-his-name. Pick you up tomorrow at six?"

"You're on."

"And you're bringing the chairs."

"I knew there'd be a catch."

"I can bring them. Except you'd have to put them on my tab."

"I've got it covered. Though you might wind up in a kid-sized one at the rate they're flying off the shelves. By the looks of it, you'll fit. You eating much?"

"First Lottie says I'm scrawny. Now you're taking potshots at my weight."

"No offense. Everyone is small compared to me. As for Lottie, she could and would call you worse. Loves her gossip as much as her romance novels," Merle said knowingly.

Abigail thought about that for a long moment. "You're saying she did it. She's the one who spread the rumor about me being a widow, wasn't she?"

"Wanted to tell you sooner. But after Franklin made you that offer to paint the cottage, I was worried you'd go and choke the life out of Lottie. That would throw a significant monkey wrench into the renovation plans."

Fuming, Abigail balled her hands into fists. "After everything I've done for her? Were you aware that all her other rental units except mine come with towels and toasters and televisions? It's shameful, appalling, reprehensible, unfair!" She ticked off the words on her fingers, ready to unleash every libelous adjective she had. "When I see her, I'm—"

"Hold on, hold on. This is the reaction I was hoping to avoid. Look at the big picture. Strangling Lottie would feel satisfying in the short term. Waiting until she does what she's promised, *then* strangling her, will be far more rewarding."

As usual, Merle's advice was right on the nose.

"How did she find out? Did you tell her?"

He put his huge hand up in a Boy Scout–style oath. "No, on my honor, I didn't, Abby."

"That leaves only Ruth."

Merle shook his head. "Doesn't track. She likes you too much."

"Then how would Lottie know?"

"Got me."

The twin mysteries of how Nat had learned about her bargain with Sheriff Larner and how Lottie had discovered the truth about her past plagued Abigail. Where was Nancy Drew when she needed her?

"Why would Lottie tell everybody something so private?"

"She probably didn't. Lottie probably confided in one person, who told another, and so on. She didn't mean any harm. There's book smarts and there's people smarts. Just because Lottie's got a high IQ doesn't mean she knows her ass from her elbow when it comes to folks' feelings."

Ironic, Abigail's brain piped in. *The same could be said about me.*

For all the knowledge and reams of definitions that resided in her mind, she didn't understand human nature. Including her own.

"I'm going to give these back to prevent me from using them on Lottie." Abigail put the gloves and metal shears on the counter. "Thanks to you, I've retained all my fingers. I'd say, *I owe you,* but I'm terrified of what that would entail."

"How about this? You go and see if Denny Meloch's at the Wailin' Whale, then we'll call it even. His dad phoned in for a part for the ferry and I set it aside for him. Ask Denny to swing by on his way home."

"I can handle that."

"And don't do anything rash."

"Me?" she replied, heavy on the sarcasm. "Act impetuously? Wherever would you get that idea?"

"Abby," Merle cautioned.

"I promise. Straight to the Wailin' Whale."

The bar was packed for happy hour, air-conditioning on high. The blue light radiating from the jukebox gave the impression that it was cool in the Wailin' Whale. Only it wasn't.

Abigail didn't spot Denny amid the crowd of revelers knocking back beers, so she asked the bartender in the suspenders if he'd seen him.

"Denny was talking to Caleb earlier. They might still be to-gether."

That lifted Abigail's spirits. Perhaps Larner had opted to recruit Denny after all.

"Hey, Guppy," a guy at the other end of the bar shouted. "Grab me another cold one."

The man in the suspenders was happy to oblige.

"Guppy?" Abigail repeated.

"What? You didn't know that was my nickname?"

She hadn't been aware of his nickname *or* his real name.

"No," Abigail said, covering. "It's cute."

He blushed. She did too. For a different reason.

Abigail scrolled through the dialed numbers on her cell and hit SEND, assuming she was calling Larner's private cell phone. Then she heard ringing in the bar. However, Sheriff Larner wasn't there.

"Hey, everybody," Guppy hollered. "That phone I found out front is ringing. Should I answer it? Could be a good-lookin' lady who has a thing for men in suspenders."

While the patrons, locals, and tourists alike were having a laugh, Abigail realized that Ruth had called Larner for her that morning. It was Tim's number Abigail had dialed. And it was Tim's phone that was ringing.

"Guppy, that phone belongs to my friend. I'm the one who's call-ing it." She held her cell phone up to show that the rings were in sync.

"Got it out of the gutter. Tell your pal I didn't make any calls. At least no long-distance ones."

That egged another laugh out of his audience.

"I'll pass that message on if you'll tell Denny to see Merle about a part for his dad."

Guppy agreed, but before Abigail could thank him, Tim's cell phone rang again.

He turned to the regulars. "Should she answer it?"

To escape the running joke and the blare of the jukebox, Abigail ducked out of the bar. The number on Tim's phone had a New York City area code.

What if it's his young daughter trying to reach him? You'd want some-
body to pick up if it was your son.

On a whim, Abigail answered. "Hello?"

"Who is this?" a woman asked brusquely. "Where's Timothy?"

Reeling, Abigail lied. "I'm the, uh, handyman."

"A handy*man*?"

"I'm working on the house that Tim—I mean Mr. Ulman—
rented." Abigail was stumbling over her words and flubbing it. "I
mistook his phone for mine."

"Listen here, missy," the woman growled. "Timothy is my boyfriend, that is my house he's staying in, and it most certainly doesn't
need fixing from some two-bit hussy 'handyman.' He hasn't returned my calls in days, and I am . . . I'm . . ." She searched for the
words. "Pissed off! Tell him I'm—"

Abigail hung up on her.

Boyfriend?

Now Abigail was pissed off too.

V

Ventose (ven′tōs), *adj. Archaic.* given to empty talk; windy; flatulent. [1715–25; < L *ventōsus* windy, equiv. to *vent(us)* <u>WIND</u> [1] + -*ōsus* -<u>OSE</u>]

◆ ◆ ◆

Abigail stood in front of the Wailin' Whale threading through her mind for the most suitable noun to describe her anger—because *anger wasn't angry enough. Rage, irascibility, wrath, fury, choler, ire:* None of them captured her full fury. The sun beating down on her was as harsh as the blistering truth that Tim had lied about being single. She wanted to hurl his phone across the square and watch it shatter into pieces.

Could he also have lied about talking to his daughter on the phone the time Nat overheard him? That would imply that Nat was right. Which was never Abigail's favorite conclusion.

Has Tim been lying to you about other things too? Does he have a *daughter? Is he even divorced? Has his whole persona been a sham?*

The crowded square was like a living, breathing, walking, talking embodiment of her mental state, the swirling throngs of tourists heading off in every different direction the way her thoughts were. Obviously, the house wasn't Tim's. Then again, he had said it was a "friend's place." It was the *girl* prefix he'd left off.

Abigail was so preoccupied with trying to stitch together the facts that she belatedly noticed Nat parked on the opposite side of the street, watching her for the fourth time in as many hours.

"Enough is enough."

Livid over the sudden turn of events with Tim, she strode over to Nat's truck and laid into him. He couldn't even switch the truck into gear to escape, because she was yelling at him through his open window from yards away.

"What? What do you want from me? Why are you following me?"

Every time Nat attempted to respond, she cut him off.

"When I'm kind to you, you're an asshole. When I'm civil to you, you're an asshole. When I'm rude to you, you're an asshole."

She could tell he was biting his tongue.

"You can't have anything to say to me that's worth listening to. But answer one question," Abigail ordered. "How did you find out about what happened with Larner after Hank's death? You said you knew it was me who got you out of jail. How? Might as well fess up. It's not as if we'll see each other again after you move away."

A strong, hot wind was blustering in from the bay, blowing Abigail's hair across her face and mimicking the tumult she felt inside. Nat clearly didn't recall mentioning Sheriff Larner. His stern façade cracked and his cheeks reddened.

"Must've told you when I was drunk. I'm sorry I did."

"It's too late for that."

"If it was, you wouldn't have brought it up."

"See. There. That's it. The arrogance. The conceit. You have to have the last word. Then, fine. It's yours. Enjoy."

Abigail was about to storm away when Nat went on.

"Caleb still thinks I'm responsible for Hank's . . . passing. He believes it to this day. So somebody had to have talked him into setting me free. Who else could it have been but you? Nobody on this island would have vouched for me. You didn't know me well enough to hate me."

"Yes, I did."

Every pent-up emotion she'd held in came tumbling from her mouth in a hateful outburst. She insulted Nat, his reputation, his abilities, his cocky attitude. With each spiteful sentence, Abigail heard herself shouting not at him but at the fire, at fate, at herself.

The emotions that had sat in her soul for months had been slowly simmering, waiting for her to take the lid off and let herself boil over. However, fighting didn't come naturally to Abigail. She'd had only two quarrels with Paul during their entire relationship. They were over the same thing. Books.

The first spat had occurred when Paul asked her to donate any duplicates she owned before they moved in together during grad school. Abigail refused. They argued. Then the extras wound up in her parents' attic. The second squabble had happened when Paul asked her to give the recently accumulated extras to charity before they moved into their house. She refused again. They fought harder.

"Why do you have to have two copies?" he'd asked, exasperated.

"The house is big enough. Why do I have to give them away?"

"You're ducking the issue."

"What if I need them someday?" she'd shouted, protective of her brood. "What if I lose one and can't get another?"

"But there are bookstores, resellers, places online."

Abigail had broken down crying and Paul caved, allowing her to keep the books. They were the exact same set that now resided in the study at the caretaker's cottage. She'd won the dispute and lost everything else.

"What kind of friend are you?" Abigail demanded.

Nat's nostrils flared at the insinuation.

"The opposite of a friend would be an enemy," she went on. "But you're worse than that. All you care about is yourself."

For a change, the look on his face was one Abigail could recognize—an expression of abject hurt. Nat gunned the truck's engine and drove away, leaving Abigail in the dust, literally and metaphorically. The wind had died down and the impact of what she'd done settled on her with grim gravity.

Her world had been as capricious and unpredictable as a breeze. She hadn't been able to put her faith in life doing right by her after the fire, nor could she trust her own judgment about men, the ghost, or her own well-being. Bitter that emotion had gotten the best of her, Abigail returned to her car. This time, the long trek to where she'd parked seemed to take seconds. The tourists were blurs of color. The humidity wasn't even there. She wanted to keep walking to put everything behind her.

This is an island. There's only so far you can walk.

Abigail had never missed the mainland so much.

The heat trapped inside her station wagon was concentrated to the point that it was scalding. Abigail had to let it air out for a minute or else she wouldn't be able to sit on the seat or touch the steering wheel. She was standing beside her open driver's-side door when Sheriff Larner pulled up in his cruiser.

"Afternoon, Abby."

She was afraid she would start to bawl if she opened her mouth to speak.

Mistaking her lack of response for annoyance, Larner attempted to smooth things over.

"Keeping busy, I see. Been busy myself."

He chatted on and on at her about the provisions for the fireworks display, the logistics, the hassles, the headaches, totally unable to read how distraught she was.

"Tough to maintain tight security on a two-man team. Our sub's still got the flu and the second recruit's on his honeymoon in Florida."

Abigail was so irate she was shaking. She wasn't sure who she was madder at: Tim or herself. Clueless, Larner finally asked if she had seen any more signs of the intruder.

"Be honest," he urged.

"I'd take a pack of barbarian picklocks over that liar Tim Ulman any day of the week."

About to burst, she informed Larner of the call she'd intercepted from Tim's "girlfriend."

"I'm such a moron," she said in closing.

"You're not the dumb one. I am." Larner removed his sunglasses and looked her directly in the eyes. "Guess I should be eating my hat. I talked the guy up to folks when they saw you two were getting close. Merle didn't care for him. Neither did Bert. Or George. Or Nat. I told them to leave you be," he admitted sheepishly. "Despite their misgivings."

"Ruth seemed to think Tim was more than all right."

"Yeah, she liked the *looks* of him, but she didn't want you picking out wedding china."

"You're saying nobody liked Tim from the start?"

"Pretty much. A lot of people didn't really like you when you first got here, so I figured that might change."

"Thanks."

"All's I mean is that nobody here takes to strangers easy. You don't live on an island 'cause you're a 'people person.' At the end of the day, there's summer folks and then there's us. You're one of us now. Tim ain't."

Hearing Larner say that, the hole that had gaped in Abigail's heart for almost a year seemed to close a little at the edges.

"If you'd o' liked him, Abby, the rest, they would have come around eventually."

The more the pieces fell together, the worse Abigail ached over her argument with Nat. Maybe he'd been following her to protect her. Maybe he really was the friend she'd accused him of not being.

"I feel bad for what I did," Larner said. "Sticking my nose where it didn't belong. I thought I was doing you a solid. You held up your promise about the burglaries last fall. I wanted to pay you back for being true to your word."

"Because of this, you owe me double."

"I had a feeling you'd say that."

In light of how keeping secrets had caused such confusion, Abigail decided to put this secret to virtuous use.

"I can think of a way you could pay me back."

"I'm not going to like this, am I?"

"Does it matter?"

"Go on."

"You're hiring Denny as your new police sub. You obviously have considerable influence in this town. People respect you, they do what you say, even when they may not agree," she added, milking her advantage. "If you deputize Denny, the locals are going to view him in a new and brighter light. You'll be giving him your seal of approval. And you're going to stand by it."

Larner took her point and grudgingly agreed. "Denny'll start tomorrow."

Abigail gave him a resolute look.

"Tonight," he corrected himself. "He starts tonight."

"You want to shake on the deal the way we did last time?" she asked, offering her hand.

"Don't need to. Your word's good with me."

That carried more weight than a thank-you or an apology ever could. It was what she'd been dying to hear.

"You're wrong, ya know," Larner added. "You said you were an idiot."

"When it comes to men, apparently I am."

"If you were, then you wouldn't confront him."

Larner had, at last, read her correctly. She wasn't planning on ever seeing Tim again or taking his calls. Her instinct was to cut him off completely. In her mind, he didn't deserve another iota of her energy.

"Do it," Larner pushed. "You'll feel a helluva lot better."

Abigail had just finished screaming at Nat. She wasn't certain she had it in her to go another round.

"As the local law-enforcement authority on this island, you're advocating that I *start* a fight?"

Sheriff Larner slid on his shades. "Just don't say I was the one who suggested it. Wouldn't want to write myself up in the report."

Back at the caretaker's cottage, Abigail readied herself for her date. It was the perfect time and place to meet Tim head-on. She sat in her favorite wingback chair and carefully knitted together her case,

purling words and phrases together into a tight, irrefutable con-
demnation.

A stunning view of the ocean was framed in her front windows.
The seemingly endless panorama of sea and sky appeared to prove
the concept of eternity. However, Abigail knew it wasn't true. The
water ended on the other side of the Atlantic; the heavens turned
into space. Few things went on forever, limitless or unchanging.
Abigail felt there had to be an end for her too.

She went upstairs and began to pack her things.

Clothes went back into her lone suitcase. It was harder to zip
with all of the new additions to her wardrobe. She considered leaving them in the drawers.

"It's not as if they fit."

Except she didn't want to leave a piece of herself behind.

Next, she took her makeshift hamper and upended its contents
on the bed. The box would hold some of the new books she'd ordered. She'd have to get more cartons from the basement to pack
them all. For now, the hamper box would have to do.

As she emptied the bookshelf in the study, Abigail thought this
was just what she needed in order to be able to return to Boston.
Being lied to hardened her resolve. She couldn't rant at destiny for
taking Paul and Justin. This was her chance to pin the blame on the
right person—Tim—and have *her* say on *her* turf, the caretaker's
cottage.

"Because soon it won't be yours anymore."

Wight (wīt), *n.* 1. a human being. 2. a) *Obsolete.* a supernatural being, as a witch or sprite. b) any living being; a creature. *adj. British Dialect.* 1. strong and brave, especially in war. 2. active; nimble. [bef. 900; ME, OE *wiht;* c. G *Wicht,* ON *vēttr,* Goth *waiht;* 1175–1225; ME < Scand; cf. ON *vīgt,* neut. of *vīgr* able to fight]

❖   ❖   ❖

The frenetic attempts at primping for dates with Tim were a thing of the past. This go-around, Abigail was a pillar of tranquillity.

She ran the bathwater and watched the tub fill. Before moving to the caretaker's cottage, Abigail hadn't been a "bath" person. Decades had gone by without her setting foot in a tub. Showering was simply faster. But with no shower in the cottage, it wasn't an option.

The first time Abigail had tried to wash her hair in the bathtub, she almost blinded herself with shampoo. She'd lathered up her hair, only to realize too late that she would have to dunk her whole head to rinse it, then come up for air into a face full of suds. Conditioning was almost as dangerous. Abigail had gotten a crick in her neck as she craned to submerge the back of her head to sluice away the product. The sudden pain sent her jerking upward, nearly conking her skull on the rim of the cast-iron tub. That inaugural experience had been a comedy of errors that was light on the comedy.

Over the months that followed, Abigail relearned how to bathe and came to appreciate the ritual. As the tub steadily filled, water pouring from the faucet in a lulling rush, she contemplated what it was going to be like to shower again. Leaving Chapel Isle meant returning to a thoroughly modern world. She pictured herself at her parents' house after the long ride—they'd be happy to see her, relieved to have her home, telling her to relax, get settled in and freshen up after her trip. Their guest bathroom had a separate shower stall and a sunken tub. Abigail could imagine herself standing in the bathroom, having to pick.

She would take a shower. She had no doubt about it. There was heartbreak in that knowledge, as if she would be washing away everything about Chapel Isle with a single choice.

Abigail shut off the water, the tap squeaking to a stop. She was about to go and get a book to read but opted not to. This was a closing ceremony of sorts. She ought to honor it.

The longer she soaked in the tepid bathwater, the more of herself she saw in everything around her. Each inch of the tiny bathroom was as familiar to her as the back of her hand. She'd painted the walls, standing on the toilet to reach the ceiling, lying on her belly to get behind the tub, kneeling under the sink to properly coat the length of wall below the pedestal basin. She'd scoured the porcelain and polished the fixtures. Abigail had even regrouted the floor. Or, more specifically, Nat Rhone had.

Her endeavor had gone awry when she'd left the grout on too long and it had dried, hardening into prickly peaks. Nat had fixed it for her when he stopped by to check her wiring, and the job he'd done looked terrific to that day. The new white grout made the dingy tiles gleam.

Nat was impossible to figure out. He could be an inveterate pain in the ass. Then he'd go and do something kind that totally belied his bad-boy rep. Which was the real Nat Rhone? The nice guy or the selfish jerk?

"Now you'll be leaving before he does. He'll probably think you did it to one-up him."

She gently soaped her sore arms and legs, then splashed water on her face. The washcloth was too rough on her bruised cheek. Clean, she sat back and recalled hearing *bumps* and *bangs* when she initially used the bathtub and being terrified because she'd thought it was the ghost of Mr. Jasper.

"You really had me going there," Abigail admitted, as though the ghost were an old friend who'd played a prank on her.

What would she tell people about the island when she retuned home to Boston? That she'd been on a mental sabbatical, living in a purportedly haunted house and occasionally conversing with a ghost? It was a contradiction in terms. Then again, so was she.

Abigail had wanted to escape her past, yet she'd confined herself to it in her mind. She wanted to be a part of Chapel Isle but had isolated herself from virtually everybody in town. She wanted to be embraced by the locals yet she rejected their attention. She hadn't wanted to open her heart, but she had—if only a sliver. Then Tim had lied to her. Abigail couldn't bear to leave the island, except she could no longer stay.

She pulled the plug out of the bathtub and let the water drain.

A towel wrapped around her head, Abigail sorted through the clothes she'd half packed. A plain shirt and shorts seemed fitting for the occasion, the lack of flash or femininity fine by her. She wasn't going to waste a dab of tinted moisturizer on the likes of Tim Ulman.

His flowers, which Abigail had transferred to an empty milk carton, acted as the centerpiece at the dining-room table, which she'd set in an intimate grouping for two. Paper towels stood in for napkins. There were no place mats to lay the pitted dishes and dull utensils on. None of the tableware matched like Tim's—or, rather, his girlfriend's—yet it had character. The fact that the spoons had been dangling from the windows hours earlier made them all the more apropos.

The stark modesty of the cottage had never been as clear to Abigail as at that moment. Certainly the antiques added richness, the paint personality, the drapes warmth. But there was no art on the walls, no sounds of laughter, no family mementos. The home struck Abigail as emphatically empty.

Am I empty too? Is this house a reflection of me?

The comparison made her want to flee, to pack the car that very minute. It also made her mad. Tim had said he wished he could dump his hectic workaday world for the simple existence she led. Abigail was offended that her life could be mistaken as enviably easy. It took a litany of Latin verbs to soothe her.

When that didn't work, Abigail defaulted to Lottie's romance novel. There were only a few chapters left. The Bedouin and his foe, the merciless Arabian king, were about to duel in the middle of a dusty town square, their curved swords drawn. Unbeknownst to either of them, the chambermaid who'd stolen both their hearts was ensconced in the crowd of onlookers, still clothed in the guise of a eunuch. The men parried and sparred. The king was besting his rival. With a swift slash, he wounded the Bedouin, an ostensibly deadly blow. The winsome chambermaid threw off her masculine garb, exposing who she was, and hurried to her beloved's side. Tears streaming, she gave an earnest speech to the smug king, ending with the insult: "You make a coward seem like an honorable man."

As if healed by her ardor, the Bedouin sprang up. He'd been faking his injuries. In a flurry of swordplay, he slayed the king, and the two paramours could be together at last. Another happy ending. There weren't any other kind in romance novels.

"You fictional characters have all the luck."

Abigail closed the book, ready for a duel of her own. Then, from upstairs, she heard a *thud*.

You did just take a bath. Is the tub getting backed up now too?

Only it sounded as if the noise had radiated down from the lighthouse.

She made her way up the wrought-iron stairs to the turret, strangely unafraid. What better time for the spirit of Wesley Jasper to make an appearance? This would be his last chance.

"Lottie will have no problem getting a new tenant," Abigail proclaimed. "Especially now that the place looks great. I'll be out of your hair, Mr. Jasper. Give me an *arrivederci* or forever hold your peace."

Abigail lingered on the winding steps, gazing upward into the lighthouse spire, waiting.

"Nothing? Okay. I took a shot."

The view of the sunset was truly magnificent from the top of the lighthouse. The sky was banded with acid tones of orange, yellow, and pink, a testament to the intensity of the summer heat. Wondering what it would be like to watch the fireworks from here reminded Abigail of her date with Merle. It had slipped her mind.

Although she would have preferred to take the next morning's ferry over to the mainland and mail Lottie a check for the remainder of the rent on her one-year lease, Abigail couldn't. She had to go to the fireworks with Merle. The issue was whether or not to tell him she was moving away.

"You shouldn't just take off without saying goodbye."

She would miss Merle, Ruth, Bert, Denny, everybody she'd met. Sheriff Larner too. Even Nat Rhone. Abigail wasn't certain she could stand missing anybody else. After months of pining for her husband and son, adding more names to the list felt insurmountable. While it would be callous to up and leave her friends without a word, it would be far less stressful. But as somebody who'd been deprived of a goodbye from her family, she couldn't bring herself to walk away from the island like that.

From the turret, Abigail could see Tim's car approaching.

"Game on."

She climbed down the spiral staircase, answering the door much as he had when she'd gone to his house—out of breath.

"Dinner is served." Tim was smiling and holding up a picnic basket full of leftovers.

He tried to give Abigail a hug. She dodged it by taking the basket.

Not a chance, buster.

"What a lovely picnic basket. Is it yours?"

"Uh, no. Something I found at my friend's house."

"This friend of yours has impeccable taste."

Only not in men.

"I brought wine too. You said it was obligatory, and I follow orders."

We'll see about that when I order you out of my house.

"Great. Why don't you pour us each a glass? I could use one."

Abigail brought the food into the kitchen and set it on the counter. She didn't plan on actually eating with Tim. He'd be out the door in a matter of minutes.

"You could reheat it or just nuke it." Tim was standing in the doorway to the kitchen, gesturing at her microwave. He'd surprised her. "I'm a guy. That's my answer to any cooking dilemma," he kidded.

Abigail thought fast. "Wish I could, but the microwave is broken. I'll preheat the oven."

She nervously set the dial to three hundred, then switched it off when Tim wasn't looking.

"No biggie. Gives us more time to talk."

"Yes, it does," she sang.

They sat at the dining-room table, and Tim noted the flowers in the milk carton. He looked a little hurt. "What happened to the watering can?"

"There was a hole in the bottom," she lied. "And I didn't have anything else the flowers would fit in."

Other than the trash can.

"Well, I like your version of a vase." Tim raised his glass. "I made the last toast. Your turn."

She had a few choice ideas. Instead, she said, "Before that, I nearly forgot. I found your phone." Abigail removed it from her pocket and slid it across the table to him.

"You did? That's terrific. Where—"

"I also happened to talk to the woman whose house you're living in. She said you were her boyfriend."

"You answered my phone?" A flash of betrayal streaked across Tim's face.

"As manners go, a minor indiscretion. Compared to lying and cheating."

"Abigail, hold on," he said firmly. "That woman is not my girlfriend. She was. We dated. Briefly. Now we're friends. All right, I *as-*

sumed we were friends and that everything was in the past. Maybe she's holding on to the relationship, wants more, but I don't."

Was Tim well rehearsed or was he legit? At the very least, he was insensitive, shacking up at the home of a woman who clearly felt close to him, letting her believe they were together. Unless the woman was the one who had misconstrued their relationship.

"I dated her right after my divorce proceedings began. Tacky, I know. I hated that my marriage had fallen apart. It was humiliating. Then this woman comes along. She's divorced too, and her ex-husband is a multimillionaire whose money she's dying to spend on a guy like me to spite him. I hadn't had a vacation in three years. When she told me I could come down here and stay at her place, I jumped at the chance. Even after I broke it off, she insisted I take the house for a week. 'No hard feelings,' she said."

Tim put his hands in his lap, repentant.

"I shouldn't have stayed at her house and I shouldn't have told you I was 'renting' it. Not altar-boy behavior, granted. I was so desperate to get away from the drama and to have a minute of peace to think—think about what to do next, who I wanted to be—that I made a crummy decision. After what you've been through, Abigail, you should get that."

"Is there anything else you've lied about?" she asked dubiously.

"No, I swear. Here." He proffered his cell phone. "This is my ex-wife's number. You can call and ask to speak to my daughter yourself if you don't believe that she's the one I was talking to the other day. Please, take it."

Tim gripped the phone hard, thrusting it forward for her to accept, and grimaced as it pressed against the bandage on his palm.

"Hurts, huh?" she said wryly.

"This is what I get for using the hot tub on the roof deck. The edge of the lid split my hand wide open."

Wait. Didn't he say he'd cut himself on a broken dish?

In an instant, everything came together for Abigail, like a mousetrap snapping shut.

She replayed her arrival at his house in her mind—the dirt on his wheel wells that was identical to hers, the panting as he got to the door. Had he set the fire in the field across from the lighthouse and sped home to greet her on time? Tim could have been the intruder as well as the arsonist, his wound inflicted by the knives Bert had rigged in the basement.

Or it could simply be your imagination in overdrive.

Abigail wasn't going to chance it. Acting as cool as she could, she took the phone from him and faked a grin, pretending to believe his explanation.

"I'm not going to call her. But I *am* going to consider it. Let me check on the oven."

She went into the kitchen, where she slipped his cell into one pocket and pulled hers from the other. Abigail was dialing Sheriff Larner when the room suddenly went dark.

Xeric (zĕr´ik), *adj.* of, pertaining to, or adapted to a dry environment. [1926; < Gk *xēr(ós)* dry + *-ic*[1]]

◆　◆　◆

When Abigail opened her eyes, everything was still dark. She wasn't at a hospital and she definitely was not at Ruth's house. She couldn't tell where she was. However, she had absolutely no doubt that she'd been hit on the head, because her forehead was throbbing.

All she could recall was a hazy dream of being in the desert and watching two men fight with swords, their faces unclear. She'd been dressed in men's clothes, her hair under a tight-fitting turban, and she looked on as the men clashed.

The Bedouin in the book. You were dreaming about Lottie's romance novel.

Then why could she hear the clanking of metal echoing around her?

Her head pounded and sweat was rolling down her temples. As she tried to raise her hand to wipe it, she couldn't move. She'd been tied up.

Tim, she thought. *As if being a cheater and a liar wasn't nasty enough.*

She'd never felt this stupid in her entire life. Her identity was built on being intelligent and in control. Her misjudgment of Tim—and how that reflected on her—galled Abigail to the point that, instead of being afraid, she was outraged.

How smart do you feel now?

Wherever she was, there was almost no light. It took a few seconds for her vision to adjust. Soon she saw something familiar.

Stairs.

She was in her own basement, and her arms were bound behind her with the same twine she and Bert had used to construct the booby traps.

Irony, table for one.

The twine was secured to a plumbing pipe attached to the foundation wall that fed down from under the kitchen. Since the pipe was smooth, there was no way for Abigail to loosen the bindings with friction. Unwilling to give up, she rubbed until her wrists were chafed. The twine remained tight.

Water gurgled inside the pipe from which the clanging had emanated. They were the very same pipes that had been draining slowly from the bathroom and causing her such problems with the tub and toilet. If water was flowing through them, that meant the tap had recently been run.

For what? Abigail wondered. She hadn't turned on the faucet since long before Tim arrived.

He's still here.

Abigail wriggled and struggled. At first, the pipe seemed to want to shift away from the wall, yet it held fast. A sliver of moonlight was shining in through the tiny basement window. She estimated that she'd been unconscious for a while.

Footsteps resounded from upstairs. Tim was moving around the first and second floors. Searching, perhaps.

He's the intruder. He started the fires. He didn't find the map the first time. He won't find it now.

She could feel that his cell phone was no longer in her pocket. Abigail racked her brain, desperate to keep her wits—and logic—about her. Presuming Tim was after the map to the *Bishop's Mistress,* all she had to do was tell him what Duncan had said about the location of the wreckage drifting south of the Ship's Graveyard. Then Tim should let her go.

Or so she hoped.

I am going to kill Caleb Larner for talking me into going out with this guy.

More footsteps. Tim was coming down the stairs. She saw the shadowy outline of his legs before she slammed her eyelids shut to act as if she was knocked out cold.

A burst of water hit her face, jarring even though she was already conscious. Tim had done it to rouse her.

"Abigail, Abigail," he chided. "Things were going so well. We were really connecting. If you hadn't been the jealous type, you wouldn't have wound up like this."

"Jealous?" Abigail was incensed, tussling against her restraints.

"Glad I tied you up. You're a feisty one."

"And you're an egomaniacal imbecile."

"Quite the potty mouth from a woman with such an illustrious background in lexicography."

Nat hadn't been the only person researching her on the Internet. Tim clearly had too. All he needed was her name, which Larner had provided when they were first introduced. After that, Tim could learn almost everything about her—her personal history, her career, the fire.

"Let me get this straight. When you're not trading stocks, you're a half-assed treasure hunter?"

"There's nothing half-assed about what I do."

Abigail had a flash of Tim's laptop open on his kitchen table. The trading page on display now struck her as a ruse.

"You're not even a trader, are you?"

"This is why it never would have worked out between us. I don't go for smart women."

Tim's passion for statistics and his claim of being a math geek had been fabricated from Paul's professional background. Newspaper articles about the house fire had listed his occupation as well as Abigail's. Tim had created a persona she would be attracted to, one she missed. That disgusted her. Except she wanted to keep him talking until she could figure out how to free herself.

"Well, I can see why you lied about being from New Jersey."

Tim glared at her. "I *am* from New Jersey."

"If you were going to fib about anything . . ."

He got out the twine, preparing to secure her ankles. "This really is your fault."

"My fault?"

"If you'd only told me you were leaving, we wouldn't be in this predicament."

He was upstairs. He saw the packed suitcases. Doesn't matter as long as he's still talking.

"I brought being tied up in my own basement on *myself*? That's rich."

"Just being honest."

"Better late than never."

Tim spun the twine around her ankles and pulled tight to knot it. Abigail winced at the pain. Backlit by the light from upstairs, his handsome features morphed into harshly angled cheeks and a menacing brow. He'd gone from gorgeous to hideous. She no longer recognized him.

Buy more time, her mind was bellowing.

"You'll never find it."

"What's that?"

Abigail almost mentioned the map. She stopped herself and said, "The *Bishop's Mistress*."

"Wasn't planning to bother. Not when I could have somebody else do it for me."

The man in the straw hat.

"You were going to steal whatever the real treasure hunter found."

"It's much less of a hassle that way. Only some people aren't as skilled at what they do as I am."

Nat had told Abigail that he and the wreck diver—the man in the straw hat—weren't having much success in the Ship's Graveyard.

"If you want something done right, gotta do it yourself, as they say."

Confused as to whether Nat was in on tipping Tim off, Abigail blurted, "But how would you know what the treasure hunter did or didn't find?"

Once the question had left her lips, the answer appeared to her.

Tim had broken into the man's bungalow as he had her home. That was why the man was stunned to see her in his kitchen. He was aware someone had been snooping around.

"I cut a slit in his gas line during my last visit," Tim informed her. "Wouldn't seem as suspicious if the house caught fire. And the mysterious arsonist would be blamed but never found."

In a horrible torrent, Abigail realized that Tim wasn't merely responsible for the fires. Each was a buildup to a far more catastrophic event intended to cover his tracks. The final pieces of the puzzle slid together ominously. The first fire that the teens had started by accident must have given him the idea—that and Abigail admitting how she'd lost her family. She had been the target from the start. It was a crushing epiphany, a day too late.

"If the other treasure hunter can't find the *Bishop's Mistress,* you won't either."

"Fortunately for me, I have a map. It was lying right on my kitchen floor, like a gift. Handy, huh?"

He produced her version of Wesley Jasper's map from his pocket, the one Duncan had added the arrow and *X* to. Abigail's heart faltered. It must have fallen out when she'd removed her cell phone from her pants at dinner.

That's what you get for not doing your laundry.

In Nancy Drew books, the bad guy confessed only when he was certain he'd get away with what he'd done. Tim didn't need her anymore. She had become a liability.

Think, think, think. You have to get out of here.

"Nobody will take you to the Ship's Graveyard," Abigail insisted. "Not a single captain. The islanders don't want the treasure found. And you won't be able to sail there yourself."

"I appreciate your concern. I'm not the one you should be worried about."

A sickening thought caused Abigail to tremble to her very core: he could be planning to set fire to the lighthouse with her in it. The idea of dying in a fire draped her in a shawl of anguish. Had she been spared once just to suffer the same fate as Paul and Justin? For a split second, she had a flicker of solace. She would be reunited with them.

Tim didn't look at her as he secured the last knot. Then he stood and turned to climb the stairs.

"You make a coward seem like an honorable man," Abigail shouted. Though she couldn't believe she was plagiarizing the last words she might ever utter, they were fitting.

Tim shut the basement door.

Her thoughts raced as she listened to him upstairs in the kitchen. She pictured him tampering with the oven. She could practically hear the pilot light clicking.

Suddenly her mind screeched to a stop. There was water flowing in the pipes, the noise growing louder and louder, as if to make her notice. Abigail tried pulling at them again. Could there really be water lingering in there after her bath, or was it a sign from Mr. Jasper?

Abigail braced her feet against the floor and squirmed to gain leverage so she could use her body weight to pull. Yanking with all her might, she managed to dislodge the rusty pipe from the wall. She shook it and rattled it and jerked it, unrelenting. Weakened by age, the metal cracked, sending water gushing everywhere and soaking her as she scrambled to escape.

As she untied the twine bindings, the noise of tires snarling against gravel came from outside. Tim was driving away, leaving quickly. Aware that she had precious minutes, at most, Abigail bolted upstairs.

Rather than heading for the front door, she went straight to the kitchen. Bucking reason, logic, wisdom, as well as her own safety, she was hell-bent on turning off the oven.

Except there was no acrid smell of gas permeating the air, no *tick-tick-tick* of the pilot light trying to ignite like a bomb counting down. Abigail checked the stove's knobs, prepared for the worst, only to remember that the oven was broken. That was why the food hadn't heated up properly on her first date with Tim.

She realized that Tim hadn't been trying to kill her. He'd tied her up to buy himself time to get to the *Bishop's Mistress*. Again, she'd jumped to the incorrect conclusion.

"You have *got* to stop reading those romance novels. They're turning your brain to mush."

Relieved beyond reckoning, Abigail slumped to the floor, grateful to be alive, grateful that the house hadn't exploded, and unsure if she should be grateful to a ghost for saving her.

Y Yerk (yûrk), *Chiefly British Dialect.* — *v.t.* 1. to strike or whip. 2. to stir up; arouse; excite. 3. to jerk. 4. to move (a part of one's body) with a jerk. 5. to pull (stitches) tight or bind tightly. 6. to kick. 7. to rise suddenly. 8. to enter into something eagerly.—*n:* 9. to kick or jerk. 10. a thud or blow, as from a stick. [1400–50; late ME < ?]

◆   ◆   ◆

Dazed yet safe, Abigail dialed Sheriff Larner's personal number from her landline. Her cell phone was gone, as was the money in her purse and her credit cards.

That was why he was so educated about the antiques. Thieves are only interested in anything that will fetch a high price. But these are too big to fit in his convertible.

She ran her hand across the mahogany console the phone sat on, happy it and the rest of the furniture were still there. As the line rang and rang, Abigail chewed over how she could describe what had happened without sounding ludicrous.

"Pick up, pick up."

Larner didn't.

Initially, she thought he wasn't answering because he recognized her number. Soon she grew anxious that he was busy attending to something else, something critical. What if Tim had set another fire?

Short-staffed as the force was, the fastest way for Abigail to get help was to hop in her car. Tim had a twenty-minute lead, and she had a bad feeling about what he was planning next.

◆   ◆   ◆

Abigail burst into the sheriff's station, where Denny was manning the desk, dressed in a loaner uniform that was a size too large for him. The shirt sagged around his torso. The collar gaped at his neck. He wore it proudly nonetheless.

Panting, she said, "I'm double-parked outside, but don't write me a ticket, because——"

Thrilled to share his big news, Denny ran over and grabbed her in a bear hug, cutting her off. He began talking a mile a minute and wouldn't let her get a word in edgewise.

"You'll never believe it, Abby. Caleb asked me to join the force. Me! A deputy! 'Course, it's temporary, 'til I can get the necessary certifications. The training. The uniform. This is Caleb's old one. It's huge, I know. He said I couldn't wear civilian clothes to work here. Sounds important, don't it? Civilian clothes. I couldn't believe he asked me. This is a dream come true. It was totally out of the blue, Abby!" he said, giddy. "Totally!"

Despite everything she'd endured that evening, Abigail had to give Denny his due. He was so thankful to have the job, so blissfully thankful. She was thankful for other reasons, but Denny was able to express it more exuberantly than she could. He was speaking for each of them.

Seeing as the natives had keeping secrets down to a science, Abigail opted to take a page from their playbook and stay mum about her role in Denny's new job.

All she said was, "Maybe Caleb sees something in you that other people haven't."

"Maybe they will too."

Abigail's thought exactly. The gawky kid she had met on her ferry ride over to the island had taken on the mantle of a man. Although the uniform didn't fit him, it suited him well.

"So what's new with you, Abby?" he finally asked.

She didn't have time to fill in the details, but after she gave him the broad strokes of what had ensued over the past few days, Denny couldn't believe his ears.

"They haven't given me a gun yet. If they had——"

"We don't need a gun, Denny. We need to figure out when the last ferry off the island leaves and find out if any boats have been reported missing or stolen."

"Dockmaster's gone home for the night, and my dad's about to run the last trip to the mainland."

"Call your father and find Larner."

Denny tried the sheriff on his two-way radio. New to the equipment, he bungled the transmission and feedback blared in his ear. Eventually the frequency cleared.

"Sheriff? Sir? It's Denny. We've got a, um, situation here at HQ."

"What *kind* of situation, Denny?" Larner answered, jaded.

Abigail snatched the walkie-talkie from Denny and said, "The bad kind."

She and Denny sprinted down to the piers. Clammy gusts of wind were hurtling in off the bay, flapping Abigail and Denny's clothes and slapping her hair across her cheeks. Boats sloshed in the water, testing their moorings. The dockmaster's shack was locked up for the night.

"Can we go to his house and get him to come check the logs?" Abigail asked.

"Don't need to. In the summer, locals only use those last two docks," he explained, pointing. "We leave the rest for the summer people. They have to pay in advance, and with tomorrow being the Fourth of July, every spot's always spoken for. Look."

A series of sleek pleasure cruisers were tied off along the second dock. There was a single gap in the line. One was missing.

"We have to track down who owns that boat, Denny."

"Now we call the dockmaster."

When they returned to the sheriff's station, Merle, Bert, Franklin, Larner, and Nat had converged there. Abigail couldn't help but feel how much the men had come to care for her. The feeling was mutual. They were all looking at her as though they wanted to hug her. Except Nat. His gaze was riveted to the floor.

"My dad's holding the ferry and one of the summer folks' yachts is gone. Probably had a decent engine on it," Denny informed them. "Dockmaster's en route."

Larner sprang into action and started delegating.

"I have Ted on his way over to this guy Tim's place of residence. Denny, you go meet your father. Search the ferry. Should be empty, but get any passengers off first in case this guy is armed or tries something."

He didn't go into further explanation, and everyone in the room seemed to be waiting to see if Denny would ask why.

Denny surprised Abigail as well as the rest by saying, "Already had my dad tell anybody on board that there was a technical problem."

Abigail shot Larner a glance. Denny had proven his value and proven her point about him.

"Franklin," Larner said. "I'm putting the word out to the Coast Guard. Get ahold of your contact there. Explain the situation," he told him, intimating that Franklin had some sort of pull.

"Will do." Franklin was dialing his cell.

"Merle, you go to the lighthouse," Larner instructed. "Sit watch in case this guy comes back. Bert, you go over to the firehouse. Check that the fireworks supply is safe. And tell the guys to be ready if that alarm sounds."

"Didn't care for that Tim from the get-go," Bert remarked. "I saw him taking the rental plates off that Mercedes and figured something wasn't right."

Merle elbowed him to keep quiet. It was too late.

"Why didn't you tell me?" Abigail demanded.

"I tried, Abby. You didn't want to listen."

She remembered Bert stopping her to talk and her blowing him off. He was right. Abigail had been paying too much attention to the wrong things rather than listening to her heart or the people she trusted.

To cut the tension, Merle said, "That it, Caleb?"

"One more thing." Larner had left Nat's assignment for last. "You willing to go to the Graveyard and look for this son of a bitch?"

Nat glanced at Abigail, as if to say he was doing this for her, then nodded that he would.

"Chop's kicking up," Franklin warned.

"Don't do anything heroic, " Larner added. "This is for the authorities to handle."

"Wouldn't dream of it, Sheriff."

Abigail was itching to apologize to Nat, but he was out the door before she could. The rest of the men took off, too, aside from Franklin. He angled his wheelchair into a corner and got back on the horn, talking intently. Larner dialed the Coast Guard, leaving Abigail standing alone in the center of the station.

"What about the man in the straw hat? The real treasure hunter? Somebody should make sure he's okay."

"I'm fresh out of men," Larner told her, covering the receiver. "I mean bodies. You can drive over and get Duncan Thadlow to go with you if you don't want to go alone."

"At this hour? His wife really will think we're having an affair."

He shrugged as someone picked up on the line. "This is Sheriff Larner with the Chapel Isle authorities. I have a fugitive to report."

As Abigail knocked on the door to the bungalow the man in the straw hat was renting, she had to resist the urge to stand at a safe distance.

Where would that be? On the other side of the island?

After repeated knocks, the man answered the door in a robe and pajama bottoms. When he recognized her, his expression solidified with distrust.

"Is your stove running?" she asked, jittery.

Puzzled, he replied, "I thought the joke went: *Is your refrigerator running? Then go get it.* Or something like that."

"No time for jokes."

Abigail barged past him into the house, went to the kitchen, and hurriedly checked the oven. Shoving her fear aside, she fanned the air, sniffing it. No scent of gas. She switched on the burners. They still weren't working.

The man stood there, arms folded. "Would you care to explain what you're doing waking me up to frisk my oven when you specifically said you couldn't fix it?"

"About that."

As Abigail enumerated the various incidents, plots, and machinations that had led up to that moment, the man's face softened, going from annoyance to sheer shock.

"The guy almost killed you," he said.

"Not really. I just thought he was trying to. But you—you were in real danger."

The man sat heavily on a chair at the kitchen table. His signature straw hat hung off the back. He pushed aside a stack of books and maps charting the local waters and invited Abigail to join him at the table.

"We've bumped into each other enough that we're overdue for a formal introduction. I'm Ray Anderson."

She spied his name on two of the marine treasure-hunting books on the table. He was the author.

"Abigail Harker. I see you have more than a passing interest in treasure."

He laughed. "You could say that. I've been doing this for years. Nearly drowned in the Bahamas once. Almost ran out of air in my scuba tank near Borneo. Had a hurricane destroy my boat in the Keys. Got a flipper caught in the wreckage of a Navy fleet ship and thought I might not make it. Mother Nature's taken a couple of swipes at me. But another human being—who'd have imagined?"

This was a man who risked his life on a regular basis. Abigail had never come even close until tonight.

"Why?" she asked. "Why live so dangerously? Are you an adrenaline junkie? A thrill seeker?"

"A little. But it's not the peril that appeals to a fellow like me. It's the magic, a faith in the unknown. If you don't believe the treasure is out there—believe it with every fiber of your being—it could be right under your nose and you wouldn't find it."

It was a sentiment that resonated strongly with Abigail.

"The *Bishop's Mistress,* she's elusive. I doubt she's going to give herself up to any of us landlubbers."

Abigail thought of Wesley Jasper and decided that if he'd been trying to save anything tonight, it was the ship. They each deserved to rest in peace.

"Think they're going to catch this guy?" Ray asked.

"For everyone's sake, I hope they do."

"Are you afraid now?"

Now?

Abigail had been scared for almost a year—by her past, her present, and the future that was unfurling in front of her. What was left to be frightened by?

"No," she told him. "I'm not afraid anymore."

Sheriff Larner had an update when Abigail returned to the station. He was the only one there.

"Treasure hunter's all in one piece?"

"One peeved piece. I can relate," she told him, flopping down in Denny's desk chair, completely spent.

"Tim wasn't on the ferry, but George Meloch said the guy had approached him about wreck diving when he came here."

"So that's why George wouldn't stop glaring at me."

"May not be the only reason."

"I know, I know. He doesn't like anybody. *Nobody* here likes any-body."

"That's not true, Abby. You saw who all came out tonight. None of those boys would've if this wasn't on account o' you."

"Wow, I haven't seen your 'old softy' side, Sheriff. It works for you."

He sniffed, self-conscious. "Coast Guard hasn't spotted the

missing yacht, but I have turned up a lot on Tim Ulman in the police database. It's an alias. One of many. He has priors for burglary, larceny, assault, fencing, and passing bad checks, as well as warrants for bilking old women for their fortunes. He's a con artist. A violent one."

"That's why the woman I spoke to on his cell phone was mad. He was running a scam on her too."

"This guy has a female accomplice, his real wife, who's also wanted."

Abigail figured that was who Tim intended to call in order to pretend he was getting ahold of his fictitious daughter. He had orchestrated this operation down to the very last detail. Although she was loath to admit it, the guy was clever. If he hadn't lost his phone, she wouldn't have caught on to his scheme. Fortune, it seemed, was as essential as reason. Whether Abigail liked it or not.

Larner's walkie-talkie crackled. Nat's voice came over the airwaves.

"I've got nothing 'cept ocean. If the guy was here, he saw the rough weather coming and took off. Coast Guard may catch him trying to dock somewhere. That or he didn't make it out of the Graveyard."

"You come on in," Larner radioed back.

"Copy that."

She wasn't sure how to feel about Tim's disappearance. He had been prepared to do away with Ray Anderson to get the treasure. If the boat he'd stolen had sunk in the Ship's Graveyard, was that a fair punishment?

Abigail mulled over the concept of equality on her drive to the lighthouse. The term *fair* originated with the Old English *fæ̃eger,* signifying something as beautiful or pleasant, and the Gothic *fagrs,* meaning fit. The word had evolved to connote freedom from bias, meaning morally unblemished and pure.

"Morally unblemished. There's a concept."

She didn't know a single person who fell into that category, herself included.

Merle was waiting for her at the house, sitting on the stoop like a giant sentinel.

"You all right?" he asked.

"I will be."

"I feel awful, Abby. Caleb told us specifically not to say anything about your beau. He wasn't askin'."

"I'm aware. I guess I don't understand how that stopped you."

"I'd rather be wrong and see you happy than be right. Being right isn't everything it's cracked up to be."

Wise words, she thought.

That was how Abigail felt about Nat as well as about Mr. Jasper. She may not have been right about them. Perhaps Nat was a decent guy. Maybe Mr. Jasper was real. Being wrong about either wouldn't be the worst thing in the world.

Zounds (zoundz), *interj. Archaic.* (used as a mild oath). [1590–1600; var. of ˈSWOUNDS]

❖   ❖   ❖

Abigail awoke the next morning to discover it wasn't morning. It was just after noon. Despite the heat, she'd slept for hours.

Her bedroom was a wreck from her hasty packing efforts. Tim had added to the damage. He'd left the closet and dresser drawers open after rifling through them for items to loot. Tim had also ransacked the study. Books lay on the floor and were splayed atop the desk. Surprisingly, none of the desk drawers was open, including the one that held Wesley Jasper's map. Abigail hadn't tried them to see if they were stuck. She preferred to chalk it up to Mr. Jasper rather than the weather.

The previous night, before falling asleep, Abigail had pledged to clean up the mess the next day.

"Today *is* the next day," she told herself, pushing the covers and loose clothing aside.

And that day was the Fourth of July, Independence Day. The significance wasn't lost on her.

After Abigail made the bed, she rehung and folded the clothes she'd heaped into her suitcases then replaced her cardboard-box hamper beside the nightstand.

"I suppose this means you're staying?" she asked herself.

Abigail shut the refilled dresser drawer in answer.

Downstairs needed tidying too. She put away the dishes that were set for the meal she'd never shared with Tim. The flowers and leftover food went directly into the trash. No reminders of him were allowed to remain in her house.

The picnic basket.

It wasn't Tim's. It belonged to the woman he had conned. Abigail didn't feel right throwing it away.

"You should return it."

She didn't want to go back to that house. Ever again. But she had to.

The phone rang, startling her.

"Abby, is that you? Are you alive?" a voice squawked, loud and clear as a siren. It was Lottie. "I called your cell and nobody answered."

"Yes, it's me."

"Heavens to pigs' feet, I prayed and prayed and you're all right. I am crossing myself left, right, and center."

"I'm alive. And I have a question for you."

"Anything, dear."

"How did you know I was a widow?"

The line went silent.

Eventually Lottie said, "I didn't. I guessed. Out loud sorta. To a gal here in town. Pretty woman like you, single, alone, no visitors. I apologize, Abby. From the bottom of my heart."

Abigail was relieved. Though she shouldn't have been. Something about the way she carried herself broadcast her darkest secret to anyone who cared to look. Yet Lottie's off-the-cuff conjecture had saved Abigail from having to continue carrying the burden alone. In a way, Lottie had done her a favor.

If it had been anybody else, Abigail might have thanked them. Only it was Lottie. "I apologize too. Because I'm quitting. Bye!"

She hung up as Lottie sputtered.

Gathering the trash and the picnic basket, Abigail locked the front door. Then opened it again.

After putting down the stuff, she headed to the car to retrieve

Wesley Jasper's journals. Abigail returned them to the basement, where they'd been safe for so many years.

"Here you go," she said, as if replacing borrowed property. "Back where you belong."

Upstairs on the main floor, she went from window to window, opening the panes. Some fought her. Others slid up effortlessly. A limp breeze fluttered the drapes.

"That's more like it."

Abigail had the garbage bag under one arm and the picnic basket on the other when Nat Rhone rode into the driveway in his truck. She could think of a hundred things she wanted to say to him, yet she was at a loss for words. It was an uncommon occurrence.

Nat got out of the truck, walked over to her, and stared. "Glad I wasn't invited to whatever picnic you're going to. You serving trash?"

"I was taking out the garbage."

"Need help?"

"No, I can—" Abigail stopped herself before she could start bickering. "Yes, thank you."

He took the bag from her and placed it in the trash can at the side of the cottage. Afterward, they stood face-to-face, each alternately silent, then stammering or interrupting the other.

"I was—"

"I didn't—"

"You go first."

"No, you were saying?"

Abigail finally managed to unspool the many emotions she had rolled tightly inside her.

"I'm sorry for assuming you were up to no good with the wreck diving. And I'm sorry for hurting your feelings yesterday, especially since you were following me only to protect me from Tim."

"Um . . ." Nat seemed flummoxed. "Actually, I knew everybody on the island didn't want the *Bishop's Mistress* found. Out of respect, I made sure the guy didn't. That was why I couldn't discuss it with you."

She shook her head, impressed. Nat had done for the natives what Abigail had done for Denny. She admired him for that.

"That wasn't why I was following you. Sure, I didn't like Tim, but I had no idea he'd do what he did."

"Then how did you know Tim had been at my house?"

"'Cause you aren't the greatest cook. No offense. All you eat are peanut butter and jelly sandwiches, and you had a car full of groceries. Doesn't take a genius to deduce that you'd invited him over for dinner."

Now who's the logical one?

"Okay, so why were you following me?"

"I was working up the nerve to—" Nat fidgeted, gathering his resolve. "To tell you that you're one of the only people who's ever done anything decent for me. You took up for me when nobody else would. What I was trying to say was thank you."

While moved, Abigail felt the pinch of disappointment.

What were you hoping he'd say?

"What is it?" Nat asked. "You look upset."

"Nothing," she insisted. "Fires, near-death escapes, con man on the lam—that tends to make a gal grumpy. It'll wear off. If you'll excuse me, I have a picnic basket to return. Oh, and you're welcome."

"There is one other thing."

Eager to put an end to this excruciating conversation, Abigail sighed. "What is it?"

"I think I'm falling in love with you."

Her mouth fell open. "Uh, come again?"

Nat took a deep breath. "I don't know why. All we do is argue, and you've made it crystal clear that you hate my guts six out of seven days a week. I told you I was moving away from Chapel Isle only to see if you'd care if I left. I read about what happened to you, to your husband, your little boy. I didn't think you'd be ready to date again, but when I saw you with Tim, I started to hope. Then Larner told us you were falling for the guy. I didn't . . ."

Taken aback by Nat's admission, Abigail's mind was frozen in neutral. Despite the feelings churning through her brain, she couldn't throw her voice into drive. Her mouth refused to move or shape a single syllable.

Believing he'd overstepped his bounds, Nat began to backpedal. His usually conceited demeanor dissolved into timid mumbling.

"I didn't mean it. To be forward, that is. Listen, forget I mentioned it. Forget I brought it up. Hell, you can forget you ever met me. Maybe moving away isn't such a horrible idea."

"No," Abigail said at last.

"No what?"

"No, I don't want to forget about it. All I do is remember—remember the way my life was, how it was supposed to be. I've been stuck alone out here remembering and not being. So I'm more than willing to forget we ever met."

Nat lowered his head, absorbing the blow.

"Which means we have to *remeet*," Abigail added. "Right now."

With the wind wafting softly through the trees, she extended her hand.

"I'm Abigail Harker."

A rare yet recognizable smile bloomed on his face.

"I'm Nat. Nathan Rhone. Pleased to meet you."

"The pleasure is mine."

They were shaking hands and gazing at each other, standing close, with only the picnic basket between them.

Uh-oh. He's going to kiss you. And you're going to let him.

Suddenly a horn honked, announcing a line of trucks and cars spilling onto the driveway. More horns blared and tooted, a symphony of arrival. Denny, George, Merle, Bert, and Ruth were pulling up to the house en masse.

"Guess I failed to mention the *other* other thing."

Nat pointed to the cans of paint and ladders on his flatbed.

"Afternoon, Abby," Merle said, getting out of his truck with a toolbox and plumbing parts.

"Got your color just right," Denny announced as his father nodded in Abigail's direction, brushes in hand.

"Plenty of food," Ruth said, while Bert unloaded a cooler from her trunk. "Bug spray too. Never the twain shall meet, hon. Promise."

"We're here to paint your house and fix the broken pipes," Nat told Abigail. "Franklin thought you could do with some cheering up after nearly being—"

"Blown up?"

"Those weren't his exact words, but something like that."

Language was the thing that Abigail understood best. But she was beginning to believe that there was a lot more to life than words. Feeling them might teach her more than studying them would.

While everybody pitched in to paint the caretaker's cottage, resurrecting it from dilapidated to perfect stroke by stroke, Abigail experienced a swell of pride. If there was a Mr. Jasper, he would have been proud too. If there wasn't, she was proud enough for them both.

That evening, Abigail found herself sitting on a folding chair on Pamlico Sound Beach with Merle and countless tourists. Kids lit sparklers, while families settled on blankets and ate snacks by flashlight. The sound of the ocean competed with the noise of excited chatter about the fireworks.

"This is a nice spot," Merle said.

"I came early. I had to drop off a picnic basket, then it was straight to the beach to claim the best plot of sand."

"You were going to move away, weren't you?"

"How you're able to read my mind amazes me, Merle. Maybe you missed your calling."

"I'm not Kreskin. I have a spare key to the caretaker's cottage.

When Caleb sent me to watch the place, I went inside. At first I thought you were a lousy housekeeper. Then I saw the suitcases."

"I'll admit I toyed with the notion."

"And?"

"Tabled it. Anyway, I wouldn't get far. Tim stole all my cash and my credit cards. I'm stranded."

"That's too bad."

"Merle!"

"Franklin ordered you that lawn mower. If you moved away, I'd get it," he teased.

"Sorry to disappoint you."

"You couldn't disappoint me if you tried. I'm honored you're my date tonight, Abby. Speaking of which, I hear you've got another one tomorrow. With Nat."

Abigail smacked the arms of her folding beach chair. "That fast? The rumor spread *that* fast?"

"Nope. I was only hazarding a guess. Thanks for confirming." He smirked at her. "Abby, my friend, most gossip is pure speculation— people telling other people what they want 'em to hear. Consider that when you catch wind that Lottie is buying new televisions and towels and toasters for *all* her rentals. Somebody must have gossiped about you, saying you would leave for another rental unit if she didn't."

Merle patted her hand, then a teenager yelled, "The fireworks are about to start!" Merle shrank back.

"Are you really okay with this, with being here?" Abigail asked, turning serious.

"I have to be," Merle said, resolute. "So I will."

Me too, she thought.

A red streak of light shot up, screaming into the night and bursting into shimmering rays of color that cascaded down from the sky. The crowd cheered and clapped. In the glow of the falling fireworks, she saw their faces, smiling, expectant, mesmerized.

For days, Abigail had viewed the summer people as selfish and unruly, running amok on her island. But she'd seen them through the lens of her own dissatisfaction. The tourists were tourists, there to enjoy the beauty she loved Chapel Isle for too. She couldn't begrudge them for having the same great taste she did.

Feeling the sand between her toes, smelling the salt air, seeing the array of colorful fireworks, Abigail could instantly conjure dozens of adjectives to describe the scene. Instead, she resolved that verbs would be more her style moving forward. She thought of the first ones she'd learned in Latin.

Rideo. To laugh.

Amor. To love.

Ago. To live.

Acknowledgments

Without the loving support and encouragement of family and friends, this book simply wouldn't have been possible, so a heartfelt thank-you to: Sarah and Fred Baldassaro, Ann Biddlecom, Ruth Blader, Claudia Butler, Jennifer Colt, Anne Engelhardt, Beth Foster, Debra Keeler, Amy and Brad Miller, Alex Parsons, Kerry Quinn, Grace Ray, Dana Schoenfeld, Barbara Sheffer, Heather Stober, Marni Kinrys Velarde, Caroline Zouloumian, and Sue Zwick.

Much gratitude also goes to my terrific agent, Rebecca Oliver, as well as my gifted editor, Caitlin Alexander.

THE

DEFINITION

OF WIND

Ellen Block

 *A Reader's Guide*

Gone But Not Forgotten

by Ellen Block

When I was seven, I saw a ghost. At least, I think I did.

I was at my grandmother's house. For the record, it wasn't some creepy old mansion on a dark and stormy night. It was a run-of-the-mill row house across from the Allegheny River in Pennsylvania, and that particular afternoon I was rummaging through the top drawer of the dresser in the guest room, which was where my grandmother kept her costume jewelry. Brimming with rhinestone baubles and beaded trinkets, the drawer was a veritable treasure trove, and I used to love to pretend I was a princess, readying myself for some imaginary imperial gala. With a wreath of sparkling necklaces draped over my shoulders, multiple clip-on earrings dangling from my lobes, and bangles stacked to my elbows, I looked up from the drawer to see something in the mirror above the dresser.

A man was standing in shadowy silhouette by the window.

I turned. There was nothing there.

Truth be told, I wasn't scared. Not in the least. I marched to the front door, assuming it was the mailman passing by the window.

But there was nobody on the porch or on the street nearby.

In retrospect, I should have been frightened. I'm not sure why I wasn't. As I recall, I returned to the dresser in the guest room unfazed, where I went on adorning myself in rhinestone regalia, and the incident faded from memory.

That was—until a few years ago.

By then, the girl who liked to make believe she was royalty had grown up to be an award-winning author and an inveterate night owl. One evening I was flipping through the TV channels, searching for something to watch that would put me to sleep, when I landed on a show about assorted haunted locations throughout America, including a lighthouse called Fairport Harbor. Though the program's lamely spooky music and murky camerawork were intended to be scary, what unfolded was categorically hokey. Given a choice between the country's ghostly hot spots and endless infomercials, I didn't bother changing the station.

The lighthouse featured on the show was built in 1871 on the eastern shore of Lake Erie, a Great Lakes beacon that boasted a tragic past. A former keeper's five-year-old son had died of influenza, and shortly afterward his wife had taken ill as well. Grief-stricken, the husband had bought his beloved a number of cats to keep her company, then her favorite one disappeared mysteriously. The wife's death quickly followed. Ever since, the ghost of a black cat had been seen roaming the keeper's quarters. Decades later, in modern times, a plumber repairing a leak under the keeper's house stumbled upon the mummified body of a cat.

Cue the eerie music.

The program depicted a reenactment of a man in overalls unearthing a dusty prop skeleton. Was it corroboration of the haunting or merely a macabre coincidence? The show's stilted voiceover script remained impartial. I watched the rest of the episode, unimpressed by the flimsy evidence, the far-fetched claims, and the skeptic-turned-believer eyewitness accounts. Once I'd gone to bed, the story of the spectral feline was mentally filed far back in my brain. Years later, right before I began writing the first draft of my novel *The Language of Sand,* the cat came back.

I'd decided upon a setting for the book—a fictionalized version of the Outer Banks island I'd visited during my childhood—and finalized the main characters, but I was short a major plot point. One might imagine that my own phantom encounter would immediately spring to mind. Instead, it was the lighthouse from the late-night program I'd watched. I began researching and was astounded to discover how many allegedly haunted beacons dotted our nation's shores.

The first of many stories I came across was about the Pensacola Lighthouse. Nestled in a corner of the Florida panhandle and looming over 150 feet in the air, Pensacola's tower was painted black, the color almost alluding to a chapter in the property's past. Long ago, the keeper's wife had stabbed him to death after an argument, and from then on a stain marred the floorboards where the murder had occurred. According to the lighthouse staff, regardless of efforts to clean the stain, it would reappear without fail. During tours, visitors told of having their clothes tugged on and feeling as if they were being trailed. One day, a young girl insisted she'd seen a woman in white on the catwalk. A guide had checked the lighthouse turret and found it locked from the inside.

Similarly supernatural tales abounded at other lighthouses, so many I almost lost count. However, there were standouts, like Owl's Keep in Maine. Situated in the pine-covered cliffs off misty Camden Harbor, this lighthouse was rumored to have had wet footprints materialize on the spiral staircase when no one except a lone employee was on the grounds. Equally peculiar was when the staff would arrive at work to find the brass fittings and glass lens in the turret polished to a high shine, even though none of the personnel could take credit.

Farther up the Maine coast was another notable haunting at Prospect Harbor, the purported home of Captain Salty, who was said to be in ghostly residence at the neighboring keeper's quarters called Gull Cottage. He was supposedly responsible for turning on lights at all hours of the night and moving the set of hand-carved statues of sailors that stood on a window ledge. By day, the figurines would face the water. By evening, they would face land. Was Captain Salty turning them in the direction a fellow seafarer would know they'd want to go?

Still knee-deep in data, I hadn't been willing to hazard a guess. I could only marvel at the large number and variety of ghost stories associated with lighthouses. Often the reference material would chalk up sightings to nostalgia-steeped folklore or a forlornly romantic mood. It was as though every one of these lonesome stone sentinels was fated to be haunted.

The more I read, the more I focused on the specific types of experiences people had reported—being touched, hearing noises, smelling the odor of perfume or candle smoke. In my notes, I'd jot things like: "Intimate the ghost is there by having Abigail sense an unseen presence" or "Have the lights turn on and off without cause." Admittedly, I was mechanizing the paranormal to fit my plot, studying firsthand accounts without any of it really sinking in. Then I learned of a trio of lighthouses clustered along the Oregon seaside.

The Yaquina Bay beacon had been known for having the shortest tenure of all the lighthouses in the entire country. It was built in 1871 and operated for a brief three-year stint before being replaced by its big brother in Yaquina Harbor. It also had a reputation as being haunted by the ghost of a teenage girl named Muriel, who's father—an avid sailor—had once left her on land with friends so she could go sightseeing.

Muriel vanished that day, and an exhaustive search turned up no sign of her body. Thereafter, the ephemeral figure of a teen in nineteenth-century garb had been sighted regularly in the lighthouse turret and even appeared as a vaporous form in the background of tourists' photos.

Nearby at Yaquina Harbor, inexplicable voices were said to resound throughout the lighthouse, and a former keeper swore he'd heard footsteps climbing the spiral staircase every night for twenty-two years straight.

As I continued cataloging strange occurrences such as these, trying to determine how I'd weave them into the narrative of my novel, I hit upon the legend of Heceda Head lighthouse. Perched on a wedge of rock jutting out into the Pacific, the Queen Anne–style edifice was home to the sad saga of a lighthouse keeper's wife whose child had reportedly drowned. Unable to go on, she took her own life. To this day, both visitors and staff attest to seeing the ethereal apparition of a woman wandering the property—especially in the attic. I was about to skip to the next lighthouse on my list when I read that in this very attic a handyman who had been wiping a window was startled by the reflection of a woman behind him in the glass. When he spun around, no one was there.

The handyman's experience was virtually identical to mine.

Despite hours of combing through literature on hauntings, it wasn't until then that I remembered what had happened at my grandmother's house. I pictured my younger self in the mirror over the dresser, decked out in a cascade of pink paste rhinestones and fake gold, playing princess. I could still picture the figure as well. A flash and it was gone, yet not completely forgotten.

I can't prove that what I glimpsed in the mirror that day was a ghost. But I'm comfortable in the absence of certainty. Because, for me, the best part of any mystery isn't unmasking the bad guy, cracking the riddle, or revealing the truth. That just means the end of the story is near, the fun almost over. Solving the mystery is what I like to savor. Luckily, when it comes to ghosts and haunted lighthouses, these are cases that aren't liable to be closed anytime soon.

Questions and
Topics for Discussion

1. Why do you think Abigail doesn't tell anyone on Chapel Isle about her husband and son? Why is she so anxious when people start finding out?

2. Why is Abigail upset by her home-repair problems? Discuss the ways in which the author uses them to mirror Abigail's emotional and psychological journey through the novel. Do you think a different set of crises would have been as effective?

3. How is Abigail's former career as a lexicographer important to the novel? Why do you think the author chose that particular profession?

4. Discuss Abigail's reservations about Tim. Did you have similar reservations? Were you surprised at the ultimate revelations about his character?

5. Why do you think Abigail agrees to help Lottie with her tenants? What do you think she ends up getting out of this role?

6. Why is Abigail so concerned with fitting in with the locals on Chapel Isle? Do you think she's ever able to achieve that? Discuss a situation in which you've tried to fit in—in the end, was it worth it?

7. Abigail finds good friends in Ruth, Merle, Bert, Denny, and eventually Nat. Discuss Abigail's relationship with each character. How do you think they are able to help her? In what ways does she have an impact on each of their lives?

8. Abigail seems at times to be both scared and protective of Wesley Jasper. Why do you think that is? Have you had any experiences of your own with ghosts? How do you think you would have reacted to Wesley?

9. Why do you think Abigail becomes so invested in the drama surrounding the *Bishop's Mistress*? What does the ship come to mean to her?

10. Do you think Nat is a good fit for Abigail? Why or why not? What do you think the future holds for them?

11. What reasons does Abigail give for choosing Chapel Isle? Do you think there are additional motivations that she doesn't state? In what ways has the island met her expectations? In what ways has it surprised her?

Ellen Block lives in Los Angeles.

www.ellenblock.net

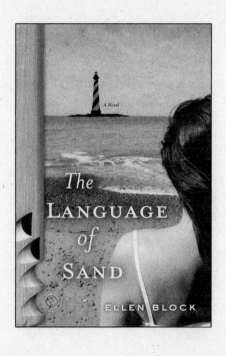

If you enjoyed *The Definition of Wind*, read more
about Abigail Harker and the residents of Chapel Isle
in *The Language of Sand*, available now
from your favorite bookseller.